NEVER
F

She first noticed it as a fuzzy lump reflected in the compact's mirror, then she slowly turned her head to her left to get a better look. It was hulking at the inner lab's entrance, its shaggy bulk all too clear and recognizable through the glass pane that made up the top half of the door. It pawed mindlessly at the glass, leaving oily streaks, and showed its teeth. Anyone else might have been frightened but Dr. Cynthia Wardoe was simply annoyed. No wonder the window looked so dirty. She was done with these creatures for the day; couldn't they leave her alone? The beast at the door watched as she slowly approached, and when she got halfway it even cocked its head in the manner that she might think was cute if she weren't so tired.

It looked weak, like virtually all of them did. Its eyes were open at half staff and its ears were limp. A tiny bit of its pink tongue pushed between its yellowing teeth. It didn't look like one of the subjects she'd seen today. It was probably one from days ago that had just found its way out of its room and into the halls, feeling very furry and very sick under the waxing moon. In its condition, there was no way it could get through the reinforced door. All she would have to do is call Jim, and he could probably take it out without even needing the tranquilizer gun. Then they'd figure out how it got loose in the building. Dr. Wardoe turned to reach for the phone when the creature surprised her. Its face suddenly brightened, its ears rising erect and its eyes narrowing to slits. It almost seemed to be laughing. One hairy paw rose slowly into view, holding an access card.

NEVER TAKE A WEREWOLF OR GRANTED

Also by Brett Davis

The Faery Convention

HAIR OF THE DOG

BRETT DAVIS

HAIR OF THE DOG

This is a work of fiction. All the characters and events
portrayed in this book are fictional, and any resemblance to
real people or incidents is purely coincidental.

A Baen Books Original

Baen Publishing Enterprises
P.O. Box 1403
Riverdale, NY 10471

ISBN: 0-671-87762-3

Cover art by Bob Eggleton

First printing, January 1997

Distributed by Simon & Schuster
1230 Avenue of the Americas
New York, NY 10020

Printed in the United States of America

To Preet

Thanks to Sarah Sturch for the title.

ONE

Carl Johnson looked like a demon. His longish hair was so tangled he resembled a brunet Medusa, and his eyes were stippled with red from staring at the tiny numbers that danced across the computer screen. He had a Ph.D. in cell biology and extensive knowledge of computers, making him perhaps one of the most highly advanced human beings on the planet. For all that, he looked little more intelligent than a caveman as he stared miserably at the squiggly creatures on the screen.

At last he pressed his index fingers to his eyes and slowly rose from his chair with a sigh. He looked as if he might stay there, frozen from exhaustion, but he managed to summon the strength to turn and stumble over to the nearby table where his boss was sitting. The esteemed Dr. Cynthia Wardoe hunched in a chair on the other side of the table, peering through her red-framed glasses at a test notebook that was dogeared, stained and battered although it had been generated only that morning. A casual

1

observer might have said that the blonde-haired doctor
looked like a college student as she earnestly pored
over the charts and graphs in the three-ring binder,
but the charts and graphs she was examining showed
nothing that any student had ever seen before. She
watched from behind the corners of her thick glasses
as Johnson shambled over to the table, but she waited
to look up until he was standing before her.

"Doc, I've had it," he said, his voice a rasp.
"Everything is about as good as it's going to get right
now, and I've got to get some sleep. These numbers
are starting to look like hieroglyphics. Mind if I pack
it in for the night?"

She let go of the notebook cover and it closed with
a thud. She gave him a cold glance.

"Why should I mind being the only one here again
tonight?" she asked, watching his face closely for any
signs of shame. He must have been too tired; she saw
none.

"I'm sorry, doc, but I can't do it. I'm afraid I'll miss
something and we'll be even more messed up than
we are now."

"Couldn't you just get Jim to get you some coffee,
Carl? We've only got a week left. You know we need
to get this right."

Even as the words left her mouth she realized they
were useless. Johnson looked like he would need a
veinful of uppers to keep going, and they didn't have
access to that particular cabinet tonight. She tried to
soften her expression, but wasn't sure it worked.

"Go home, Carl. Goodnight. I'll see you tomorrow.
Early."

He swayed before her like a weary ape, but didn't
move to go.

"I hate to say it, but I've been checking and rechecking these figures and they just aren't budging. I don't think they'll be any different tomorrow. I don't think we can make it."

She looked at him coldly but said nothing.

"Have you thought any more about what we talked about?" he asked.

She glanced around the room and set her teeth together, almost in a snarl.

"Not in here, Carl," she said as quietly as she could. "We don't discuss that here."

"Where else can we discuss it?" he asked, dropping his voice to match her low volume. "We practically live here. We *do* live here, we only go home to sleep. Where else can we talk about it?"

"We still have time to succeed. Don't give up yet."

Johnson snorted and straightened up. His voice got louder now, causing her to flinch.

"Yes, I forgot, we will succeed where the Army failed. We will make a fortune. You've already put a down payment on that house, haven't you? I told you not to do that."

"Good *night*, Carl. Get *out* of here. I'm not kidding."

His weary eyes turned into bloodshot slits.

"Don't threaten me, doctor. We're in this together."

"I know that, Carl. Don't you do anything without me. But don't do it yet. We still have time. There's no need to jump the gun."

"Soon, doc, soon. We'll have to make our move soon."

"Good night, Carl."

He stood a moment longer and then uttered a goodnight and walked out, leaving his computers on. The automatic file protection software would lock their

data up tight. She could hear the control panel on the
door beeping as he punched the code to leave, then
the door swished back to a close and locked her inside.
Once sure he was gone, she pushed the notebook aside
and walked down the center aisle of the lab, past the
measuring devices that were assembled like loyal
servants on the left side and the clinical computer
equipment that had conquered the available desk and
shelf space on the right. She grabbed the white plastic
phone and punched up the inter-office line, tapping
her foot impatiently as she waited for a voice on the
other end.

"Jim, is Steve still down there? He's off duty? Could
you tell him to get back *on* duty for a little bit? Yeah,
there's something extra in it for him. Tell him that
Dr. Johnson is leaving, and that he's really tired and
I'm worried about him. Get him to follow Dr. Johnson
and make sure he gets home all right. You know his
car. Yes, thanks. Oh, and tell Steve to call me if Dr.
Johnson goes anywhere other than home. No, it's
nothing like *that*, Jim, you joker. I just need to know
where he is in case any emergency comes up. Thanks
again."

She plopped back down at her spot and picked up
the book with its parade of unsightly images, ready
to work for a few more hours. She had only been at
it for a quarter of an hour when she had to pull off
her glasses and rub her eyes. Either her vision was
going or the lighting in here was getting bad, but
either way the end result was the same. She had been
looking at the pictures for so long that she could hardly
see anymore. The tiny lines of data next to them had
faded into rectangular gray blocks, nearly devoid of
identifiable shapes. She pulled away from the book

for a few moments and glanced around. The normally spotless window in the door looked dull and soapy. Even the cheerful pattern that danced across the computer screens to protect them from phosphor burn-in now looked vaguely menacing, as if the computers were really aquariums harboring nasty fish. A shadow seemed to hang in the room, as if some fog had gotten in, which was, of course, impossible. The only fog in Las Vegas was from the dry ice in the casino stage shows, and even that could never get in this building.

"All I need is a hunchback and some moss on the walls and I could be Dr. Frankenstein," she said quietly, her voice gently echoing back.

The hunchback remark would be considered insensitive these days, but she was too tired to care. She yawned. Carl had the right idea. It was time to go home. She had an interview in the morning with that damned perky reporter for that atrocious show, *Live Entertainment*, and she wanted to look as fresh as possible, even if she didn't feel that way. Eight o'clock was going to come early.

"Igor, bring me my purse, I don't know where I left it," she said loudly, but no hunchback came running.

The inner laboratory was built as a plain square, which gave her the freedom to arrange it any way she wanted using spare tables procured from other labs in the building. It was currently laid out as a blocky U, with lots of room in the middle for the subjects and even more room along the tables for the instruments and the monitoring equipment. She would have preferred a gleaming, white, ultramodern room, but the economics of science—and the fact she had purloined much of the furniture—dictated a more humble set-up. The dark brown tops of the tables conspired with the off-white walls and the green floor to give the lab an arboreal feel, which was heightened by the dozens of power cords that descended from the ceiling at odd locations like shiny rubber vines.

After two minutes of looking, she found her purse leaning against one of the cords like a monkey preparing for the ascent. She picked it up and walked back to the middle of the U, to the lab's central feature: an oversized chair, a giant white recliner that was attached to nearly half the wires and instruments in the room. It looked like a La-Z-Boy that had been dropped out of a UFO. All the video monitors pointed at it, along with a bank of small microphones and sensors. The connectors that fed it poured from the back and were clumsily braided into a thick cable that was duct-taped to the floor. The cable was then routed under the tables like a robotic anaconda until it reached the far wall, where the wires sought their individual destinies. The chair could be tilted and adjusted over an almost infinite range. Its surface could not be scratched or dented, and its backrest and legrest featured adjustable restraints for arms, legs, head and torso. All it lacked was built-in vibra-massage.

It wasn't pleasant to think about the things that had occurred in the big chair as recently as three hours ago, but then again the lab techs cleaned it pretty thoroughly each time so Dr. Wardoe figured it was at least as clean as any furniture she had at home, if not more so. She plopped down, feeling her pants slide against its smooth composite surface. The chair was definitely not built with comfort in mind. She slipped her glasses off her face and dropped them in the breast pocket of her white jacket, cut to resemble a stylish lab coat. She never wanted anyone to forget she was a top-flight medical researcher, but she didn't want anyone to think she was a dowdy frump, either, and there were a lot of camera crews out and about these days. Feeling the strain in her lower back from her slouched position, she sat up as far as she could, but kept sliding back. She finally gave up and used the leg manacles as boosters. Once secure, she searched through her bag for the pager unit to call Jim, so he could let her out and close the lab. She was always tired when she left, and liked for someone who was thinking clearly to do the final lock-up.

But her eyes had increased their war against her, and she decided to survey the damage. It felt like her eyelids were scraping along over hunks of rock. She suspended the search mission for the keys and instead pulled out her compact, flipping it open to get to the eye drops she kept there in place of makeup. She looked at her face in the mirror; it was about as bad as she had expected. She might as well have plums jammed in her eye sockets, and the rest of her face didn't look so hot, either. Her marathon work sessions kept her fit, so she still possessed a lean, healthy face, but tonight it looked more like an unfinished sculpture. The skin on her face was almost as dry as her eyes. She wanted to bring a humidifier from home but knew it wouldn't work in the closed environment of the building, and at this point she certainly didn't want to do anything to screw up the tests any more than they already were. She put in a couple of eye drops, blinked out the tears, and sighed.

"Leatherface needs microwave dinner," she muttered

to herself, folding the tiny bottle back into the compact. "Leatherface has an interview in the morning."

And then she saw it. She first noticed it as a fuzzy lump reflected in the compact's mirror, then she slowly turned her head to her left to get a better look. It was hulking at the inner lab's entrance, its shaggy bulk all too clear and recognizable through the glass pane that made up the top half of the door. It pawed mindlessly at the glass, leaving oily streaks, and showed its teeth. Anyone else might have been frightened but she was simply annoyed. No wonder the window looked so dirty. She was done with these creatures for the day; couldn't they leave her alone? The beast at the door watched as she slowly approached, and when she got halfway it even cocked its head in the manner that she might think was cute if she weren't so tired.

It looked weak, like virtually all of them did. Its eyes were open at half staff and its ears were limp. A tiny bit of its pink tongue pushed between its yellowing teeth. It didn't look like one of the subjects she'd seen today. It was probably one from days ago that had just found its way out of its room and into the halls, feeling very furry and very sick under the waxing moon. In its condition, there was no way it could get through the reinforced door. All she would have to do is call Jim, and he could probably take it out without even needing the tranquilizer gun. Then they'd figure out how it got loose in the building. Dr. Wardoe turned to reach for the phone when the creature surprised her. Its face suddenly brightened, its ears rising erect and its eyes narrowing to slits. It almost seemed to be laughing. One hairy paw rose slowly into view, holding an access card.

This was not good. Her face was no longer dry; she felt the wet heat of sweat pushing up through her pores. Well, so he had a card. He certainly wouldn't know the code, and those claws would make it tough to punch it in anyway. She backed away a few steps and started to run for the phone, only to bang her knee hard into the leg rest of the UFO chair. She let out a grunt and dropped to the floor as a wave of pain shot through her leg. Her knee scraped against one of the leg manacles as she fell, staining her white coat.

The phone might as well be in L.A. for all the good it would do her now. She'd have to call Jim on his beeper and hope he was nearby. She yanked open her purse and began digging frantically for the pager. Why did she have so much junk in her purse? Her flailing digits pushed aside packs of gum and moldy pennies and old keys and various computer floppy disks, but no pager appeared. To hell with decorum. She dumped the purse on the floor and started rooting around in the contents like a soothsayer seeking a message in chicken entrails.

Just when her hand closed upon the pager, Dr. Wardoe realized that she'd been making too much noise. She hadn't heard the soft tones from the door lock's keypad, hadn't heard the swish as the door started to open. She looked up into a moving mountain of hair, a mountain with sharp teeth and fangs. Then she didn't hear anything else at all.

TWO

Ashly Durban was in great pain. She had managed to get one of her long blonde hairs stuck in her left eye. The hair had dragged through her mascara before setting out on its trek across the cornea, meaning it had effectively glued itself down. Her eye, which normally resembled a tiny blue sky surrounded by clear white clouds, now looked as if it was playing host to a miniature-scale nuclear war. Fat tears rolled down her left cheek, leaving tracks in the Sahara of tan powder that covered her face.

She shoved her way blindly through the small but dense crowd of early-evening partygoers, pursuing the enormous back of Bob Savik, her cameraman, a college football star gone to seed and broadcast journalism school. Savik had a Vulcan-sounding name but looked uncannily like an African-American William Shatner. He provided a decent-sized wake for her to follow, but she had plenty of elbow-throwing of her own to do. They had reached the bright yellow police tape when the raised hand of a burly cop stopped them as surely as any brick wall. He squinted at them through the gloom.

"Media? Go no further. Nothing to see here."

"Whattaya mean, nothing to see?" Durban snarled, the pain in her eye making her pushy. "We hear you have a dead woman in there."

The people who were mashed around her and Savik oohed and ahhed appreciatively. They were pleased they had stumbled across a good scene at which to rubberneck.

"Is it a heart attack?" one thin and hopelessly drunk young woman slurred to Savik, but he ignored her.

"Who have you got in there?" Ashly asked the cop, but it was no use. His lined face told the tale. He was no rookie, and he wasn't about to talk.

"You know the drill, ma'am. Formal statement to follow from HQ. Us grunts don't know anything."

"I *don't* know the drill, actually," she said. "I don't usually do cops."

He shrugged.

"I don't usually do reporters," he said absently. "Supposed to be off tonight."

This was not going at all well, and in the meantime her eye felt like it was sawing itself in half. She squinted it shut and glanced around with the spare one. The police seemed to be recent arrivals. Two squad cars, lights dancing, were haphazardly parked in the yard of a small white building that was crammed in between rows of clothing shops so upscale they only bothered to put things like driftwood and flowers in their display windows. Some sort of nightspot down the street provided the staggering and curious crowd.

Ashly Durban sighed. This trip to Las Vegas was not going well. She should be snoozing comfortably by now, readying herself for her early morning interview with Cynthia Wardoe, glamorous doctor. Instead she got a phone call at her hotel room from Savik, who had been monitoring his police scanner and had heard of a fatality at the Landon Institute, the very place they were due in the morning for the Wardoe interview. The Landon Institute was doing most of the work for the Telephone Drive to Cure Lycanthropy, known colloquially as the Werewolf Telethon. The fifth annual edition of the telethon was coming up in a week, fittingly enough on Halloween night, hosted by action movie star Monty Allen. A cure for lycanthropy was supposed to be at hand; the telethon was rumored to be the final one.

Durban and Savik worked for NBC's *Live Entertainment*, the frothiest Hollywood show imaginable, and she was happy with that, was content to try to climb that ladder to success. In fact, the voice of Reva, the anchorwoman, had been proven to cause epileptic seizures in some viewers. That was not the sort of audience reaction that *Live Entertainment* sought. Durban was hoping Reva would soon get canned and she would be tapped to take over and sit next to toothy anchorman Victor Storm.

Savik, however, had his eyes set somewhat higher in life. He aspired to work for *Cops*, so he carried his police scanner everywhere he went. This time it actually came in handy, although it meant rare late-night work. Covering murders was not her typical fare. She generally did "exclusive" interviews about new movies coming out. She had done a couple of pieces in the past about Monty Allen and his werewolf action movies. With the Werewolf Telethon approaching, *Live Entertainment* decided to do something a little different, and have her do a series of reports about people who were werewolves but tried to live normal lives. "Living with Lycanthropy" had so far turned out pretty well, and had gotten some decent reviews. With the telethon coming up, NBC decided to fly her to Las Vegas for a final week of shows before werewolves ceased to exist.

Las Vegas had been her stomping ground years ago, the scene of her indoctrination into broadcast news. It was the place where she met the love of her life and then grew to hate him. She couldn't bear to see it all at once, from the air, and had closed the plastic window cover until the airplane had landed. She wanted to get back into her old life one step at a time, not to see it pinwheeling beneath her like a county fair run amok.

Now she was right in the middle, and it was as if she was right back at Channel 12, the local NBC affiliate, once again barreling out into the nippy night air and running over to some crime scene to wait around for the police to come out and lie to her.

"Film whatever you can," she muttered to Savik, and started skirting the crowd, moving along inside the yellow police tape. The footage might come in handy for "Living with Lycanthropy," although she couldn't immediately imagine how. No one was moving in or out of the building, but she thought she could see shadowy forms stalking back and forth inside. This was probably just nothing, a waste of time.

There was a young policeman holding back the rubberneckers on the left side of the crowd, keeping them about thirty yards back from the building and the yard. His overly stern frown on an otherwise playful face made him look like a kid playing dress-up in a policeman's suit.

"What's the deal?" Durban shouted over the tape, but before he could respond their attention was diverted by the arrival of an ambulance, siren snorting, pushing the crowd out of its way. It parked in front of the police cars, leaving about fifteen feet of open space between its back door and the white building's entrance. Two short but sturdy trees in the yard prevented the ambulance from coming any closer. The driver didn't bother to turn off the engine or the lights, and its red stabs mixed in the night with the flashing blue coming from the police cruisers and the lone white beam of Savik's camera, making the scene resemble an ad hoc outdoor disco. Given the altered states of some in the crowd, Durban wouldn't have been surprised to see them start dancing. When the ambulance had finally stopped and the paramedics jumped out, Durban turned back to the young policeman. He took one look at her and pulled her under the police tape.

"My god! What happened to your eye?" he asked, his face almost a comical mask of concern.

She realized that she had been given an opportunity. Through her pain and annoyance, she decided to take it.

"Someone elbowed me a while ago. It hurts really bad. Does it look bad?"

His eyes opened wider.

"Lord, yes. It looks awful. Come here."

He led her past the edge of the crowd to a stoop at the building next door to the one the paramedics entered. The police had roped off the buildings on either side of the one they were interested in, just to give themselves room to work. She sat down on one of the brick steps and hugged her knees to ward off a sudden chill.

"You sit here and we'll get one of the paramedics to look at you in a minute."

"Won't they be busy with the woman in there?"

He frowned and shook his head.

"Not for long, they won't. She's not in a recoverable condition, you might say."

"Pretty bad shape, huh?" She dabbed at her bloodshot eye as she spoke, just to keep up the charade. The hair had actually come unglued while he had maneuvered her to the stoop, and her eye felt much better. She didn't have much time to get her information. In another couple of minutes her baby blue would be back to normal and the ruse would be over.

"Worst I've ever seen, and I used to ride highway patrol," he said. "I've seen some people come out of twelve-car pileups in better shape than the woman in there."

"I thought it was just a robbery attempt," she said, going on early police speculation Savik had gleaned from the scanner.

"If it was, they were stealing internal organs," the cop said, smiling at his own joke before he realized how gruesome it was.

One of the other cops barked, and he turned and stood up.

"Stay put. I'll be back in a minute," he said, and she dabbed at her eye and nodded.

He entered into a parley with some of the other policemen and one of the paramedics, who apparently had agreed that the job inside was hopeless. Durban sat still, facing the crowd, straining to hear what was being said.

... working ... for the ...... telethon

16 Brett Davis

careful with the ...

... yick! slobber ...

The young policeman returned, interrupting her thoughts. Before he could say anything, before he could ask about her eye, which was now fine, she blurted out: "What was her name?"

Surprised, he said haltingly, "Uh, Wardon, I think, or Wardill. War something."

Well. So much for her interview in the morning.

"Say, how's your eye?" the cop asked, a trace of suspicion evident in his voice for the first time.

"It still hurts," she said, not looking up.

Then she heard a gruff voice and heard heavy footsteps crunching across the institute's lawn.

"Dickinson! Dickinson! Dickinson! What the hell are you doing with that woman? Don't you ever watch TV? Don't you know who she is? Get her out of here!"

It was a grizzled older cop, but apparently one who kept up with Hollywood gossip. The young policeman flinched as if he were being shot every time his name was called. She suddenly felt sorry for him.

"I'm sorry, sir," he stammered. "Sir, her eye was—"

"I don't care if it was hanging out of its socket! You shouldn't have let her through here! What have you told her?"

"Just the name, uh, of the victim . . . not much, really. . . ."

The young cop looked as if he was about to cry. Durban rested her forehead on her knuckles, but then snapped her head up when the older police officer barked at her.

"And you! I ought to take you in! You know that you—"

He interrupted himself in mid-rant when he saw that she wasn't looking at him. She was looking past his hip, watching as the paramedics went back to the ambulance and returned with thick white gloves on their hands, gloves that looked more like casts used to set broken arms. The crowd couldn't see the gloves, which the paramedics held close to their stomachs. From her privileged perch, however, she could make them out easily.

She squinted at them in confusion for a second. Oven mitts? Then she knew what they were. She had never seen them in person before, but she knew what they were. They were used to protect against the transmission of werewolf saliva, believed to be the means of the disease's transmission. They were used to handle the bodies of werewolf victims.

The older policeman watched as the paramedics entered the institute, still hiding the gloves by hunching over as if they had all eaten something rotten and had stomachaches. When they were inside, he walked directly in front of her and looked down.

"Are you happy now?" he said over the racket from the crowd behind him, his voice sounding raspy from the strain.

"Do we have a werewolf loose?" she asked, rising slowly to her feet.

The younger police officer was looking closely at her face, looking for a trace of the injured eye that had seemed so bad before.

"Are you happy now?" the cop repeated, but she stared him down.

"Do we have a werewolf loose?"

The older policeman sighed and shook his head.

"We have lots of werewolves loose, miss. We feel

bad for them in their condition. That's why we're trying to cure them."

"But now a researcher for the werewolf vaccine has been killed by a werewolf herself."

She had hoped that he would cave in before her fearless questioning and tell her the whole long story, like cops always did in TV shows. The look on his face said that wasn't going to happen.

"Miss, the doctor involved looks like she has been run through a meat grinder. You yourself have seen paramedics entering the building wearing gloves to ward off werewolf spit. Now, clearly something has happened in here, but you draw conclusions at your own peril. And you cannot attribute any of this to me."

"Or me," the younger cop chimed in, but it only earned him a grim look from his more experienced colleague.

More cars had pulled up now on the other side of the crowd. More media lights had added their eerie glow to the darkness, too, but Ashly Durban knew that none of them could see what she had seen.

"I think you have your little scoop, miss, so why don't you move along? You want anything else, get it through headquarters."

"Thanks for your help," she whispered to the young cop as she passed, but he stood still as a statue on the Landon Institute lawn as the crowd outside the police tape continued to grow.

THREE

He was obviously terrified, this cleancut young man in the dirty black and white soccer shirt. He had been walking home from practice, along a little-frequented urban pathway, when suddenly he found his progress blocked by a snarling, hunched-over werewolf, clad only in ragged blue jeans. The wolf creature was wiry, even skinny, but everyone knew that werewolves could be much stronger than they looked.

At first the young man tossed down his gym bag and adopted a karate stance, right arm protecting his left ribs, left arm waving lazily in the air like a cobra ready to strike. Werewolves were just animals of a sort, and sometimes they could be bluffed. It didn't work this time. The werewolf merely snarled and lashed out with its claws and the soccer player's left arm suddenly gushed what looked like buckets of blood. The soccer player shouted in fright and quickly abandoned the fight. He looked desperately for somewhere to run, jerking his head to the right and the left.

He was at the opening to an alley between two buildings, and above him hung a skeletal fire escape. Its lowest rung was several feet above his head, further than he should have been able to jump, but fear lent urgency to his legs and he managed to catch on to one of the metal rungs despite the fact that his left arm was still dripping blood at a furious rate. He kicked his feet at the advancing werewolf and tried to pull his whole body onto the fire escape, but it was too late. The werewolf was upon him. As he dangled there like a rack of ribs, the wolf creature started slashing. Buckets of blood and guts splattered the alley. The werewolf, its mind completely gone in a blood fury, let loose with a chilling howl.

"Jesus, somebody get over here!" the soccer player suddenly shouted. "He's cutting through the blood packs!"

A man wearing thick black gloves with silver studs appeared and shoved the werewolf three times. The werewolf snarled but backed off, and then stood panting quietly. The eerie blue light that had suffused the alley faded and was replaced with the dim flickering glow of fluorescent tubes, which sputtered from the low ceiling of what was now revealed to be a small warehouse. The alley entrance wasn't an alley at all, merely two slabs of a fake brick wall pushed close together in one corner. The fire escape was a ladder, painted black and wired to the ceiling. Two men with large floor cameras slowly wheeled back from the scene and a thickset man holding a boom microphone wiped sweat from his forehead and leaned the mike against one of the fake brick panels.

"All right, let's take a break," shouted a tall, thin

man who was sitting twenty feet away on a ratty-looking stool that was raised up so far it resembled a child's highchair. He walked up to the soccer player who stood, hands on hips, in what appeared to be a pile of his own intestines.

"I wish you could have gone two more seconds," the tall man said. "I wanted to get that whole thing in one shot with camera one."

The soccer player did not look happy. He grimaced in the direction of the werewolf.

"Well, you'll just have to do an *edit*, Steve. I know you hate that. But I'm not getting paid enough to let Spot over there rip my guts out for real."

Steve patted the soccer player on the shoulder.

"All right. I'm sorry."

"And that fire escape is too damn high! What do I look like, Superman? I can barely get up there."

"All right, all right. We're done with that anyway, don't worry about it."

The soccer player started to stalk off, but the director grabbed him by the arm.

"Hold on one second. Hey, Mack! Come here."

The man who had been holding the boom microphone reluctantly left his leaning spot and walked over. The director held up the soccer player's left arm and shook it a couple of times, sending blood flying. The director apparently didn't mind getting it on his tan knit shirt, which was already stained with various unidentified substances.

"Mack, did you fill the blood pack on this arm?"

The heavyset man nodded slowly.

"Did you see how much blood came out of it when wolfie boy tore it open?"

The man nodded again.

"Did you think to yourself, that sure is a lot of blood to be coming out of an *arm*? Did you think that?"

This time the man shook his head, but even as he did so he seemed to realize that this was the wrong answer.

"You didn't think that was too much blood?" Steve said, leaning his head forward into the heavyset man's face. "Mack, when you cut someone on their forearm, they simply *do not* release *gallons* of blood! They don't! You don't have to go to med school to know that!"

The man nodded sheepishly.

"Yes, sir."

"It's okay for now, but don't let it happen again. Use your head. The packs are marked. If you see one that says, say, 'arm,' then don't put so much in it. If it says 'head' or 'stomach,' then knock yourself out, put as much in as you want. Got it?"

"Got it," the man said quietly.

"Good. You screw up again, maybe we'll get our little werewolf friend to show you where people bleed and where they don't."

The man nodded and smiled, but his face was ashen.

In the meantime, the werewolf in question had stumbled over to a small cot that was set up along the side of the real warehouse wall, behind the fake ones. The man with black leather gloves accompanied him, keeping a keen eye on his movements, the silver-studded gloves held at the ready. Silver had no effect on werewolves, which was one area in which the old movies were wrong. Still, the makers of werewolf exploitation films figured they could use all the help they could get, and several pairs of specially studded gloves were usually on hand for any film. They weren't needed for this particular werewolf right now. He looked like a gust of wind could have knocked him over. He collapsed on the cot with a sigh, and the hair on his body slowly started to fade away, revealing what came more and more to resemble human skin, until finally he was just a pale, skinny kid with long, matted black hair.

"You all right?" the man with the leather gloves asked.

"Yeah," the former werewolf said weakly. He put one thin arm over his eyes.

"You want your shirt? It's a little cold in here."

"Yeah."

"Raise up your arms."

The man pulled a wadded-up black t-shirt off the edge of the cot and pulled it over the skinny youth's head. It was like dressing a mannequin. The man had to pull the kid's arms down when he was done.

"Well, rest up, Bobby. We'll need you again in about fifteen minutes."

"Okay."

Bobby Chaney closed his eyes and started to drift off to sleep when he noticed that an annoying sound was being piped into his ear. He propped himself up on one arm and looked around. A small black and white TV was on the floor. The sound coming from it was not loud enough to let him make out the words, but just audible enough to be irritating, like the whine of a mosquito. He slowly flopped around until he was on his stomach, and then reached out to turn the set off. Then he paused and squinted at the screen.

The face of the news anchor had suddenly been replaced by the photograph of a woman who looked vaguely familiar. It was a woman in her mid-thirties, wearing glasses, her hair pulled up into a severe bun.

Her hair was white on the small screen of the cheap TV, but he knew in life it was blonde. He squinted at the face, but couldn't remember where he had seen it. It was always so hard to concentrate right after making the change. What were they saying about her? He turned up the volume, but he was too late. The anchor was back, and the news was over.

"This is Ashly Durban, with a special report for Channel 12. Stay with NBC for all the latest news and entertainment."

Bobby turned off the TV and rolled onto his back. He put his arm back over his eyes and drifted off to an uneasy sleep. It was his usual dream, one he must have picked up from an old movie. A tidal wave smashed into a pier, sending wood planks flying. The ocean seemed to writhe with anger. He could almost feel himself rocking with its furious waves. Then he realized he *was* rocking; the man with the black leather gloves had returned and was poking him, saying he was needed. His master's voice.

"Don't poke me so hard with those things next time," Bobby said as he slowly groaned his way to a seated position on the cot. "I was all there. You could have just yelled at me."

The man smiled.

"You kiddin', slugger?" He smiled, revealing a couple of holes where teeth were supposed to be, and gave Bobby a playful nudge on the shoulder. "You were an animal out there. Thought we were going to have to bring out a cannon to take you down. You looked like you were ready to turn that soccer player into spaghetti. Not that it would be such a great loss."

Bobby smiled weakly back.

"I'll try to go easy on whoever's next."

The man put one arm around his small, sloped shoulders, being careful not to touch him with one of the studs.

"Come on. They only need you for one more scene, and then tomorrow you can rest up."

They trudged back to where the alley had once stood. In its place now was a cheap facsimile of a high school cafeteria, with two tables with folding metal legs backed by a fake lunch counter. The heavyset man who had been holding the boom microphone was now costumed as a female lunch room attendant, complete with a stringy wig descending from a shapeless white hat and small pillows stuffed up in the top of his smock. A thick coat of tan makeup failed to completely hide his moustache, and as Bobby took his place the man was sneezing repeatedly as the powder went up his nose.

Steve the director was slouching again on his stool, running one hand through his long, thinning, hair.

"How we making it, slugger?" he asked Bobby.

"Good."

"What's that in *Spanish*, Bobby?"

"Buenos. Bueno. Goodo, whatever. Let's do this."

"I'm glad everyone working on this movie has such a good attitude," Steve said with uncharacteristic sarcasm. He gave Bobby a cursory pat on the shoulder, one hard enough to sting. "Fine art takes time, my friend. Don't rush things. And I wish you would brush up on your Spanish once in a while."

Bobby curled his upper lip, a reflex action that he knew made him look even younger than he was. This time he couldn't help it. He was too tired for restraint.

"So dub me if I mess up."

"I will. I *have* to. And it costs me money each time."

Steve snapped the crew to attention. Someone else

was handling the boom mike now, someone new who hadn't screwed up the blood packs and therefore didn't need to be punished. Bobby was always amazed at the people who could be found to work crew on these things. There never seemed to be any extraneous people hanging around the warehouse, but the turnover among the help was almost constant and there was never a shortage of semi-capable hands.

Bobby was guided to his place on the set by the man with the black gloves, who then stepped out of camera range but remained nearby. Bobby was supposed to stand between the lunch matron and two other high school students, but he wasn't sure why; they hadn't shown him that part of the script yet. They wanted to get as much of the wolf stuff as they could out of the way before they bothered with plot or characterization, the two things that were the least valued features in this sort of movie.

Bobby was the only person who could pass for an actual high school student in the movie, or at least in the parts he had seen filmed so far. The two cheerleaders who were his co-stars in this scene were played by women who were at least thirty, and whose faces were so caked with tan makeup that they looked like dull clowns. They were most likely refugees from the porno mill that took up the other half of the warehouse. One of them smacked her gum like a horse, and neither one even glanced at Bobby.

"All right, you know the words, let's hit it," Steve said, with a moist clap of his sweaty hands.

Bobby pretended to enter the lunchroom from the left, shuffling with all the dignity of Stepin Fetchit.

"Buenos dias, senoritas," he said to the powdered cheerleaders. He knew a few words of Spanish, so they tried to write his parts to feature them. The harder stuff would be dubbed, often by two or three different people, so Bobby's voice frequently changed several times in the course of one movie. "Como esta?"

"CUT!" Steve shouted. "Damn it, that boy's face is shining like the full moon up there, pardon the pun. Johnny, I thought you were supposed to put some makeup on him! We're not shooting a zombie movie here. I want him to look like a high school student!"

A thin man who Bobby had never seen before scampered onto the set, wielding a crumpled makeup pad. He approached so forcefully that Bobby flinched involuntarily, but it was too late and Bobby's face was soon enveloped in a cloud of tan dust that made him sneeze five times in sharp succession.

"I know how ya feel, kid," said the forced transvestite behind the fake lunch counter.

"You ready?" Steve shouted.

Bobby waved some of the dust away and nodded, capping the nod with a sneeze. He started the scene again, and this time got through his meager lines without incident. After he finished speaking, the "girls" gave him what were supposed to be innocent flirtatious glances, but which more closely resembled the predatory stares of experienced pornographic actresses. They then began chatting, but Bobby couldn't make out what they said, and it was probably just as well. He had been told that this scene was supposed to be at night, before a big high school dance, although why such a scene would be set in a cafeteria was anyone's guess. He didn't have time to wonder about it, though, because Steve gave the signal, and suddenly an eerie blue light hit Bobby full in the face. It was time. He was on.

He twitched, jerked, took two stuttering steps back and leaned on the counter. His face was shaking with sudden spasms, but he could see through slitted eyes that the porn queens had moved away from him, had slid to the edge of camera range and were looking back in horror that was supposed to be mock but might very well be real. He could feel the hair coming out of him, pushing at his clothes, sliding through his skin, coming on as quickly and inexorably as an erection, growing with that strange rushing of blood that almost rendered him deaf to the world. His jaw clenched as his elongated teeth started to push their way down, and the top of his head felt tight as his new long ears reached for the sky.

The strange silent peacefulness was coming over him. His body continued to twitch, but Bobby's mind was slipping away, sliding under mental sheets, going to sleep.

"The sounds, Bobby! Make the sounds!" Steve shouted through cupped hands. Bobby could barely make him out through the light and through the noise, but there he was, shouting words of guidance like some annoying guardian angel.

Bobby had almost forgotten. Turning into a werewolf was actually a peaceful, silent affair, but the moviegoing public was largely not aware of that because the truth was not interesting to watch. To please the demands of the marketplace the directors of werewolf exploitation movies had therefore decided that here, too, they would still go by the form dictated by the older movies: turning into a wolflike creature had to look painful.

Bobby began moaning and snarling. He hoisted up his furry right arm and looked at it as if in disbelief, more hokum from the old movies. When he had reached a stage of appropriate hairiness he threw back his head and let loose with a chilling howl, one that prompted the porn queens and the faux lunch matron to get out of camera range for real.

Suddenly there was a lot of shouting behind the blue light. Bobby stopped howling and squinted back to where Steve was shouting at someone else, waving his stick arms around like a heron trying to take flight.

"Dammit, Sal, it's a werewolf movie! We've got to make noise!"

This happened on a fairly regular basis. Sal the pornographer, who shot his quickies directly onto video on the other side of the warehouse, had come over to complain about the noise. Bobby's eyesight was keener as a werewolf, and he could see that two naked women were lying on a mattress at the other end of the building, looking over expectantly to where Sal was arguing with Steve. The two women who were playing cheerleaders in the werewolf flick trotted over to talk to them.

"Just dub in their moans, you idiot!" Steve was shouting. "My boy can't fake his howls, not like your girls can!"

"It's not the dubbing I'm worried about!" Sal shouted back.

He was the opposite of Steve. Where Steve was tall and gangly, with long, thinning hair, he was short and stocky with no hair whatsoever. He wore tortoise-shell glasses that might have made him look distinguished if they weren't ill-fitting and didn't spend so much time perched precariously at the end of his stubby nose.

"I've got to play some mood music for my girls, and they can't hear it for Fido over here!" Sal shouted.

"Those sluts don't need mood music, Sal. They could do it on the runway at McCarran. Don't come over here interrupting my art for your sleaze all the time!"

There was more, but Bobby wasn't listening. Ordinarily, the blue light wasn't kept on him for more than two minutes at a time. This time there must have been a new person operating it because it was still hitting Bobby full force while Steve was involved in his latest altercation with Sal. It was still working, and he was still changing. He couldn't concentrate anymore. He was slipping away, and something else was taking over.

"Turn the blue light off!" he heard the man with black gloves shout, but it was too late.

Bobby was gone. He was an animal. With a muscular snarl, he twitched his powerful legs and launched himself over the fake lunch tables, overturning one of them with a crash in the process. He flew over the crew and landed on the unfortunate Sal, who watched his descent in sheer terror, his mouth opened like a bottomless pit. The snarling beast that was once Bobby knocked Sal to the ground, sending his glasses flying, and burrowed sharp finger claws into the soft flesh under Sal's ribs. Sal was trying to scream, it seemed, but the creature that once was Bobby couldn't hear him. This beast was interested only in the fleshy tube of Sal's throat.

Just before it was to taste that throat, it realized it had made an error in judgement. It had let the urge to feed come on too strongly. It had attacked too quickly, without getting potential enemies out of the way. This thought occurred to the beast after the man with the black gloves walked up behind it and smacked it so hard on the side of the head that it rolled half a dozen feet away from the wheezing Sal. Before the werewolf had a chance to respond in kind, the man with the gloves walked over and smacked it again, delivering another blow to the head that left the creature coughing on the floor.

The man with the gloves knelt down next to the werewolf, which now resembled a large, sick dog dressed in human clothes.

"Sorry, kid," he said, before brutally punching the werewolf's forehead.

The next howl that went up in the warehouse was a howl of pain. The creature rolled slowly to its hands and knees, coughing small spatters of pink foam on the bare concrete floor. It wasn't quite so hairy now. Its hair became less shaggy, more stringy. Its clawed fingers, which had so recently been exploring Sal's interior, now just looked like the thin, dirty digits of a teenager. Bobby looked around and gave a weak cough. He was back.

"What happened?" he asked softly.

The man with the gloves leaned into his face and held out the gloves for inspection. There were spots of blood on the silver bumps, small clumps of hair stuck to the knuckles.

"Told you you were getting a little rough out there, slugger. I thought I was going to have to take you down for real."

Bobby looked across the floor, to where the rest of the crew was gathered around Sal. Even the two naked women had left their mattress to come over to look. They stood like gangly birds, impulsively brushing their long blonde hair out of their eyes so they could see better.

Sal wasn't doing so well. He looked like someone

had fitted him with too many blood packs, except Bobby
had the sickening feeling that the blood that covered
Sal's stomach was for real. He was twitching, and pink
foam was coming out of his mouth. The crew for both
the werewolf movie and the porn flick gathered around,
perhaps a dozen in all, but no one seemed to know
what to do. Steve bent over Sal, running his hands
across his tormentor's bald head, gibbering words of
comfort that Bobby couldn't make out and which didn't
seem to be helping all that much. The two cheerleaders
sniffled. The man with the black gloves looked over
at Sal, shook his head, and muttered, "Jesus."

   Bobby rested his aching head on the cool concrete
floor and blinked out tears.

FOUR

Carl Johnson flicked across the TV channels. Nothing put him to sleep faster than late night broadcasting, with its parade of infomercials and boring talk shows. The Henry Hull show was just going off on Fox. The host waved goodbye to the cameras as the credits rolled, then turned to make small talk with some virtually unknown guest he had managed to convince to come on. The papers said the Henry Hull show was not long for the airwaves, but Johnson did not care. It would just be replaced with something worse.

He flicked over to CBS, which had photos of the latest carnage from Eastern Europe. ABC had a long shot of a woman watering her plants. Johnson didn't have the sound turned up, so he couldn't tell if it was supposed to be a comedy or a drama.

Johnson was smoking like a fiend and wearing his old green medical scrub suit from his days at George Washington University hospital, and actually looked about the same as he used to then, when he was pulling

long shifts in the knife-and-gun club emergency room
and a cigarette was about the only thing that would
perk him up. He had actually stopped smoking years
ago, but after he left the Landon Institute and the
exhausted Dr. Wardoe he had stopped off at the Zippy
Mart to get two packs for old time's sake. Dying of
cancer was the least of his worries these days. He
popped another one in his mouth and sucked the smoke
down like gaseous candy. Its corpse soon joined the
others in the cheery frog-and-lilypad ashtray, also newly
bought for the occasion.

He flicked to NBC, which was rerunning its earlier
version of *Live Entertainment*. That damn thing seemed
to be on all the time now. He would have preferred
an infomercial. Johnson's thumb was poised above the
channel button when suddenly the show disappeared
and a blonde woman appeared on screen, speaking
breathlessly. The TV then showed a rather glamorous
picture of his boss. He hit the volume button instead.

"This is Ashly Durban reporting, live from Channel
12, your NBC news affiliate in Las Vegas. Dr. Cynthia
Wardoe has just been found dead at the Landon
Institute. I was an eyewitness to the scene and can
report to you that she appears to have been killed by
a werewolf. The Landon Insti—"

She was still talking but he hurled himself out of
bed and ran for the living room, fear making his lungs
fight against the cigarettes he had inhaled. He had
the fax machine pre-programmed, so all he had to do
was hit the button. The pages were in there, ready to
go. He heard the burst of salutory static from the fax,
and also heard a noise from outside. He was getting
sloppy; he had put his pistol down somewhere and
now couldn't see it. He spotted it just as a hairy paw

knocked the front door of his house halfway off its hinges. There was a deadbolt and a chain on the door, but they didn't seem to matter. The paw ripped through the chain as easily as if it were golden licorice. Johnson's loaded pistol was on an end table on the other side of the couch. It might as well be on an end table on Mars. He sucked in a lungful of air and made a dive for it, cracking his chin on the couch's arm, but the beast reached it first and batted it out of the way, table and all.

"Where are they?" the werewolf said thickly.

He was a big one, with a huge chest and arms and thick, shiny gray hair. Johnson didn't recognize him. Not one of the Landon Institute patients, that was for sure. None of them could move that fast, and none of them were that strong.

"The cigarettes? They're back in the bedroom," Johnson said, gasping.

That was clearly not the answer the man-beast was seeking. The werewolf appeared to want to say something else, perhaps engage in some snappy repartee, but its mouth wasn't up to the task so it just snarled in frustration and waved its claws menacingly in his face. Johnson smiled and tried to look ignorant, but all the while his left arm crept toward some of the junk that had been on the table the werewolf upended. Among the detritus was a letter opener a friend had sent him from Senegal. It was small and finely formed, with delicate African carvings on the hilt and lower part of the blade. It was also sharp.

The werewolf leaned its snout in close to his face, so close its whiskers brushed his stubble. Its breath was hot and far from minty fresh.

"Where are—"

Johnson sat up and raked the werewolf across the face with the letter opener, aiming for the eyes. He missed, instead cutting a channel across the bridge of the werewolf's nose. Blood spurted from the wound and the werewolf howled with rage and pain. It raised a handful of claws to retaliate.

Then the fax issued a grinding noise and the paper started to go through. The werewolf's head snapped around. It dashed to the machine, where the top of the first page was just coming out the other side. Dripping blood from the werewolf's deep cut made interesting patterns on the paper. The enraged creature put a stop to the transmission with the thrust of a hairy hand, turning the fax into a collection of random chunks of plastic and metal. It snatched up the paper and squinted down at its mangled, bloody prize. The first page was a list of names, typed double spaced and alphabetized. Through pain-filled eyes, the werewolf was able to read the first name: Bobby Chaney. An address followed, also neatly typed.

With the werewolf suitably diverted, Johnson made a run for the door. He made slightly less noise than a rampaging elephant, and the werewolf heard him. Johnson didn't make it.

FIVE

"I take my medicine. I haven't changed into a full werewolf in fifteen years. When the moon comes out full, I usually am just lying on the floor, sick. My husband knows how to help treat it, he puts a blanket down for me and tries to keep me cool. Then, when the moon's not full, I'm okay. Sometimes when the moon is waxing I feel a little sick and get a little hairy, but then usually I just take a few of my pills again and I feel all right, kind of sleepy. But I want to tell you that because I am a werewolf, I am discriminated against. I am no different than anyone who occasionally gets a little sick, but I am discriminated against."

The woman's voice was shaky, but a steely edge of strength was shining through. She was in her mid-sixties and her face was wrinkled, but her brown eyes locked firmly on the camera, stared firmly out through the TV screen and into the placid eyes of Bobby Chaney. The TV reporter's voice was steely, too, steely and without a hint of wavering. It hit the high notes and the low notes as surely as if it was a musical instrument,

37

and spoke above the video face of the old woman like the voice of a god.

"Denise Flanderman says she has been trying to buy a house in the historic district of Las Vegas for three years now. She has the money, and she is willing to live within the guidelines that have been established by the Historical Society. And yet she has been turned down repeatedly. She says it is because she is a werewolf."

"They are afraid I will turn into a beast and rip the house apart," the woman said. "I have had one member of the historical board tell me that to my face."

The next face was of a painfully pale woman with glasses so enormous that it looked like they had been handed down to her from Elton John.

"I am familiar with Mrs. Flanderman's claims, and they are without merit," the woman said, her voice robotic. She looked at the camera nervously as if it, too, might turn into a werewolf and attack her. "In the time period in which she has been looking, no houses in her price range from the historical district have appeared on the market."

The reporter's voice resumed speaking from the heavens, over shots of three massive houses.

"But that's not true. *Live Entertainment* checked the records of Clark County, and discovered that five houses were up for sale in the past few years. Mrs. Flanderman made bids on three of them, and all three bids were turned down. We made a further check and discovered that in two of the cases, the bids that were accepted were lower than what Mrs. Flanderman offered."

The old woman was back, her brown eyes open wide and firm.

"It's not right. I caught lycanthropy twenty years ago while I was on vacation overseas. I have been treating it for years, and I haven't hurt anybody in a long time. I am not an irresponsible person. When the cure goes on the market, I will take it and gladly be rid of my disease."

"A cure is expected soon, and, for the first time in the history of medicine in America, it will be paid for through the proceeds of a telethon. That's the Telephone Drive to Cure Lycanthropy, hosted by Monty Allen, airing on Channel 12 here on NBC, the major networks and several cable channels on Friday. Mrs. Flanderman says that when she is cured, she will try once again to buy a house in the historic district."

"It won't make any difference," said the woman with moon-sized glasses. "It has not made any difference yet."

You could tell the reporter thought she was lying.

"This is Ashly Durban reporting. NBC Nightly News is next, and tune in tomorrow for another installment of 'Living with Lycanthropy,' right here on *Live Entertainment*, coming to you this week from beautiful Las Vegas, Nevada."

The tall woman with the bad lipstick came out to the waiting room and turned the TV volume down so Bobby couldn't hear it anymore. He had been watching the TV because all the magazines were old, and anyway he had read them all the first time he had waited out here. He had been watching it loud to drown out the noise; the Jean Grenier Society was outside, staging another protest.

There were half a dozen young men, barely older than him, in their usual uniform of gray suits and

maroon loafers, tossing their long hair, waving placards
and shouting slogans in front of the warehouse. The
Jean Grenier Society was devoted to werewolf pride,
and its members had come to Las Vegas to protest
the Werewolf Telethon and other things they found
offensive, including the cheapie lycanthropy videos
shot in the warehouse. Bobby could see one of the
protest signs from the grimy window: WEREWOLF MOVIES
BITE, BUT THE COPS DON'T CARE. That, Bobby would
readily admit, was true.

"Steve said come in," the woman said, and the thin
youth gave her a shy smile. She didn't smile back.

He slowly walked past her and went into the inner
office. He had sacked out not long after they took Sal
away to the hospital. Despite his revulsion at what he
had done, he was so exhausted he had slept for nearly
the entire day. The crew was gone when he woke up,
so he had waited in the front office for Steve to return.
He wasn't looking forward to facing him.

"Hey, glad to see those Gren-yahoos out there didn't
scare you off," Steve said, waving him to a seat. "What
a buncha whiners. I'm glad you stuck around. You know,
you really gave us a scare there last night, Bobby. You
damn near turned Sal into a pile of lasagna."

Bobby tried to say "I'm sorry," but all that came
out was a wheeze.

Steve the director conducted business from an office
that looked like it had been stolen from the set of a
stage play. It was paneled in fake dark wood so
haphazardly assembled that several long gaps were
visible, showing skinny bent nails, as if the room had
undergone an operation and its scars were still healing.
There were three plants, waist-sized miniature trees
that were in various early stages of death. The yellow

tips of their leaves were the only spots of bright color in the room.

Steve looked at Bobby across a plastic desktop that was covered in wallpaper to make it look like woodgrain. Its fake woodgrain did not quite match the fake woodgrain of the walls.

"Are you going to call the police?" Bobby asked in a quiet voice, and Steve frowned.

"Why should I? Sal isn't dead. You did quite a job on him, though, I must admit. Those werewolf fingers are stronger than I thought. Sal lost a kidney and his liver is damaged."

Bobby winced and looked down at his fingers, which were now pink and hairless and harmless and intertwined, twitching nervously.

"The kidney is not that big a deal. Fortunately, he's got a spare. For a heavy drinker like Sal, though, losing the liver is a big problem," Steve said, and it wasn't until he laughed that Bobby realized the statement was intended to be humorous. "He's going to need a new one. I, personally, don't have the money. I wish I did. It would be spare livers all around, for everyone."

Bobby looked up, his eyes showing flashes of fear.

"I don't have the money, either. I don't have any money."

"Don't you have the money we paid you up front?"

Bobby frowned, and looked back down at his fingers.

"I . . . have some of it. I spent some of it."

"Look, that's okay. I wasn't asking you to buy Sal's liver. I personally don't care whether he can drink again or not, but he does need a new one. An agreement has been reached with his people. My film company will pay for the liver, but we have to finish this movie in order to do that. My distributor is all ready to ship this one to Mexico, and we're going to try for the Argentine market as well for the first time. I hear this stuff is getting pretty hot down there. This werewolf cure business that Monty Allen has going may screw our business up pretty soon, but right now werewolves are *happening*. Everyone is thinking about werewolves, talking about werewolves, all over the world, Bobby. There is money to be made, but we have to make it *now*. We have to finish the movie. I still need you to work. We've just got to control you better."

Bobby stared at Steve. From under his waterfall of stringy brown hair, Steve looked like a prehistoric predatory bird coming to claim his prey.

"You're not firing me?"

Steve fluttered his stick arms.

"*Fire* you? No! I need you! I need you now more than ever! Did you think I would call you here to fire you?"

"I *wanted* you to fire me."

There was a long, awkward pause. Steve's eyes opened wide, the predatory bird backed away in surprise.

"Why? Those Greniers didn't get to you after all with all that werewolf pride shit, did they?"

Bobby shook his head, and watched his fingers twine and twist nervously around each other like oversized worms.

"No, it's just . . . I thought . . . I thought if you fired me, I could get unemployment for a while."

What followed next from Steve was a complicated series of reactions, starting with quick barking laughs that trailed off into wheezes that stopped altogether when Steve the director realized that Bobby the werewolf was serious.

"Bobby, it doesn't work that way. You get unemployment if you get laid off, like your job doesn't exist anymore. Not if you get *fired*. If the government paid everyone who got fired, everybody would intentionally screw around and get fired and nobody would be working."

Bobby opened his mouth. He was trying to speak but the words were jostling for position on the tip of his tongue and consequently none of them escaped.

"Listen, Bobby, don't worry so much about what happened in there with Sal. You didn't do anything wrong. We left the light on you too long. That idiot Sal came over and distracted everybody is all, but you can bet he won't be doing that again anytime soon."

"But," Bobby managed to say before Steve's bark cut him off.

"We left the light on you too long, is all. We won't do that again, Sal or no Sal. In fact, from now on we'll cut the time in half. One minute with the light after you've changed, tops. Deal?"

Bobby watched his fingers some more, and then was surprised to hear himself say, "No."

He wanted to be like the woman trying to buy a big nice house. He wanted to be able to say he hadn't made the full changeover in fifteen years. He wanted to say that.

"I can't do it anymore," is what he did say. "It's too hard."

Steve waved his stick arms around again, a giant marionette losing control of its limbs.

"Kid! Kid! You're a natural out there! Look, I've seen some werewolf guys who change and then just stand there, like big hairy knots on a log. But you, you get out there and you've got the whole facial expression thing going and you take direction well, it's like you're born for video. The kids down in Mexico love your stuff!"

Bobby could barely see Steve now, because he was shaking his head quickly and the hair was flying back and forth, blocking his view.

"I can't anymore. I'm sorry. I . . . want you to fire me, you know, even if I don't get the money. I can't anymore."

Steve was around the desk quicker than Bobby would have thought possible, those long arms coming at him like tentacles.

"Kid, you don't understand something here. *I need you*. I have to pay for that liver that you punched a few holes in. I don't know if you checked the prices of usable livers these days, but they cost a little more at the hospital than they do at the meat counter."

He was shaking Bobby now, his thin face shoved up so close that Bobby could see the muscles twitching under the sallow skin.

"Look, Sal has some guys that could make a *lot* of trouble for me if he doesn't get his bright shiny new liver. I am not eager to see Hoover Dam from the bottom up while wearing heavy shoes, if you get my drift. And don't think they'll be nice to you, either. They can make things very rough. Let's stick together. You help me, I'll help you. Don't bug out on me now."

He was shaking Bobby still, and Bobby's stringy brown hair had fallen to the point that he really couldn't see anything. His universe was reduced to only the two contact points where Steve's clawlike hands were clamped on his shoulders, and after five seconds Bobby twitched in his chair, twitched and shoved Steve away and shot to his feet.

"I can't do it! I told you!"

Steve advanced on him and Bobby took a wild swing with one skinny arm. He was surprised when it connected. Steve stumbled against his desk, and Bobby turned and started to race from the room. Steve recovered quicker than Bobby had expected, but all he had time for was a poor attempt at a flying football tackle.

"Don't go, kid!" Steve shouted through great heaving breaths. "Please! You owe me!"

Bobby was down on one knee, but unfortunately for Steve he still had one sneaker-clad foot free. The sole of the sneaker was quickly made acquainted with Steve's red face, and Steve the director lost his hold. Bobby started to shout at Steve again, but his lungs made the choice for him. He had to save his breath. It was time to go. He sped through the front office, leaving a startled secretary in his wake, and blasted through the front door into the night and into the knot of startled protesters.

"You want a sign, man?" one of them asked.

Bobby would have laughed at the incongruous headgear, but he didn't have time. Steve appeared at the front door, his face now so red it almost matched the baseball cap.

"Stop him!" he shouted to the two plainclothes security guards he kept stationed at the warehouse, partly to keep an eye out for the cops and partly to keep the protesters away.

The guards were lounging by the front door on metal folding chairs, reading dogeared copies of *Guns & Ammo*, listening to music on headphones to drown out the shouting. They exchanged glances until Steve yelled again, and then took out their earplugs to hear what he was saying.

"GET HIM!" Steve screamed, his face even redder than before.

The guards suddenly hopped up and trotted towards Bobby, their hands reaching ominously into their pockets. They were both skinny, grizzled biker guys wearing camouflage pants that appeared baggy enough to hold a variety of weapons. Either that, or they were turning off their Walkmans. Bobby decided not to find out which. The Jean Grenier Society members tried to form a knot around him to protect him, but he dropped to his knees and squeezed out between their legs. The protesters pushed at the guards with their placards, not realizing the person they were trying to save was rapidly scuttling away. Still, that bought him time. He darted to the left and cut in front of the self-storage building, then ducked back to the right and crossed through a Chik Fil-A parking lot. A huge pickup truck was just pulling out, its driver poking around in a takeout bag, and Bobby ran as fast as he could alongside it and then jumped on its broad silver bumper. The driver, lost in chicken aroma, didn't notice. Bobby looked back. There were a lot of agitated figures back there, but he couldn't tell anymore which ones were Jean Grenier and which ones were Steve's guards, and he didn't care. The wind in his hair felt like freedom.

SIX

It wasn't until she drew close to the fairly new Universal Monster Grand casino that Ashly Durban was able to make out what the crowd was chanting. They were ten deep along the front of the casino, with the thickest knot gathered under the fifty-foot-tall fiberglass Dracula that leered out over Glitter Gulch. The Dracula wasn't much to see in the daytime, at least by Vegas standards, but at night it was truly eerie— its eyes glowed blood red, its huge mouth opened and closed revealing yellow neon fangs, and every quarter hour its fingernails emitted a web of blue sparks. Dracula wasn't the reason for the crowd that had gathered this Tuesday morning, however, as Durban realized when Savik threw the car into park in an illegal spot on Emerson Avenue.

"Monty Allen is unfair to werewolves!" some of the people shouted, as they waved placards bearing various messages, several of them misspelled. WE'RE NOT WEREWOLVES OF LONDON, WE ARE REGALAR PEOPLE, one proclaimed in letters so big that Durban could

47

read it from the other side of the Las Vegas strip.

She wondered why they weren't gathered under the thirty-five-foot-tall fiberglass werewolf that snarled over Sands Avenue, but then realized that it was out of commission, with scaffolding covering its toothy face and a sign around its furry feet warning of dangerous high voltage wires.

Savik slammed the door so violently that the rental car shook, and shouldered his camera like it was a heavy bird of prey. He had dressed down for his new role as hotshot cop reporter; gone were the khakis and hideous blazer, replaced with a black Gap pocket T-shirt and what appeared to be checked surfer pants. Durban was still attired as if she had a grown-up job. The scoop on Cynthia Wardoe's werewolf killer had simultaneously upped her journalistic profile and created more work than she would have liked. She and Savik were now on temporary loan to the NBC Nightly News and were also doing spot news work for Channel 12, the local NBC affiliate. That was plenty, but they were still expected to grind out episodes of "Living with Lycanthropy" for *Live Entertainment*. They had several already in the can, with more to come. She hoped her ex-husband, a reporter at Channel 9, was watching; it would kill him to see her face so often.

"You sure you know how to work that thing?" Durban asked.

Savik had been given the best camera NBC Nightly News had to offer, which was much better than the cheapie *Live Entertainment* equipment. He flipped a couple of its switches like he knew what he was doing.

"It's not exactly brain surgery, dear."

He bounded across the street with the fearless zeal exhibited by a child with a new toy, oblivious to the traffic or to whether the light was red or green. A couple of tourists in a rented convertible honked and flipped him off for his trouble. Durban waited patiently for the light to turn green and then slowly crossed the strip. She didn't like crowds and was in no hurry.

Once on the other side, she saw that what she initially thought was one homogenous protest was actually more of a cluster of protests, as there seemed to be at least three factions operating in the crowd. She pushed her way through a thick knot of people gathered at the base of the Dracula statue, people who seemed to have a complicated series of complaints against the Universal Monster Grand. One young woman, dressed in a black cloth coat that was far too thick for what passed for winter in Vegas, got right up in her face and started shouting.

"You're that woman from on TV, aren't ya?" she shouted, and Durban nodded, against her better judgement. "Why don't you interview me? The vampire statue is much too big!"

"What?"

"The Dracula is too big! It's bigger than the werewolf! That's not fair!"

The woman had long, stringy hair the color of corn and wore enormous glasses that made her eyes look like veined saucers.

"So what?" chimed another woman from the crowd, who had heard the exchange and pushed her way over. She carried a sign that said VAMPIRES NEED HELP, TOO. "It's all exploitative."

"Well, we want to be exploited *evenly*," the woman said, her voice rising in pitch as her sentence continued.

"I'm a lycanthropy survivor and I'm proud. The werewolf should be much taller. Have you seen the Frankenstein statue on the other side of the building? It's eighty feet tall! *Eighty* feet! And the werewolf is less than forty! It should be three times as big."

"No, it shouldn't," the vampire supporter said. "What do you care? You're all going to be cured anyway. What about us? What about vampires?"

The lycanthropy survivor held her thin arms up to the heavens as if asking for patience.

"All you have is a little blood disease! You have that romantic mystique bullshit going for you. People think we're just animals. You have Bela Lugosi and Lestat and all we have are cheap werewolf exploitation movies. Even the Faeries and Elves and all that crowd are legalized these days, but we're still victims. So quit complaining!"

Durban tugged herself out of the conversation, which was getting worse because several of the woman's friends had come over and were shouting werewolf pride slogans at the suddenly outgunned vampire.

"Hey! Aren'cha going to interview us?" the lycanthropic woman shouted, but Durban shook her head furiously and yelled back that she was off duty.

She managed to swim through the crowd past the Dracula statue but was then caught between the other two groups that were swarming around outside the casino. Judging from the raggedy chants that got going every few seconds only to die away in the general din, she gathered that these groups also fostered disagreements among their members. EXPLOITATION IS STILL EXPLOITATION, said one placard that was shoved so close to Durban's face that she could clearly make out the grain of the plywood.

"Monty Allen makes his living off of us," shouted one young man, whose hair was so closely cut that it was almost too short for a skinhead. "We don't need sympathy, we need a cure!"

He quickly got into a shoving match with another young man, this one sporting enough hair for the both of them and two or three other people besides.

"We wouldn't have a cure without Monty Allen!" the shaggy-hair shouted, waving his own placard about menacingly.

Durban thought the two were about to swordfight, but other members of the crowd pulled them apart. She ducked as one of their signs passed over her head, and then she saw Savik, waving his camera above the crowd and motioning to her.

"Hurry up!" he shouted. "Get inside!"

Several members of the mob had advanced upon him, placards in hand, demanding to have their views disseminated by the media. Durban rushed to get to him before he had to start using his camera as a defensive weapon.

"I got a shot of you a minute ago!" Durban heard him shouting at one angry-looking woman.

Once she had fought her way to his side, he grabbed her elbow with his free hand and pulled her through the crowd.

"You're good at crowd-surfing," she said in praise.

"It's part of the job," he replied, but she could tell he was pleased.

They pushed and swayed to the front door of the casino, where five stern looking guards waited. One of the guards held up his palm, as if he could stop their forward progress through the power of suggestion. Maybe he could; his yellow skin and pointed ears showed that he was an Elf. Elves were not common in Las Vegas. A few had once worked as croupiers, but their ability to do magic had led to a couple of lawsuits from gambling patrons who claimed the supernaturals were using magic to stack the decks even further in favor of the house. The few supernaturals who worked in Vegas now tended to have jobs away from the gaming tables, like this guard. He was young, and would have had a pleasant face if it hadn't been fixed in so stern a frown.

"Nobody's getting in," he said.

Bob held his camera in front of his chest as if it were a baby and he and Ashly were the proud parents.

"Do we look like protesters?" he asked gruffly. "We're media. We're here for the Monty Allen press conference."

Durban flashed the guard a smile and held up the laminated plastic tag with the bold yellow Werewolf Telethon logo. The guard stood aside, but his face never broke out of its frown.

"In the Black Lagoon Room," he said. "Down the hall, past the slots, to the right. And hurry up."

They walked through the door. A couple of protesters from the crowd tried to follow in on their coattails, but the guard popped quickly back into place and held up his palm once more. This time it worked.

Compared to the fracas outside, the interior of the casino was relatively quiet. The gamblers who had gotten into the Mummy Room before the protest started were happily plunking their tokens into the one-armed bandits. Durban and Savik walked down the length of the corridor, the shouts of the crowd outside having been replaced with the endless chiming of the machines and the occasional rattle of coins in the slot trays. The only young people in evidence were the women who served free drinks, all of whom were dressed as mummies that had lost a good bit of their wrappings. There were no rich playboys lounging by the slot tables, no Robert Redford types laying down any million-dollar bets. The place looked like an AARP convention.

"Any big winnings they get will be spent on pacemakers," Savik cracked, and Durban poked him in the ribs.

They reached the end of the hallway and saw another branch of the casino heading off to the right like it was some secret cave, complete with five guards that looked like clones of the ones at the casino's front door.

"Press," Bob and Ashly chimed together, and the guards waved them through, where they were greeted by the sight of an enormous green monster head, with slot machine lemons and cherries for eyes. It was the Black Lagoon Room, dedicated to Universal's CREATURE FROM THE BLACK LAGOON series. This was ordinarily a regular gambling room, with gorgeous young drink dispensers wearing slimy-looking (but low-cut) Gill Girl costumes, complete with shapely green lace "gills" on their necks, but it had been roped off for Monty Allen's press conference. There was an impressive mob already present, and Ashly and Bob edged their way into the middle of the throng.

And there he was, center stage, on a dais slightly to the left of the giant Gill Man head, dressed simply in razor-creased tan chinos and a blue shirt. The Gill Man's mouth had been replaced by a red electronic ticker that repeatedly proclaimed, JACKPOT NOW APPROACHING A QUARTER OF A MILLION, but even such a hideous

commercial construct could take nothing away from
the legendary Monty Allen.

His occasional movies weren't doing much at the
box office anymore, but everyone still knew his name.
He was the black comedian who had worked his way
up from blaxploitation films in the early 1970s to star
in huge blockbuster comedy-action werewolf flicks like
Hairy Death Machine and *Long Moon Rising*. The
latter had proved to be his high water mark, the best
vehicle for combining his curious blend of highbrow
comedy and hyperviolent, bone-crunching lycanthropic
action. The finale alone had put him in the film history
books: a giddy and hysterical chase scene across a public
works project where he had pummeled and slashed
the bad guy while snarling lines from T.S. Eliot's "The
Love Song of J. Alfred Prufrock." He had finally
dispatched the evildoer into the roaring white waters
of a dam, and then had paused for the faintest moment
before turning his hair-covered face away from the
camera and hitting the tag line—" 'til human voices
wake us, and we drown." His movies had been
simultaneously attacked and applauded for their use
of werewolves as subject matter. They were attacked
because they still showed the creatures as violent
predators, and applauded because they often showed
them as intelligent and resourceful violent predators
rather than the mindless slashers of old.

Now Monty Allen was a fixture in Las Vegas and
did a light comedy show, minus fake werewolf fur, in
the Universal Monster that was still packing in the
blue hairs. Durban hadn't seen him in the flesh for a
while, but it was clear he was still in the excellent
physical shape that been his hallmark during the heyday
of his film career. He was impressive, even in his

boringly normal clothes. His arms were like sculpted
tree limbs, and his chest swelled out his light blue cotton
shirt so much that it looked like he was packing an
automobile air bag that had already inflated. His face
was the only point of departure from the muscular
look; it was benign, slightly goofy, with the ragged
moustache that he used to twitch in that world-famous
manner when he wanted to get a laugh. His black hair
sported a few gray strands, but that seemed his only
bow to the aging process.

"My friends, if you'll settle down, we'll get started,"
he said, raising both arms, palms outstretched, like
some Egyptian pharaoh.

"I'm sure you have some questions," he said, wiggling
his moustache, and the assembled throng laughed on
cue, "but if you'll just wait one moment, I have a few
words to say. We are here today to both mourn a tragedy
and to celebrate a pending breakthrough, and I am
sorry that we have to do both at once. Of course, I
am saddened by the unfortunate deaths of Dr. Wardoe
and Dr. Johnson. Dr. Wardoe was invaluable to the
fight against lycanthropy, and her efforts will be missed.
Likewise with Dr. Johnson, without whose help we
would not be here today. These two valiant and brilliant
researchers were always willing to work long hours,
and we need more like them in the medical field."

He stiffened on the podium, raised himself ramrod
straight like an old Southern Baptist preacher about
to call down fire and brimstone.

"These murders clearly show that *someone* out there
is satisfied with the status quo, satisfied that nearly
200,000 people in this great nation have to suffer the
sickness of lycanthropy. But I am here to tell you that
Dr. Wardoe and Dr. Johnson did not die in vain. Thank

God, their work was finished when they passed on. The final testing was as complete as we could have hoped. We can proceed with the Werewolf Telethon, and do it safely."

There was faint murmur in the crowd, and Savik looked at Durban and tilted an eyebrow. Monty Allen reached in his shirt pocket and pulled out a piece of paper, neatly folded into a small square.

"I have here a letter from Food and Drug Administration director Siodmak which says that based on Dr. Wardoe's tests, and the unique nature of this illness, the Food and Drug Administration has agreed to waive some of the normal certification procedures and to speed up the delivery process. This means that the cure that Dr. Wardoe and Dr. Johnson gave their lives for will be available to people who need it. Our fifth telethon will start on time on Friday, only three days from now, in this very casino, and by the time the twelve hours are up we expect to have raised enough money to give the lycanthropy cure to all werewolves. Free of charge. This is one of Director Siodmak's rules. If the cure is not FDA certified—and in my opinion, that process takes too long—then no tax dollars can pay for the cure. So be it. I have learned that the werewolf community is a generous community. There will be enough money. And this will be the very last Werewolf Telethon we will ever need to have."

Savik nudged Durban; the show was starting. Monty Allen was starting to weep the famous tears he would display numerous times during the telethon, the tears that had gotten him lampooned endlessly on late night talk shows. He let them flow down his face unchecked. His voice started to break.

"I don't know if you can imagine what this means

to those poor people who suffer from lycanthropy. No longer will they have to fear the full moon. No longer will they lie sick on their couches or floors, moaning in pain. No longer will they have to be tied down to keep from turning into hideous, unnatural creatures. The curse will be broken. The curse will be broken!"

He finally pulled a handkerchief out of his back pocket and wiped away the tears, which had started flowing around that famous moustache and into his mouth. As he replaced it, he held out his other hand to someone standing behind him, someone obscured from the crowd by a door that led to the private employee's entrance.

"Come here, come here," he could be heard saying tenderly into the microphone. Ashly couldn't quite see what was going on, but a few seconds later a prolonged *aaahhh* went up from the crowd of supposedly tough-minded journalists.

A tiny boy, no more than two years old, toddled out onto the makeshift stage. Monty Allen took his hand and then hoisted him up on his massive shoulder. The boy was dressed in a white sailor suit with blue trim, and he looked about as pale as the suit for a moment as he surveyed the crowd. Then he broke into an instant baby smile and hid his face behind his chubby hands, and the crowd *aaahhhed* again. Monty Allen beamed at the child and then beamed at the journalists.

"This is Trevor," he said. "Say hi, Trevor. Say hi."

Trevor peeked out from behind his hands, but then quickly hid his smiling face again. Allen laughed for a moment and then became serious.

"This is all fun now, but I have something to share

with you. This boy, this gorgeous young man, suffers from lycanthropy. Not the fake stuff I used to have in the movies, but the real thing. His uncle has the disease and accidentally bit him one night. Trevor's okay, he recovered from that, but now every full moon he suffers agonizing pain and becomes hairy. He snarls and spits. He's confused and he hurts and he lashes out in pain. That's not much trouble now, but when he grows up . . . well, you've seen my old movies. You know the risks."

He brought the boy down to face level and crinkled up his nose, and Trevor ran a tentative hand through his moustache and then gave a sparkling laugh. Then a pretty young woman came onstage and took Trevor away. Trevor waved bye-bye, and most of the journalists waved back. Ashly looked at Monty Allen; the tears were back, making his face shine in the lights from the cameras.

"I tell you, he is the reason we're doing what we're doing. He and other little boys and girls like him, boys and girls and men and women who currently suffer under this terrible, terrible curse. If we raise ten million dollars—just ten million dollars—during the telethon this Friday, people, I'm telling you that I have an agreement with the FDA and with medical labs around the country that we can start giving out the antidote right away. The cure! The cure for lycanthropy, paid for by the caring people of America."

The powerful hand moved across the famous brow and moustache, wiping away the tears and the sweat that had joined the tears, even though the Gill Man room was cool enough to cause condensation to form on the glasses of several of the reporters.

"No longer will they have to change into horrendous

beasts whenever the full moon shines down. Now they can be like us. Now they can walk out at night and look up at the full moon and smile, and hold hands, and watch its reflection in the lake. All we need is a successful telethon, and they can be just human once more."

Durban looked at the floor, and crinkled up the left corner of her mouth. She never did those things now, and she wasn't even worried about turning into a wolf. Her reverie was disturbed by an angry voice from the rear of the room, near the dollar-a-pop slot machines.

"That's bullshit!" someone shouted. "We *are* human! We're even *better* than human! We don't need a cure!"

The assembled reporters snapped their heads around so quickly that Durban thought they might hurt themselves. The camera lights left Monty Allen and whirled to focus on whoever was shouting. Durban stood on tiptoes to see over the people behind her, and could barely make out a long-haired young man wearing a neat gray pin-striped suit.

"I understand your pain," Allen started to say, but the shouter didn't seem to be mollified.

"Why don't you release the results of the tests? We've tried to get them and they aren't available! No one knows what really happens with this cure of yours!"

Allen frowned.

"Now that's a misrepresentation. It's true that some aspects of the tests have been kept from the public to protect the privacy of the victims—"

"There are no victims! I'm from the Jean Grenier Society, and we don't put up with your pitying rhetoric! Werewolves do have a role to play in society, a role that's needed now more than ev—"

Whatever else the young man wished to say was drowned out, as a bevy of guards had descended on him and dragged him kicking and twisting out of the room. Durban caught a glimpse of his maroon loafers, so polished that they reflected back the camera lights. Once he was gone, the reporters' heads swiveled back around to Monty Allen.

"What do you think of the Jean Grenier Society?" someone shouted out. He smiled.

"They seem a bit excitable, don't they?"

A couple of the reporters laughed, but then Allen got serious.

"Well, they're entitled to their point of view, I suppose. I've seen their leader, Paul Moreau, on the TV, on the talk shows and such, and he seems very intelligent and talks a good game, but I don't think he has much credibility among the people who suffer from the illness whose alleged virtues he trumpets. I don't think it's reasonable to take his position that being a werewolf is okay, or even admirable. It's a disease, people, as simple as that. We've proven that time and again. Paul Moreau popped up a decade or so ago and formed his little society, but he can't go against the experience of thousands of years of history. I would debate the man at any time or any place on this issue, and I would win. Lycanthropy is a disease, and it's highly contagious. It leaves people miserable. It leaves people dead. It's nothing to be happy about. Victims of werewolfism are actually lucky to live in the United States. You know that some countries still quarantine them or just kill them outright. We don't do that. We give them drugs to help ward off the worst of the symptoms, and let them live a life that's as close to normal as possible. Now we're about to give them a cure. That's more than Mr. Moreau has to offer them."

"The Jean Grenier Society says the cure probably isn't safe, and you say you don't have FDA approval for it," a reporter asked. "*Is* it safe? Can you give any guarantees? Why not just wait until the FDA signs off on your cure?"

Most people in New York, L.A. and Washington, D.C., knew Allen's position on this matter. A fake grass-roots group he had created, Citizens Against Lycanthropy, had taken out full-page ads in major newspapers consisting only of a set of cartoonish fangs snarling out at the reader. Underneath the teeth, the ad's text said only, *Thanks to the FDA, these may be the last things you will ever see.* The Jean Grenier Society had protested the ads, to no avail.

"Gentlemen and ladies, life involves risk. The United States of America has not gotten to where it is today without taking risks. The cure we will present has had impressive test results so far. No, they don't fully satisfy the FDA, but I feel the FDA is being too conservative in the face of this dreadful plague. The people I've talked to say they can't wait another five or ten or fifteen years for the bureaucracy to make up its mind. We will make the test results available to all victims of lycanthropy, and let them choose whether to take the cure or not," Allen said. "I think I know which way they will go."

"Will you release a list of people tested?"

"Maybe. I'll have to talk to the lawyers. Clearly, with the brutal murders of Dr. Wardoe and Dr. Johnson, there is security to think about. But we'll do whatever we can to reassure everyone."

"Some members of the Jean Grenier Society claim

they won't take the cure even if the telethon raises enough money to pay for it," someone else shouted to Allen. "What will you do then? Can you get some court order forcing them to take it?"

Allen stroked his moustache, the movement causing his arm muscles to flex like snakes in a bag.

"I would hope it wouldn't come to that. I mean, I would think that if people are given the option to improve their lives, they will."

"But what if they don't?"

He shrugged, and twitched his moustache.

"Then we'll do what we have to do. But I'll make the following prediction. Within the next two weeks, we will cure all the werewolves in this country, and the Jean Grenier Society will fade away and everyone will be safe and happy."

There was a momentary silence, and then more questions.

"Let's get up there after this is over and offer to air a debate with Paul Moreau," Durban whispered to Savik. "We need to fill another 'Living with Lycanthropy' segment."

SEVEN

Chesty Moore clicked past the 11 o'clock news in favor of a rap video that featured several thin and angry-looking young men cavorting on a beach with a throng of bikini-clad women. Bobby had sort of wanted to watch the news, but he was also interested in the video, so he let it slide.

After his escape from Steve the director, Bobby had holed up in the North Las Vegas apartment which he shared with a drug dealer named Stoke. Bobby had always suspected it was not his real name, but he didn't pry. They had met through a mutual acquaintance, a maintenance man at the warehouse who had a powerful craving for the things Stoke was selling. Stoke needed a place to live, the fewer questions the better, and Bobby was low on money, so they were a natural pairing although they had nothing in common. The apartment was in Bobby's name but Stoke paid most of the rent. Things worked out. Stoke was a pleasant enough young man with powerful arms, although Bobby never saw him lift anything heavier than a tallboy beer can.

Bobby hoped that Steve the director didn't remember where he lived. He couldn't remember filling out any forms when he had signed on to work. It wasn't the sort of job that required anyone to be scrupulous about paperwork. Bobby had been a little worried about that at the time, but was glad of it now. Anyway, he had been home for hours and nobody had called or come by, so he figured he was safe. He felt safe, but not particularly good; he had stopped by the 7-11 on the way home and picked up a quart of St. Ives malt liquor, which he had quickly slugged down. It had made him feel like he was floating for a while, but all too soon the cheap booze coalesced into a cannonball in his stomach and brought him back down to earth. Now the rap video was starting to bother him, as was the arrhythmic swaying it prompted from Chesty, who was slouched three feet away on the tattered couch.

Chesty Moore was Stoke's stripper girlfriend. She worked about three hours a day in the wee hours of the morning and spent the rest of the time in front of the thirteen-inch television which had such bad color that all the Caucasian actors looked overly tanned, stop signs were a nice robin's egg blue and the sky usually had a greenish tinge. Bobby had gone to see her work once, at the Kit Kat Lounge. The lights in there made everything look about like it did on the TV at home, so Bobby figured that Chesty thought the colors were just normal.

Chesty herself seemed to be painted with all the hues that the TV had difficulty showing. Her hair was a shocking bleached blonde, her eyes looked like black pits dug out of her skull, and her blue veins stuck out on her thin arms like deep rivers flowing through snow. For all that, she was strangely attractive. She wore first little and then nothing when onstage, but around the apartment she favored off-white buccaneer shirts and black leather pants, which made her look like a cheerleader who had gotten trapped in Never-Never Land. Underneath the buccaneer shirts, she lived up to her name, her amazing upper torso helped along a little bit by well-placed silicone gel.

She had come Stoke's way only two months before. Her home was Kansas City, she said, but she intimated that she had run into some kind of family problems there and so she had left, hitchhiking her way across the country. She had intended to go to Hollywood to try her hand at acting, but her money ran out before she could make it and so she was in Las Vegas, and that was close enough. Stoke had met her at a club and brought her home.

"This video is stupid," Chesty said as the rappers went away, to be replaced by three thin pink Englishmen standing in front of some kind of factory. The young men seemed to be suffering from some terrible inner turmoil, but Chesty was not interested. She changed channels with such gusto she almost dropped the remote, as if she intended the switch to be a personal affront to the anguished crooners. She had meant to switch on up the dial, but in her haste she backtracked to the news.

"Police currently have no leads in the double werewolf murders of the lead researchers at the Landon Institute, but film star Monty Allen said today that their work was finished," the blonde woman was saying, but Chesty wasn't interested in that, either.

"Tell it to the judge, lady," she said, and flipped on

to a cooking show, where a thin man was sliding snails around in a wok.

"Turn that back!" Bobby shouted, suddenly tensing up on the couch. "Chesty! I want to see that!"

Chesty looked at him as if he had asked her to perform on the table for free, and spitefully kept flipping down the dial, landing on an exercise machine infomercial which featured an unnaturally healthy woman tugging on a contraption that appeared to have been designed by Rube Goldberg.

"C'mon, dammit, Chesty! Just for a minute!"

Chesty wrinkled her upper lip at Bobby, but he moved faster than she expected and managed to wrest the remote away.

"You shit!" she shouted, and started pounding him on the shoulder while he simultaneously fended her off and flipped back through the channels to the news, which was now displaying a clip of Monty Allen, weeping into the camera.

"Allen told reporters today at the Universal Monster Grand casino that the research for the cure is finished, and predicted it will soon be widely available to victims of lycanthropy."

Chesty had wriggled around until she could almost reach the remote, but Bobby, his eyes never wavering from the TV set, gave her a shove that caused her to slip off the couch and bang her much-displayed chest against the coffee table, knocking off her beer can in the process.

"Stoke! Your idiot roommate is trying to kill me!" she shrieked, but Bobby jacked the TV volume up until a line of green bars went all the way across the bottom of the screen.

"In a surprise development, werewolf activist Paul

Moreau has agreed to Allen's challenge to debate the issue of lycanthropy. That will be aired on tomorrow's edition of NBC's *Live Entertainment*."

"Huh," he muttered to himself. That might be a good show.

Chesty shoved the entire coffee table aside and made a lunge for the remote, spiriting it neatly from Bobby's hand. He grabbed for her but she rolled away across the floor, executed a nice spin and changed the channel in one quick move.

"Chesty, goddamnit, I'm watching the news!"

Stoke kept hours unusual even for a drug dealer. He came barreling out of the bedroom, having been roused from his usual early-night nap by the ruckus. He rubbed his grapefruit-sized left bicep with his right hand as if he was pumping himself up with air for the hard deals ahead.

"I am going to shoot you both if you don't shut the hell up! Bobby, don't get Chesty all bruised up before a work night, and Chesty, damn it, it wouldn't hurt you to watch the news once in a while."

"Make her turn it back, Stoke," Bobby said, aware that he was pleading, but he didn't care.

Chesty dropped the remote down the front of her pirate shirt, which made Stoke smile.

"Now you *know* I will come in there and get that if I have to."

He started walking toward her with an animal leer on his face, but then checked his watch.

"Oh, shit! I slept too long. I got some people coming by for business. You two keep quiet for a change. Chesty, turn back the damn channel."

She grudgingly did so, but hit the MUTE command and glared at Bobby, daring him to complain. He started to call out to Stoke, who was stalking back to his bedroom, but then decided it was useless and resigned himself to trying to read lips.

The TV was showing a photograph of the two people who had been killed earlier. Bobby frowned. The man looked familiar. He had definitely seen him somewhere before. Then the face of a woman appeared, the same woman he had seen earlier on the old black-and-white TV at the warehouse. He had seen her somewhere before, too.

"Don't ya want the sound up?" Chesty asked from behind the couch, but Bobby ignored her. The woman and the man . . . where had he seen them? It had to have been at the warehouse, but the memories from there were always so foggy and imprecise.

Just then there was a scratching at the front door. Stoke came marching out of the bedroom, eyes bright at the thought of lucrative business. He had changed into a nicely pressed white shirt and looked almost presentable, like an eager college graduate about to get a big break. The scratching sound came again, long and slow. Bobby felt goosebumps form along his arms, as if the dormant wolf hair was trying to come through.

"Stoke," he said quickly. "Are you sure that's them?"

"Nah, it's the pizza guy. Of *course* it's them."

Bobby's skin felt like it was rippling, and he had to look down at his arms to make sure the hair wasn't poking through for real. Suddenly he felt a tremor of fear and jumped to his feet, just as Stoke put his hand on the chain.

"Stoke, I don't think it's them!"

Stoke gave a dismissive wave with his free hand as he disconnected the chain and turned the knob.

"I told you to chill out. It's them! Eddy said these guys have a weird knock."

He was smiling when a hairy fist shot through the doorway and halfway into his chest, and was still smiling when a long, thin canine snout closed around his neck. The clean white shirt was undergoing a very quick dye job, and by the time Stoke hit the floor it looked like it had never been any color other than dark, dark red.

The werewolf turned its snout to Chesty and Bobby, its toothy grin dripping blood. It was a big one, with a lumpy human musculature visible under the hair. It wasn't a full moon, so the werewolf was obviously using drugs to make the change. Its hair jutted out to a tasteful length, longer than it would have with the blue light at the movie warehouse but nowhere near as elongated as it would have been in a natural change under the full moon. All in all, the interloper would have been a singularly well-coiffed lycanthrope were it not for a nasty, deep scar running across the bridge of its nose.

Chesty dropped the remote, did another rolling dive and fished a big pistol out from under the couch. Stoke had once told Bobby that there were lots of guns hidden around the apartment, but Bobby didn't know where any of them were. Chesty seemed to have that information. She was crying in fear, but that didn't stop her from assuming a marksman's stance and firing off three slugs. Two of them hit the wall, taking huge chunks out of the plaster and Bobby's security deposit. The other caught the werewolf in mid-leap, shattering his kneecap, sending him shrieking to the floor.

The werewolf gasped for a moment and then staggered to its feet, leaning on the edge of the couch

for support but still clearly intent on doing them harm.
Its eyes were nearly hidden behind brows clenched
in anger and its growl was so low it vibrated through
the floor like thunder. Bobby dipped his fingers in his
pocket and retrieved his tiny folding knife, which
seemed pathetic next to Chesty's elephantine pistol.
Chesty sighted the gun in the center of the werewolf's
chest and pulled the trigger six more times. The gun
made six sickening clinks to indicate that it was empty.
There were innumerable guns hidden around the
house, but Stoke had never claimed they were fully
loaded. Chesty stood up and dashed in the bedroom
just as the werewolf put its weight on its good leg and
jumped at Bobby.

He dodged its outstretched claws, and being smaller
and faster he was able to duck down and deliver a
quick swipe to the werewolf's ribs with the knife, giving
it another scar to match the one on its nose. The beast
howled in pain and threw him back to the far wall,
sending him crashing down on the television, which
somehow disabled the mute command. Suddenly the
instrumental version of "Suicide is Painless" blared
through the room, signaling another episode of
M.A.S.H.

The big werewolf paused for a moment to look at
the helicopters on the screen, giving Bobby enough
time to regain his feet and kick him right in the snout,
a blow that Bobby knew from experience to be
particularly painful to anyone in werewolf form. His
bigger foe howled again, but this time he moved quicker
than Bobby expected and hoisted him by the ribs up
to the ceiling, shoving his face into the cheap light
fixture. The glass came loose and the bare bulb singed
Bobby's face. Bobby could feel the werewolf's claws

tightening, constraining his lungs, shutting off his air. He squirmed but to no avail. The room seemed awash in pain.

Chesty reappeared in his field of vision, upside down, emerging from the bedroom with a large and very nasty-looking submachine gun. Bobby fell through space, sprawling painfully on the edge of the couch. His tormenter took a bullet in the arm and another in the chest and then hurled out of the apartment door, thumping halfway down the steps to the building's first floor. Chesty kept shooting, angry tears blinding her to the fact that her target was gone. What little decoration they had in the apartment was shredded.

Bobby staggered upright, each gulped breath sending shocks of pain through his chest. He could hear the werewolf gasping on the stairs, and there were several thumps from downstairs as the neighbors complained about the noise. None of them had called the police, in all likelihood. This was a rowdy apartment building, and gunfire was relatively common. Chesty stopped shooting and pulled out the gun's magazine. It was apparently empty, too.

"Damn it, Stoke," she said. "Why didn't you buy more bullets?"

There was a catch in her voice, and her mascara had started running through her tears, its black lines dividing her face into three roughly equal sections. Bobby glanced out the window. Two floors up, but a small, unkempt yard, with ragged bushes, awaited them below. He hurt all over anyway; he might as well jump.

"Come here," he said, his throat thick with pain, his voice sounding garbled and scary even to him. "We have to go out the window."

"Are you crazy?"

The werewolf chose that moment to stick his head back into the room to see why no more bullets were flying. He was bleeding all over, but apparently wasn't done with them yet. That made up Chesty's mind. She and Bobby dashed to the window and flung it open and he maneuvered his rear end on the sill so he could hold her and drop onto his back. The antagonistic werewolf had other ideas. Seeing Chesty drop the gun, it stumbled its way across the room and tried to clamp its jaws on her right arm, but missed, its teeth spewing spittle against the windowpane. Bobby grabbed Chesty and dropped away into the night.

The pain of impact was much greater than Bobby had expected. The bushes that looked so round and springy when viewed from the window sill felt more like concrete blocks capped with spikes when he landed on them. Chesty hopped up immediately, but Bobby rolled off the bushes and sprawled on the grass, gasping like a fish, out of air for the second time in as many minutes.

"He's going to jump! Hurry, Bobby, get up!" Chesty shouted.

Bobby finally managed to get a little air back into his lungs and sat up, an action that sent new volleys of pain through his body. He never knew he had so many nerve endings. He looked up and saw the werewolf's head poking from the window. He held out his arm and Chesty pulled him to his feet.

"Let's get out of here," he gasped.

Stoke was the only one who had a car, but the werewolf wasn't likely to toss them the keys. They would have to go on foot. The werewolf's head disappeared from the window. With all its injuries it had decided not to jump. That didn't mean it couldn't take the stairs. They would have to go now. Fear lent urgency to their legs, and Bobby forced his body to ignore the pain. They started running, ducking out of the streetlights and into the back alleys. If those slugs didn't slow the werewolf down, they were sunk.

"Where are we going?" Chesty asked.

"To the warehouse."

Bobby felt that even saying it was an admission of defeat to Steve. He just didn't have anywhere else to go.

EIGHT

"I'll get right to the point," Monty Allen said. "Werewolves have a disease. That disease is called lycanthropy. They must be cured so they will cease being menaces to society. Any opposing viewpoint is incorrect."

"I respectfully disagree," Paul Moreau responded. "The traditional fear of werewolves is based on a lack of understanding. Werewolves represent a vital link between the rational human world and the wild, natural world, a link that will grow even more vital in the future."

Ashly Durban stepped in front of the two men and smiled for the camera.

"Welcome to another edition of 'Living with Lycanthropy,' here on *Live Entertainment*. Tonight we bring you a very special event—a debate between the two leaders on either side of the controversial werewolf debate. Monty Allen wants to cure 'em, Paul Moreau wants to represent 'em. Tonight, each will have the ability to speak his mind."

There were loud hoots from the cheering section. Both sides appeared to be equally matched, at least in numbers. Monty Allen had brought his supporters to cheer him on—mostly sycophants hoping for a movie job—and Paul Moreau had a big chunk of the Jean Grenier Society on hand. That was only to be expected, because in agreeing to a debate Moreau had specified that it had to be held at the Society's Las Vegas headquarters, a nondescript white-walled expanse that once housed a drugstore. It had been sectioned off for its new life. The front, glassy part faced the street and served as the Society's window to the world. The middle section had been cleared out for the debate, and the rear was where the Society kept its tangle of computers and printers. In short, it looked like the headquarters of any other nonprofit group, although one with a unique mission.

Durban and Savik had shown up at the appointed hour of 2 P.M., along with the camera crew for CBS, the only other network that seemed interested in the debate. Monty Allen and his contingent had appeared shortly thereafter, where they milled around uneasily near the youthful Jean Grenier Society members, who were on their best behavior but couldn't help but toss nasty looks now and then.

Durban eyed them carefully. All were clean shaven, or didn't need to shave at all. Only one or two appeared to have aged beyond twenty-five. There were a couple of African-Americans, and one Asian that she saw. Aside from those members, they were white. They were also almost overwhelmingly male; out of the thirty or so in attendance, she saw only two that she took to be female. It was actually a little hard to tell, given the preponderance of long hair among the members. They all wore it at least to their shoulders, some beyond that. All of them, even the females, were in the regulation uniform of crisp gray suits with white shirts and shiny maroon loafers. Gathered together in their nice clothes, with their skinny faces deathly solemn, they looked like some sort of perfume ad.

Allen's crowd, by contrast, appeared to be a collection of Hollywood stock characters come to life. Their ages ranged widely from the second to the fifth decade, some bodies were aerodynamic while others were ponderous, and no two had shopped at the same store. Some were well dressed, some barely dressed. If the Greniers at least seemed to share a common purpose, Allen's crowd appeared to have been pulled together at random. Durban wasn't sure which approach would come across better on camera.

After everyone was assembled, they waited for the host to arrive. Allen checked his watch several times and smiled to the cameras to indicate that he wasn't the one making everybody late. Then the back door to the building opened and Paul Moreau entered, striding past the computers, his jaw set with a sense of purpose.

If one needed to have a rebel leader, Moreau was probably a good one to have. He looked like a model gone slightly to seed, but in a sexy, decadent way. His long, uncombed hair was flecked with gray streaks, and his cheekbones would not have looked out of place on the face of a cliff. He was also at least a head taller than anyone else in the room, and surveyed them with a kind of airy dignity.

Moreau walked up to Monty Allen and shook his hand, although he didn't smile. Moreau wore a black dress shirt over black jeans, with a black belt. Allen was dressed in a muted peach knit shirt and khakis, but compared to Moreau's somber garb he looked almost garish.

"Thank you for coming. I'm sorry I'm late. Let's get started, shall we?" Moreau said, all before Allen could get in a word.

Allen nodded and then smiled to his followers as the group headed for the debate area. His group smiled back, and some of them stuck out their chins in a parody of Moreau's serious demeanor. Bob Savik was carrying a small hand-held camera, and caught them on tape. They quickly stopped.

"I'd like to challenge your notion that there is something worthwhile in the disease of lycanthropy," Allen said once Durban had made the introductions and the two combatants had made their opening statements. "Fact: People who get it turn into animals at least once a month. Fact: they often kill or wound other people."

They were seated on white chairs on a raised stage, as if they were intimate talk show hosts. Behind them, on the far wall, were several Jean Grenier Society posters. They would be in the background, but they might be visible quite often during the debate. Moreau knew how to manipulate the media almost as well as Allen did, Durban had to admit.

"People are far more likely to get eaten by a shark than to get killed by a werewolf," Moreau said.

Allen wiggled the famous moustache and scanned his side of the crowd.

"That's really not as comforting as you might think."

Allen's supporters laughed. Moreau rubbed his eyebrows, aware that he was already on the defensive.

"Okay, I guess that wasn't the best way to get into

this. Mr. Allen, I won't deny that werewolves change into animal-like creatures. Obviously they do, or we wouldn't be sitting here. But there is far more to being a werewolf, as I have discovered over the last three decades."

He leaned forward and addressed the cameras as much as he addressed his opponent.

"This is not something I have discussed before outside the Jean Grenier Society, but I feel the time is right. I have been a werewolf longer than anyone else alive. My development was accelerated because in the 1960s I was kidnapped by the United States Army and used as a subject for experiments intended to use lycanthropy as a weapon."

The Society members gave a collective gasp, although they had obviously heard the story before. Allen's supporters laughed.

"Oh, *please*," Allen said. "Everybody knows the Army did some research in the Second World War, but then they let it drop. Didn't you see that documentary *Tooth Beach*? A whole squadron of shock werewolf troops landed at some Pacific island, I forget which one, right as the full moon came out from behind the clouds. They didn't even bother with the Japanese. They tore each other up. That werewolf-as-weapon stuff went nowhere after that."

"That's not true," Moreau said. "You think it's true but it's not. The United States Army continued werewolf studies after the war. They didn't stop until 1969, when Richard Nixon made them stop."

Ashly Durban watched Moreau's face closely. Did he ever relax? The furrows under his cheekbones seemed to deepen under the camera lights. Whatever he was doing, he wasn't kidding.

"I was a runaway in the mid-1960s when I became a werewolf. I was taken to what I was told was a lycanthropy treatment center in New York City. It was really a front for the Army. They kidnapped me and took me to an Army base somewhere in Maryland, and they fed me lycanthropy drugs to try to turn me into a better soldier. Instead, they just made me a better werewolf."

Allen's half of the crowd hooted with laughter, so loudly that the sound man for CBS had to frantically adjust the sound monitor. Allen himself just stared at Moreau.

"You can't be serious," he said.

"I'm afraid I am. The doses of werewolf drugs accelerated my development beyond anything anyone has known. In a short time, I learned that a werewolf can retain his or her mind even under a full transformation. I also learned something else."

Allen seemed to suddenly remember that this was a debate, and he needed to get in his digs.

"What, that your claws are lethal?"

"No," Moreau said, over the angry hisses of the Jean Grenier members. "I learned that on some level, werewolves can communicate with animals. Don't you see how helpful that could be?"

Durban looked for a smile on his face, but there wasn't one. Allen leaned towards him slowly.

"You mean you can talk to the animals," he said slowly. His moustache was already twitching.

"Yes," Moreau said.

"You mean, just like Dr.—"

The laughs from his supporters almost drowned him out. The Jean Grenier members shoved some of them, and for a second there it looked like a fight was going to break out.

"Mock me if you must," Moreau said. "Yes, just like Dr. Doolittle."

Durban thought Allen's smile would rip through the sides of his mouth.

"You can *talk* to the *animals*."

Durban quickly glanced over to Savik to make sure he was getting it all. He smiled from behind his camera stand and made a little circle around his ear with his index finger, making sure none of the Jean Grenier Society members saw him.

"Not like that," Moreau said. "It's a mental communication on some level, I don't know what. But it works."

Allen roared and slapped his knee. His supporters and the Jean Grenier members were openly shoving each other. The place was beginning to look like the mosh pit for a punk-rock band. Durban eyed the angry crowd. ABC and CNN would kick themselves for missing this one.

"Imagine what could be done with that ability!" Moreau said, standing up and raising his voice to be heard over the suddenly noisy audience. "There was a subdivision built in L.A. recently. Turns out it was built way too close to mountain lion country. Two joggers were killed. That's the sort of thing a good werewolf could figure out. I could get in there and see through the animals' eyes and their senses. We could have found a better place for the subdivision. We could help people live more in harmony with nature!"

Allen, still emitting his famous laugh, wiped his eyes in an exaggerated show of how amused he was.

"You're going to keep a murderous illness around just because it might result in better real estate deals?"

he said at last. "My god, this is funnier than anything I had in my movies."

Durban thought Moreau was going to take a swipe at him. He towered over Allen, his fists balled up like rocks. Moreau had the height but Allen had the bulk. But then again Moreau was angry, so Durban wouldn't have taken bets just then on which one would win. Allen, perhaps realizing that such a fight wouldn't look too good for either one of them, collected himself and stood up. He put his massive hands on Moreau's shoulders and tightened his face into a solemn mask.

"Mr. Moreau, I'm sorry. This is a serious issue and we shouldn't make light of it."

Moreau, taken aback, merely nodded. His fists softened.

"You laugh, but what I say is true," he said. "A fully mature werewolf can communicate with animals."

Allen looked up into his eyes. He wasn't laughing now.

"And you learned this from the Army testing."

"Yes."

"Interesting. Let's sit back down and continue our discussion."

"All right."

They returned to their seats warily. Each sat on the edge of his chair, as if ready to spring up again should the need arise. The crowd members stopped jostling each other and stood quietly at attention.

"Mr. Moreau, it is my understanding that the only testing done after World War II was to find a cure for lycanthropy, something that has obviously taken a long time. But you say this is not so."

"It is not so. The Army was using a synthesized werewolf agent that mimicked the effect of the full moon. It can be delivered either through light or through intravenous fluid. It is the stuff now found on the black market, and the old lights are used to make illegal werewolf exploitation movies."

"Mr. Moreau, may I ask you a personal question?"

Moreau looked a little surprised, but he nodded.

"How did you become a werewolf?"

Durban couldn't remember if Moreau had ever answered that or not. She thought back to his interview last year with *People* magazine, but couldn't remember him mentioning it. Moreau frowned and looked out at his Jean Grenier Society members.

"This brings up another thing I haven't told anyone but members of the Society," he said, and ran his fingers along his eyebrows. "But I suppose now is the time. Mr. Allen, do you know where I got the name Jean Grenier for the Society?"

"Not really. I heard something about it. Some guy from back in the past who was a werewolf."

"He was a boy in rural France in the 1500s. There was a werewolf scare going on, some kids disappearing. Eventually the villagers caught this boy, Jean Grenier, acting really strangely, crawling around on all fours. He confessed to the crimes. He said that he went out into the deep forest at night and there he was visited by a tall man wrapped in shadows, sitting on a big black horse. Jean Grenier called him the Lord of the Forest. He gave Grenier a wolf pelt to wear, and when he put it on it turned him into a werewolf."

"So? Is the Lord of the Forest supposed to be an archetypal werewolf myth?"

Moreau looked directly into the cameras and paused, as if unsure what to say next. Durban had seen that look on dozens of talk show guests, who paused before announcing that their mother had beat them or they were in love with their brother's wife. It was a look that almost always led to juicy revelation.

"The figure pops up in the werewolf lore of several countries. He is reported to step in when some wrong against werewolves is being done. There have been similar sightings later on, even into our more enlightened age."

"So he's a sort of guardian angel myth."

"No, actually, he's not. He's real. I've met him myself. He turned me into a werewolf."

That did it for Allen's supporters. They howled with laughter. Allen managed to stay on his chair, just barely, but his crowd had completely lost its composure. The Jean Grenier members, outraged to have their legacy made a laughingstock, bypassed the shoving stage entirely and began throwing punches. Moreau tried to shout down the ruckus, but it wouldn't stop this time. Allen sat back in full view of the cameras and shook his head sadly, as if to show his concern for the poor deranged man beside him.

"It's true!" Moreau shouted into the din. "It's true!"

Savik managed to pull his camera off the tripod just before the surging crowd knocked it over. He would cover this fight with a hand-held camera; that always looked more immediate and dramatic. He held the camera in front of him, away from his face. That way if anyone happened to slam into it, the viewfinder wouldn't give him a black eye. It was hard to tell who was winning the fight. The Jean Grenier members were scrappy, but they were also fairly small, and there were some serious sluggers among Monty Allen's crowd.

Things were so intense that Durban, who had jumped

on the stage to escape being pummelled herself, almost
didn't notice that the police had arrived and were
steadily making their way to the front of the room.
The police waded fearlessly into the crowd, chins up
to avoid random punches, and managed to quiet the
throng down with surprising ease. Then one of the
cops stepped onto the stage and stood before Paul
Moreau. The cop was both muscular and tall, able to
stand nearly on par with Moreau. He spun Moreau
around as if he were a doll and slapped handcuffs on
him.

"Paul Moreau, you are under arrest for the murders
of Cynthia Wardoe, Carl Johnson and Bobby Chaney,"
the policeman said.

"What's your evidence?" Ashly Durban asked,
shoving her microphone under the policeman's nose.
He batted it away.

"This isn't a press conference, lady."

He quickly ran through Moreau's Miranda warning
in a robotic monotone.

"You have anything you want to say?"

Moreau, still stunned, stared at the back wall, where
his own face stared back from the Jean Grenier Society
posters.

"Who's Bobby Chaney?"

The suddenly quieted Jean Grenier Society members
cleared a path so the police could take their leader
away, but they stared bloody murder at the cops as
they passed. Allen rose to make a solemn statement
to the cameras.

"This incident clearly shows that even though there
may be some romance to the idea of the werewolf, it
indisputably turns its victims into killers. I feel sorry
that Mr. Moreau has led these young people down

the primrose path to thinking of themselves as anything more than victims of a terrible, terrible illness. I only thank God that we are on the eve of its eradication. Thank you."

He headed out the door behind the police, perhaps not wanting to stick around in a building full of angry Jean Grenier members. While Bob packed up the camera and tripod, Durban walked over to the wall that had served as the debate's backdrop. Paul Moreau, now an arrested criminal, stared down impassively from the posters. She felt a touch on her hand and twitched in surprise.

"He's impressive, huh?" said one of the Jean Grenier Society members, who had walked up so quietly she didn't hear him. "I can't believe they think he killed people."

Durban smiled politely and nodded. The kid couldn't have been more than twenty, and he looked up at the elegantly photographed face of his hero with an almost pathetic puppylike devotion.

"He is interesting," she answered, but the young man wouldn't meet her gaze.

He looked at the floor, or the wall, or Paul Moreau, but not her eyes. Ashly Durban sometimes forgot that she was beautiful, and these days the only times when she seemed to be reminded was when she interviewed shy young men. Oh, well. Better that than never, she thought.

The Society member, who stutteringly introduced himself as Bruce, pointed out the poster on the left. It was the one of Moreau staring sternly with the words "A Wild Mind is a Terrible Thing to Waste" spelled out in bright red letters underneath him.

"We got sued for that one," Bruce said. "Or at least

the Society did. I wasn't a part of it then. But the United Negro College Fund sued. We had to take it out of circulation after that. They're collectors' items. Don't tell anyone, but Paul said I could have that one once we close up shop here. I won't sell it, though. I just want to keep it."

"That's nice." Durban knew it was probably very rude to ask, but couldn't resist. "Are you a were—uh, do you have lycanthropy, too?"

That was the only time Bruce looked her right in the eye.

"Yes, I'm a werewolf. I'm proud of that."

"Uh . . . good."

Back at the local NBC affiliate office, Ashly padded across the tacky green carpet to the restroom, stripped off her jacket and tossed it over one of the stalls. As was happening so often lately, her story was too good to wait for *Live Entertainment*. She was back on deadline, but first she needed a pit stop. Her right hand was itching her to death. She had kept it balled up in her jacket pocket the whole way back, but now she wanted to check it out. She held it out in front of her face and flexed her fingers. The horrible fluorescent bathroom light made everything look sickly and yellow, including her hand; aside from that, which she expected, it looked just fine. Still, it had been touched—*she* had been touched—by a werewolf.

She didn't know what that could mean. In the time she had been doing the "Living with Lycanthropy" series, she had commiserated with victims of lycanthropy, had felt their pain, but never once had come into actual physical contact with any of them. These were people who could turn into animals. She felt as if something were crawling under her skin. Could lycanthropy be passed on by touch alone? No one had said it couldn't, as far as she could remember. Had tiny werewolf microbes leaped off that boy Bruce's skin and onto hers? She flexed her hand again, and then looked at her face in the mirror. Same thin jawline, same rounded cheeks, same small nose. No gray hair, no claws, no fangs. Yet.

The news director banged on the bathroom door.

"You fall in? We're going to have dead air in about five minutes where your story ought to go!"

She waited until he stomped off and then resumed inspecting herself in the mirror. She looked just fine, only a little sleepy, but she always looked sleepy these days.

"I'm sure this is terribly insensitive, but I'm sorry," she said softly to nobody in particular.

Then she rolled up her sleeves, hit the soap dispenser a couple of good licks, and washed her hands. She dried them when she was finished and then for good measure she washed them a dozen more times, ignoring the increasingly frantic banging on the door.

NINE

Bobby howled and leaped through the window, sending glass flying through the spartan living room. Chesty, seeing his hairy form, dropped the drinking glass she was holding and shrieked. The glass fell to the floor but hit a corner of the cheap oriental rug and didn't break. Bobby, sweat dripping from his fur, advanced on her, his snout twisted in a menacing grimace.

"Cut!" shouted Steve the director. "Get that light off now!"

The blue light switched off, returning the set to its usual dull glow. Steve had one of the technicians play back the tape, and squinted through the eyepiece to see it. He smiled as he watched.

"That was terrific," he said. "That window was the only piece of candy glass we have. I wish Chesty's water glass had shattered, but it can't be helped. That window was great. Bobby, you went through it beautifully."

Bobby smiled weakly from the couch. His head rested

in Chesty's lap, and she gently stroked his spiky blonde hair. Steve had been appalled when Bobby and Chesty had shown up the previous night, mere hours ago, trembling and spouting a story about a killer werewolf. Bobby had expected to find him shooting something, but instead he was holed up in his office in the basement of the warehouse, drinking Evan Williams straight from the bottle and watching *Mean Streets* on videotape. Steve had hustled them inside and listened intently to their tale, which had more action than anything he had ever filmed.

"Jeez, Sal must be really pissed," he muttered, taking another swig of the Evan Williams.

Drunk as he was, he had insisted on cutting and bleaching Bobby's hair right there and then.

"I want to finish the movie, but if Sal has any goons watching, I don't want them to know it's you," he explained. "And you *must* finish this movie, or things will just get worse."

Bobby complained that his new blonde hair wouldn't match the brown hair he had in the first half of the werewolf movie, but that didn't seem to bother Steve in the slightest.

"The color is so rotten in this studio I doubt anyone will even notice."

Chesty volunteered to do the work, since she knew something about bleach. While she worked, Steve returned to his movie. He had a notebook open beside the VCR, and whenever he found a mistake Martin Scorcese made, he jotted it down.

"The pros screw up almost as much as I do," he said, with a trace of pride in his voice.

Because Chesty was an unknown quantity around the warehouse, Steve did not insist that she make any

changes or do anything to her hair, which had obviously
already suffered enough. After Bobby's dye job and
Mean Streets, she was tired, worn out from stress and
lack of sleep. In her desperate state, she also agreed
to be in the werewolf movie, since Steve was now having
trouble getting the porno actresses to participate after
they saw what Bobby did.

"I'll do it if you'll let me sleep," she said, her eyes
narrowed to weary slits.

Steve dragged a tattered cot out of the corner.

"I only have one," he said apologetically. "It's the
one we use for you between scenes, Bobby. I use it
between marriages."

Bobby hesitated before answering. He pictured Stoke
busting in and finding him sleeping next to Chesty,
like two spoons, and imagined Stoke using those big
arms to pound him to a pulp. Then he remembered
that Stoke was most definitely dead, and wouldn't be
pounding anyone ever again.

"It's fine," Chesty said. "Really."

Bobby initially attempted to fit himself on the narrow
cot without coming into contact with her, which took
some doing and caused his muscles to quickly cramp
from the effort.

"You can touch me," Chesty said after several
minutes. "I'm not radioactive."

She wasn't radioactive. She was soft. He dropped
one arm over her side, accidentally brushing the
underside of her left breast. It felt sort of like touching
a basketball, but he liked it.

"You never told me," he said after a while. "What's
your real name?"

She never answered. He could hear her breathing
coming slow and regular. He had nearly dropped off

to sleep himself when he felt her shaking. She sputtered and grabbed his arm with her sharp fingers.

"I'm sorry," she said. "It's Stoke. We just left him there."

Bobby remembered Stoke lying slumped against the wall, his shirt soaked and red.

"He was dead," Bobby whispered in her ear. He could feel her tears on his arm. They gave him goosebumps.

"I know. But he shouldn't have died like that."

There was nothing more to say. She finally fell asleep not long after, but never let go of her grip on his arm and never did tell him her name. Bobby lay awake, breathing in the smell of sweat from her neck. He thought her fingernails might be drawing blood, but didn't move his arm.

Steve woke them up at noon to start a long day of filming. He had been upstairs setting the candy glass window since around 10 o'clock, working through his hangover. He had Bobby back, and a brand new actress, and he was happy.

"I hate to be an asshole," Steve said, interrupting Chesty as she cradled Bobby's head. "But could you rest off to the side? We're done with this set. We need to convert it to the morgue."

Bobby creaked his way to his feet. He had already been turned into a werewolf four times in the last two hours, and had been called upon to overturn a couch, smash through a door, fall down a flight of stairs and leap through the candy-glass window. He was clapped out, but Steve showed no sign of letting up.

"I don't remember a morgue scene in this movie," Bobby said as Chesty helped him toddle back to the cot.

"We wrote it after you took off," Steve explained. "We were going to have you die and be replaced by someone else, and have them turn into a zombie. That way they wouldn't have to be a werewolf. Because I haven't been able to find any more werewolves. Zombies are easier."

"But I'm back."

"I know. But I've already written the scene so we might as well go ahead and shoot it. This way you'll be a werewolf and then a zombie and then a zombie werewolf. I think it will be fun. This could be a real breakthrough. This could really put us on the map."

Bobby stretched out on the cot with a groan. He had scraped his arm on the windowsill while in werewolf form, and it still stung even after he had changed back. That was one of the drawbacks of the change; it made you more excitable and prone to injury, but left you the scars.

Chesty rolled up a chair and perched next to him.

"I never asked you this before, Stoke told me not to, but . . . how did you get into this business?" she asked.

He was too tired to talk about it.

"It's a long story."

The black-and-white TV was on, as usual, beaming tiny images to no one. A fist-sized head was talking. Bobby kicked up the volume lever with the tip of his tennis shoe.

"In a dramatic development this afternoon, police have arrested werewolf activist Paul Moreau for the murders of Drs. Cynthia Wardoe and Carl Johnson, and for a third werewolf murder that had not even been reported, that of unemployed drifter Bobby Chaney."

Chesty kicked her legs in surprise and nearly let

the chair roll out from under her. Bobby sat up on the cot, suddenly energized.

"You're not unemployed," Chesty said.

"I'm not dead, either. They must think Stoke is me."

Stoke was bigger than two or three Bobbys put together, but the police wouldn't know that. They'd check to see who rented the apartment, and assume the bloody dead body on the floor was the same person.

"Chaney was reported dead last night, but police have just released his name after charging Moreau with the murder," the tiny head said. "Ironically, Moreau was debating actor Monty Allen about the need for a lycanthropy cure at the time of his arrest."

The TV showed footage from the debate, including one shot where the camera zoomed in on Moreau as he was angrily making a point. Bobby grabbed the TV with both hands and held it right in front of his face, peering intently at the picture as if wanting to step into it.

"What are you doing?" Chesty asked.

"Look at his face. This was taken today."

He held the TV towards her. She frowned at the screen and then shook her head.

"So?"

"Look at his face."

"He's pretty good-looking for an old guy, but so?"

"Don't you remember the werewolf last night? He had a scar across his nose. A deep scar."

"Bobby, I don't know much about werewolves."

"Sorry. If he had a scar that deep when he was a werewolf, he'd have it on his nose today in human form."

"Your TV reception ain't so good. He could have a scar."

Bobby held the set back in front of his own face, squinting. He shook his head.

"No, it's not that bad. You would be able to see that scar. Plus, you shot him a couple of times, right? This guy doesn't look shot."

"So what you're saying is—"

"It's not him. They arrested the wrong guy."

"Are you going to tell?"

Bobby put the TV back down and stretched back out on the cot. He sighed and looked at the ceiling.

"No. I guess not. Then the police would wonder who Stoke was and they might bust Steve. I won't tell. It's just that guy's tough luck."

TEN

Paul Moreau was in a funk. He would have cried from sheer frustration if he were not so tired. The police had questioned him incessantly about his connection with the murders, and did not believe him when he protested his innocence. The way things were going, he couldn't blame them. How could he have been idiotic enough to suppose he wouldn't be framed for the murders? He was a prominent werewolf activist with a semi-shady past, in town to rail against the Werewolf Telethon. Whoever killed those doctors would be nuts *not* to frame him. He hadn't had sense of mind enough to come up with good alibis.

Even worse, how could he have a prime chance on nationwide television to debate his biggest enemy, and then blab secrets and come off looking like an idiot? He had his chance and lost everything. He sprawled uncomfortably on the prison bed and looked around at the shadows that strained through the bars. Even they seemed gloomy and dispirited, barely up to the task of sneaking in the windows to help make him depressed.

He had once thought it was only a matter of time before werewolves were accepted. After all, the Faeries and Elves and Goblins and other supernatural creatures had announced themselves to the public at the end of the 1960s, and had gradually been accepted into mainstream society. They moved out of the realm of folklore and became actors and farmers and whatever they wanted to be. If an Elf could be accepted, why not werewolves? But it hadn't happened. Even the supernaturals didn't want to associate with werewolves. Faeries were just as scared of werewolves as regular people were. His dream had never arrived.

And now everybody would be cured soon, to hear Monty Allen tell it. The Jean Grenier Society would disband. His dream world of human consciousness co-joined with animal senses would fade away. Maybe the Japanese would take up the idea. He heard they had werefoxes. They would take his idea and run with it, and America would lose another promising avenue of exploration. And it was all his fault. Deep down, he was afraid. He had let down more than himself. He had let down the one who made him.

"I'm sorry," he whispered, but there was no answer.

He thought back to the night when his life changed forever. Everything he had said in the Monty Allen debate was true, but he was annoyed with himself for saying it on television. It was a story he had previously only shared with the Jean Grenier members, and then only when they were ready. Now they would probably want their dues back.

It was, literally, a dark and stormy night. Thunder boomed frequently but there seemed to be no lightning. Raindrops drummed along every flat surface and the trees snapped and popped like the creaking joints of a giant. The enormous finned cars moved like blind sharks through the New York streets; bars and restaurants were packed with people huddling away from the elements. It was a bad night to be out, but a good night for a thief.

Paul Moreau was eighteen years old and was already very good at his chosen career. He required little food and little sleep and was blessed with a seemingly infinite patience unusual in one so young. He could watch the doorways of the townhouses on the upper East side, being careful to note who went where and when the houses were vacant. Now and then he did his pilfering in the daytime, making off mostly with jewelry and other small items that wouldn't impede his getaway. Mostly, though, he worked when the sun went down.

One night, well into a particularly successful string of burglaries, he was surprised by a homeowner who was home when he wasn't supposed to be. The homeowner heard a rustling sound outside a window and had looked out, expecting to shoo away a squirrel, when he had instead come face to face with what appeared to be a tall, thin dog. Moreau had grown his brown hair long until it swept down across his shoulder blades and onto his chest. At the time of the homeowner's surprise appearance, he was jimmying a window lock, an action that forced him to hunch on a fire escape and look down. His hair completely obscured his face and the effort of jacking the lock back and forth had eliminated any semblance it had to being combed. It looked like Lassie was conducting a break-in.

The homeowner banged on the glass, and Moreau had jumped back with a surprised yelp before scrambling away on all fours and dropping to the street below. From then on, the legend of a "dog-boy" thief roaming the streets of the upper east side had made the rounds, until even the *New York Times* did a small piece on it. Unfortunately, for Paul Moreau, the sudden notoriety also meant an increase in police patrols, which cut down on his ability to properly case his targets. A long-haired boy was noticeable in 1965, even in New York, and especially at a time when a dog-boy was on the prowl. He took to wearing a hat, but he kept on robbing.

The notoriety added something else to his modus operandi; now, when he was startled while breaking into a home—which was becoming a more frequent occurrence due to his impaired research—he would trade on his image as a half-beast by uttering a blood-curdling howl before tearing off into the night. He added to the mystery by dressing in brown trousers and shirts. He toyed with the idea of buying cheap plastic fangs, but rejected them as being uncomfortable. Nevertheless, his ruse worked. Soon the talk on the street was that a werewolf was robbing the city.

Werewolves had not been considered a problem in New York City until Moreau's crime streak. All of them took their medicine and tried to stay out of trouble. Having one of their number dedicate himself to lawbreaking cast a pall across their status as victims. As his crimes became more publicized, some members of the public began agitating against werewolves, at least werewolves in the city. In the country, it was presumed, they would simply be shot for trying to get into someone's house. A few hooligans even destroyed a shelter in Hell's Kitchen that gave out free tranquilizers to lycanthropy victims. Moreau himself did not care about that. Having the law-abiding citizens of Gotham turn their attention in the wrong direction was a boon to his activities. Business picked up.

Moreau's reputation as a wolfman preceded him by the time the dark and stormy night rolled around. He had pilfered a three-story townhouse of some valuable jewelry and a small radio and was making his way out an upstairs window onto a fire escape when the owner of the premises arrived home and rapidly made his way upstairs. The man saw the shaggy boy hanging halfway out the window and approached rapidly, snatching up a heavy candlestick on his way across the room. He was a big guy and he took a couple of practice swings on the way over; apparently he hadn't heard of the thieving werewolf on the prowl. The man was almost upon him when Moreau let out his practiced sound, a long howl that sounded like a rocket crashing to earth. He almost ruined the effect by laughing once he saw how quickly his attacker retreated.

Moreau was in a fine mood as he bounded down the fire escape and splashed through the streets, heading for the shelter of the trees in Central Park. His climbing and jumping, coupled with a skimpy diet, had conspired to put him in excellent physical shape, and the air he pumped in and out of his lungs felt cleansed by the spring rain. He bounded through the park, crossing through the first line of trees and a softball field, heading into a thicker patch of woods where the treetops were dense enough to keep most of the rain off the ground. Moreau leaned on a dry tree trunk and ran his hands through his wet hair. His run had left him tired but exhilarated, and he wasn't even annoyed to discover that the radio had gotten drenched. He tossed it under a nearby bush; he'd try to sell it anyway, if the bums didn't get it first.

It took a while before he realized that the rhythmic sound he had been hearing for the past minute wasn't his heart, but the steady clomp of approaching horse hooves. He stood up and looked around, but saw nothing. Surely the cops weren't out in the park on a night like this. He had just leaned back against the tree trunk when he felt the hairs rise on the back of his neck. The hooves were suddenly louder, and he heard the unmistakable snort of a horse. Whoever it was, they were right behind him, on the other side of the tree. His heart was racing again and he stood once more and slowly peeked around the trunk. Moreau didn't see anything at first, anything at all; it was as if a wall of darkness had fallen in front of him, as if the night had grown deeper. He blindly faced the dark wall until his eyes started to adjust.

Standing before him was an enormous man on an enormous horse, the two of them towering into the night like an evil totem pole. Moreau's initial fear was momentarily quelled by curiosity, and he stood squinting before the pair until he could see them better and better. The horse was a truly titanic beast, with neck muscles bigger than the circumference of his legs. It stood still and silent now. Its initial snort must have been a warning. The man was also still, an ebony statue. The darkness hovered over him, and the rain seemed not to touch him at all, offering no glimmering outline that would make him easier to see. Moreau couldn't gauge his age, or even his race. He was large and blocky looking, and wore a thick tunic that seemed to be made of dozens of different types of fur. The fur bristled, dry despite the rain. The man wore some kind of dark gray helmet that looked almost like a skull. Whoever he was, he was no cop, but possibly someone even worse. Paul Moreau wanted to run now, but it was no longer an option. He couldn't move.

"You are the wolf-boy I've heard about," the man said, his voice as mysterious as the rest of him.

It was resonant without being deep, raw without being scratchy. Moreau couldn't even be positive that it wasn't the horse that was talking. He stood silent and trembling before his interlocutor until he realized that a response was expected. The voice that only minutes before had issued a terrifying howl could now barely croak up an answer.

"Yes."

"You are a wolf-boy yet you are not a werewolf."

Moreau didn't know what to say; he had dropped out of school in part to avoid pop quizzes.

"Uh, yes. Sir. I mean, no, sir."

There was a long pause, and for a moment the figure seemed to fade back into his patch of deep night. Then the horse snorted once more, a short, sharp sound, and the man returned to view, a little brighter than before.

"Your misrepresentation has brought pain to those who do not deserve it. This must not continue."

Moreau just blinked.

"Would you like to be one? To become what you pretend to be?"

Moreau thought it over for a while. He didn't understand, but the man seemed to expect an answer.

"Would—would that be good?"

"Does it matter? Would you like to be one?"

His answer caught in his throat, but before he could voice it the man tossed something out to him.

"Catch."

Paul Moreau caught what he at first thought was an animal, a heavy, lifeless creature. He almost dropped it, but then realized it was just a skin. It looked like a gray rug.

"Put it on," the man said.

The skin smelled rank and felt damp, and he hesitated until the man raised one enormous arm as if to reach down and strike him. Moreau hoisted the skin over his shoulders, grunting with the effort, and almost fell to the ground under the weight of it. It must have been the hide of an unusually large wolf, or that of a whole pack of wolves sewn together.

"Well, I'm in your little suit," Moreau said after a moment, the weight of the fur and the absurdity of his situation making him indignant. "I don't feel anything. Are you happy now?"

The man's laughter surprised him. It was a strange chuckle, a little higher than he would have guessed.

"You have much to learn. You can be great if you wish. Good luck. I hope you survive."

So here he was now, in jail, the cause of promoting lycanthropy as limp and lifeless as that werewolf skin had felt when it first weighed down upon his back so many years ago. Moreau rested his head against one of the jail bars. *You can be great if you wish*, the Lord of the Forest had said. What a joke. There was nothing that could be done now. He had called his lawyer, an attorney who worked with the Los Angeles chapter of the Jean Grenier Society, but he couldn't be in Vegas until tomorrow and he probably couldn't help anyway. It was all over.

Moreau heard a rustling sound in the corridor and heard a familiar panting. He raised his head and caught sight of a K-9 drug-sniffing dog passing by, its nose held curiously in the air. It was a big dog, its eyes bright and intelligent, its coat shining even in the drab hallway. It cast a glance over him and then continued slowly down the hall, following a slow-moving knot of cops who were joking and laughing. Moreau smiled. Maybe things weren't so bad. He could prove his point. Doctor Doolittle could escape.

ELEVEN

Halloween was fast approaching, and it was getting nippy at night. Talbot Braudaway shivered and pulled his cotton jacket closer around his ribs. It didn't help much, and neither did the red Caesar's Palace baseball cap he wore backwards. Fall in Las Vegas did not have the changing leaves that he knew from Connecticut, but it did have the cold weather, at least at night. He wasn't sure he liked having only that part.

His two-way radio gave out a burst of static but then went quiet again. He was beginning to think he was being played for a chump, out at night spying on a stupid warehouse where they filmed porno flicks and werewolf movies. Maybe the Jean Grenier Society was just a waste of time, like his dad had said. Maybe he should just take the cure and get it over with. He could always write a book or something. *My Days as a Werewolf*, maybe, although he had made a full change without tranquilizers only three times, and had regretted all of them, especially the time when he killed his neighbor's dog. After that the neighbor's

daughter, who he thought was kind of cute, had
shunned him.

The Jean Grenier Society's rhetoric sounded pretty
good to him. He saw Paul Moreau on a late-night
infomercial and decided to sign up. He hated taking
the tranquilizers every month; they made him groggy
for days, which was probably the intent. They also did
nothing to relieve the horrible nightmares he got every
full moon, in which his hometown was destroyed again
and again by thundering tornadoes, so he just ended
up groggy and frightened. Moreau said he had a 12-
step program to show how people with lycanthropy
could make the change safely. Over his parents'
objections, Talbot took off for New York City and joined
its local chapter. He took over publication of the
newsletter, which was put out on a really ancient
Macintosh with an even more antique dot-matrix
printer.

He was happy for a while, but gradually grew
disillusioned. The 12 steps made reference to some
mysterious higher power, but it didn't seem to be god,
and Talbot wasn't sure he wanted to sign up for any
kind of devil worship. The training courses were also
a bust. The idea of turning into sentient, well-behaved
werewolves apparently involved injections of some kind
of illegal werewolf liquid, but Moreau didn't seem to
have much on hand and so it was rarely used and he
ended up on the tranquilizers anyway. Talbot had never
even seen any of the illegal stuff, had only heard about
it. Mostly, it was them sitting around, listening to
Moreau reminisce about how he was kidnapped by
some Army mad scientist with a German accent. Maybe
that could be his book, now that Moreau was arrested.
My Days with the Mad Werewolf Leader. Something

like that might sell, although he hadn't really seen
Moreau all that much.

"Talbot! All shit has broken loose," his radio squawked.
"The boss has escaped. We don't know where he is.
Remember, that's the story line. We don't know where
he is. And there's more. A bunch of people in a white
van have pulled out of here. I don't know what they're
doing. Over."

"Thank you, Eric," Talbot said flatly into the radio.

Eric was taking this fake spy business way too
seriously. He didn't realize they were wasting their
time. Those jokers in the van were probably just going
for dinner. Eric was keeping an eye on the Landon
Institute, and he was stuck watching this dismal
warehouse, where absolutely nothing seemed to be
happening. To make it worse, he had to perch at the
edge of a raised parking lot behind the warehouse,
which put him right in line for any cold wind that came
through. At least in the front he could watch traffic
go by and try to keep the wind off, but there was
nowhere to hide there so he was out in the dark and
the elements. Plus, the front was where the two scuzzy
guards worked. They were lazy, rarely deigning to leave
their folding chairs, but not so incompetent they
wouldn't eventually have spotted him. As long as he
was in the front, that is. The guards were presumably
supposed to guard the whole warehouse, but they never
came around the back.

All the Jean Grenier Society members had gone to
watch the debate with Monty Allen, where the great
leader had been arrested. He didn't know what had
happened to the rest of the JGS after that. They had
probably gone out to get beer.

And now the boss had escaped. Well, that was about

that. Moreau would probably disappear, leaving the rest of them to look like dumb teenagers. Eric was being weirdly cautious with his "that's our story" stuff on the radio. They really *didn't* know where he was. Moreau had never trusted his own troops enough to tell them where his hangout in Las Vegas was. They all stayed at the downtown headquarters or at rented apartments, but he had some secret pad stashed away and wouldn't let them visit. Talbot spat on the ground. Well, the boss man could rot there. It was all over. His dad was right. He could have been in college for a year now. He'd just take his cure and be done with it.

And this warehouse stakeout was really boring. It could be a chicken-packing plant for all he knew. The windows were blacked out and he couldn't see a thing that was going on inside. Moreau said they shot porn flicks on one side and werewolf movies on the other. He'd seen enough werewolves. Maybe he could peek in a window and at least see a skin flick underway. Then he remembered: they shot the porn in the day and werewolves at night. Just his luck.

Talbot almost didn't notice when a white van pulled into the parking lot of the warehouse, next to the pile of dim gray cars that always seemed to be parked there. It looked like a snowball rolling over slush. Didn't Eric say something about a white van? But there were probably a lot of white vans. Four men dressed in dark jackets got out and peered around suspiciously, touching their underarms. Did these guys have guns? Suddenly the stakeout was a little more interesting. The men walked around to what Talbot had been told was the werewolf side of the warehouse. One of them knelt and fooled around with the outside door, finally getting it to swing open. So they had guns, but they didn't have an invitation.

"Hey, Eric," Talbot said quietly into the radio, although he was far enough away that the men couldn't possibly hear him. "I think you better get over here. Now. That van you saw pulled up here. Something's going on."

Eric sounded very excited.

"I'll be there as soon as I can."

Talbot crept down the hill and edged his way around the cars, towards the blacked-out windows. Without Eric around, he wouldn't go in unless he heard gunshots. And maybe not even then.

TWELVE

A burly police officer shoved Ashly Durban to the side of the police van with one meaty arm and tapped her on the shoulder with his pistol.

"I said in the *back*," the man said, his eyes flat and cold. "In the back, not the front. We don't usually lead raids with reporters."

Durban nodded. She didn't really want to be in the front but felt it was her duty to at least make the effort. Another officer walked by, also clad in a dark blue LVPD jacket and wearing tall black leather boots. It was an unusually cold night for Vegas, in the 40s, and his breath frosted lightly in front of his face as if he were exhaling from a ghost cigarette. He frowned at Durban's lecturer.

"Larry, don't use your pistol like that. Clumsy as you are, you could blow her shoulder off."

The burly cop's Santa Claus cheeks blushed and he quickly slid his pistol into his holster.

"I'm sorry. I wouldn't have blown your shoulder off," he muttered to Ashly, and she smiled sweetly.

"I'm sure you wouldn't have."

The two police officers walked past the van and two cruisers to where half a dozen of their compatriots were gathered, all nervously standing around. Several of them were fondling their holsters. It was time for the raid. A beam of light suddenly struck her right in the eyes, turning the world red and giving her a quick shadow view of the veins in her eyelids.

"Bob, turn that thing off," Ashly snarled. "I thought you knew what you were doing. They're pissed at us already."

Several cops hissed at Bob and dragged their fingers quickly across their throats.

"See?" Ashly said. "That gesture means they're going to kill you."

She was a tad underdressed for the evening, wearing only a blazer over a thick blouse, as she had foolishly listened to Channel 12's weatherman, who had smiled and smiled as he predicted a much warmer night.

"I was just trying to warm you up," Bob said, flicking off the video camera's beam, which looked bright enough to light the moons of Jupiter.

Bob had not only ignored the local weatherman, he appeared to have tuned in to an Alaskan meteorologist. He wore a dull red parka with a tatty fringe of fake fur around its hood.

"Come on, Nanook," Ashly said. "I think it's showtime."

It looked like a football game was ready to break out, the way the cops were lined up. One of them was peering through night-vision binoculars. Durban squinted through the night trying to see what he was looking at; she thought she saw something moving, but it was so dark it looked like a shadow walking. Suddenly the man with the binoculars said, "He's in!"

and all the cops dashed off across a grassy field, their destination an apartment complex on the other side of a small square. Ashly and Bob trotted behind, Bob grunting with each step from the weight of the camera.

CBS had accompanied their footage of the Paul Moreau-Monty Allen debate with an article about police grandstanding, using their very public arrest of Moreau as one example. Apparently that did not sit well with the local law enforcement officers. When they got a tip that Moreau was going to pop into an apartment used by a known Jean Grenier Society member, they called *Live Entertainment*, which had made no snide remarks about the arrest. The police had been hideously embarrassed by Moreau's escape. He had somehow managed to trick a police dog into opening his cell and escorting him out, using its fangs to ward off other cops. The police didn't want the public to think that even their K-9 squad could be corrupt; they wanted *Live Entertainment* to witness valiant police officers recapturing Moreau, and they wanted it to be soon.

Ashly and Bob gasped their way up to the door of the apartment just in time to see the police knock the door in with a portable battering ram.

"Freeze!" the cops shouted, several times. They heard some muffled thumps and the sound of something breaking.

Ashly and Bob perched on the flat piece of concrete that served as a front porch, craning their necks to see in, but the two cops at the end of the raiding party kept shoving them back.

Durban quit trying after five minutes. She turned away from the door and leaned on the white wooden railing that surrounded the small porch and surveyed the courtyard. All the buildings in the apartment

complex looked the same, boxy and squat and brown
with simple white wood trimmings and neatly arranged
walkways. They were the architectural equivalent of
sensible shoes, and their bland simplicity somehow
made them seem more comforting under the night
sky. A few golden lights were burning, but no neighbors
had yet opened a window and poked their heads out
to see what was happening across the way. Aside from
knocking in the Jean Grenier Society's door, the police
had conducted a pretty quiet raid.

She could hear the tinny sound of one of the police
radios sending out a description of Moreau, beaming
it out to unseen police officers huddling in the night.
*Suspect is not known to be armed but is considered
dangerous. Suspect believed in possession of substances
that allow change to werewolf status even without full
moon. Be advised. Respond with deadly force if
attacked. Silver bullets are not required.*

It was actually a lovely night. The apartment complex
wasn't very well lit and the constellations were able
to muscle their way through the faint glow to show
their designs clearly in the desert sky. Durban could
make out some familiar shapes, but she didn't have
the names to go with them and so she just let her eyes
wander from star to star. She thought it was kind of
sad that the only time she had been able to relax this
month was in the middle of an arrest raid. All she
needed was a nice glass or two of wine and the night
would be perfect.

She was just about to turn back around and make
a token effort to get inside when something else caught
her eye. A white dog was standing underneath the
large tree that grew in the middle of the courtyard,
staring at her. She initially assumed that the dog was

just looking in her general direction, since there were several men on the porch with her, not to mention Bob with his bulky camera and its blinding light. After a minute she became convinced that it was staring right at her. It was one of those husky dogs, the ones that look like albino wolves, and she thought she could see its ice-blue eyes, although she knew it was too far away and she shouldn't be able to see much of anything.

"You can go in now," one of the cops said, and she could hear Bob's boots clunking on the floor, but she didn't want to move. The dog didn't take its eyes off of her, just stared at her with those tiny cold blue laser beams. One of the police officers behind her poked her gently on the shoulder.

"Uh, Miss, you can go in now. But don't talk to any of them."

She snapped out of it and smiled at him.

"Thanks."

Durban turned to look across the courtyard once more before stepping inside the apartment, but now she saw only the tall black tree. The dog must have just been someone's pet, out for its evening constitutional.

Once inside, Durban decided that either the Jean Grenier Society was made up of exceedingly sloppy individuals or the cops had really made a mess. There were papers everywhere, including the floor, so many that at one point Bob slipped and nearly busted the camera. The apartment was pretty sizable but the Society had stuffed it with so much furniture and equipment that it seemed cramped. There were five folding tables holding innumerable computers and printers, three large televisions and several black boxes that must have been VCRs. Cables and extension cords snaked everywhere. The place may or may not have been harboring a wanted criminal, but it was definitely a fire hazard.

Several members of the Society were scattered about the room, each with his very own police officer at his side. One of them was leaned up against a wall being patted down for weapons by two cops who weren't patting very gently. Durban could hear the slaps from across the room. In contrast to their usual fastidiousness, the Society members present were dressed in T-shirts or rugby shirts and shorts, and their long hair was tousled. Anyone wanting to borrow a comb in that place this particular evening would be out of luck.

"I thought you kids dressed a little nicer and did your hair up all fancy," one of the cops said. "What happened to your little gray suits?"

"We stopped wearing them because people are blaming us for those killings," one of the Society members shot back. "Two of our guys got beat up on the strip last night, not that you care."

Seeing Durban and Savik, he rolled his eyes in disgust.

"And here's just what we need, more negative media coverage. Fan the flames, incite the people to blame us for everything."

The complaining member was hunched in front of one of the computers, his thin arms splayed across the table top while one of the policemen leaned over him and rifled through a box of floppy disks.

"What you need is a haircut and a better attitude, son," the cop said, and the Society member rolled his eyes.

"Thanks, *Dad*. And you can bet you're going to pay for that printer if you broke it."

He gestured with a still clean shaven chin towards a printer that had been knocked off its stand and trailed perforated paper like a jet fighter spewing smoke. The cop moved his right hand to smack his young taunter, but, seeing that Durban was looking, he simply patted the man on his shoulder.

"Just put it on my tab, son."

The police were getting as testy as the Society members because they apparently had failed to locate their prey. Paul Moreau was nowhere to be found.

"Look, we don't just pop in on a whim," a cop named Derek said to the highest-ranking member of the Society present, an acne-ridden man in a tattered green Pink Floyd T-shirt who, after some prodding by Derek, said his name was Scott. He was also clean shaven, and Durban wondered if the Society members were now going to drop that habit as well.

"We were watching. We saw Paul Moreau come in here. He was wearing a black coat."

Scott shook his head, shaking his frizzy curls.

"*I* just came in. Not Paul. You're the ones who arrested him, keeping track of him is your job, not ours. It was me you saw."

Derek squinted at him.

"Then where's the coat? We sure didn't see any Pink Floyd shirt."

Scott began crooking his index finger in an exaggerated motion, like an old movie villain, and walked the cop down the hallway to a closet near the front door. Durban and Savik had to step back out on the porch so he could come through. He threw open the door with a flourish and there, in the midst of six or seven jackets of various sizes and shapes, was a long black wool coat.

"There ya go."

Derek fondled the coat with his fingers.

"It's not cold."

"I wasn't out long."

"It looks kind of big for you. Try it on."

Scott sighed in disgust, but dutifully slipped the coat off its padded hanger and put it on. It hung on him almost as loosely as it had on the hanger.

"It doesn't fit you," Derek said, but Scott shrugged, which made the coat ripple.

"Baggy is in, man, don't you know that?"

There was a pile of clothes wadded up on the closet floor.

"And what are these?"

"My laundry. I haven't had time to go to the laundromat lately. Want me to try them on, too? We could have a nice little fashion show."

Derek gave up on the clothing issue with a snarl and stalked back down the hallway to the living room, with Scott right on his heels and Bob following after, camera light beaming.

"Look, I told you. Paul is not here and he hasn't been here," Scott said. "We heard he escaped, but we have not seen or heard from him since."

"You know where he stays in Las Vegas, though, don't you? He is your *leader*, after all."

"You'd think so, but we don't, and that's the truth," Scott said. "He came to Vegas before most of us did, and he doesn't hang out with us all that much. He likes his privacy. He meets with us here or at the headquarters, but we do not know where he stays the rest of the time."

The police milled around for a few minutes until it was apparent that Paul Moreau was not to be found. One of them was scuffling the floor with his shoes, another looking behind doors to rooms that had already been thoroughly searched. The Society members frowned until Scott said, "Look, he's not going to come here. He wouldn't put us in danger. You might as well go get some doughnuts."

Larry lunged at him, but Derek restrained him.

"Camera's here, Larry. Shouldn't get all worked up, y'know. He's not worth it."

Larry walked to Savik and whispered in his ear, "Say, you wouldn't turn that camera off for a minute, would you? As a favor?"

Savik didn't take his eye away from the viewfinder as he whispered back.

"Sorry. Wouldn't look good, my man."

"All right," Derek said. "If anyone suddenly remembers where Mr. Moreau might be out howling at the moon right about now, such information will definitely be appreciated. If we find out later that you knew all along where he is, rest assured that you will become intimately familiar with the inside of a jail cell."

He paused for a long moment, but got no response. Ashly and Bob pushed themselves against the wall to let the police go clumping past.

"Make us look good, huh?" Derek whispered, giving Ashly a wink as he went by. "Like on that show *Cops*."

As they walked out the door, Durban saw the white dog again, this time standing on the other side of the big tree. It looked at her for a second and then trotted off into the night. It shone eerily white against the dark ground until it vanished out of sight.

THIRTEEN

His next scene called for Bobby to be only a half-werewolf, as he was supposed to be discovered mid-change by the angry father of one of his teen victims, a perky brunet he had dispatched with his fearsome claws. Steve pondered using the blue light on one-quarter power, but decided against it. It was late, Bobby was far too tired for another change and Steve was worried about fiddling with the light too much and possibly burning it out. Those things were hard to replace, and he didn't have the money for it.

They decided to just stick a fuzzy wig on his head and plastic fangs in his mouth. A stagehand bought the fangs down the street at a convenience store for $1.39. The cardboard backing behind them showed a boy pretending to be a dog, showing his canines. Up until four years ago, the cardboard had displayed a bloody-lipped vampire grimacing over the pointy teeth. A prominent lawsuit from a vampire support group had put an end to that, but

118

everyone knew they were really vampire teeth for
Halloween.

Bobby was relieved that there were no more changes
in store for the day, and happily wore the teeth even
though they chafed his gums. The wig itched, too, but
it was much better than having the light on again. It
was a first for him—a real werewolf dressing up as a
fake werewolf. The man playing the enraged father
turned out to be a burly guy who actually spoke Spanish
as his native language, another first for one of Steve's
productions. The man actually did look kind of pissed
off; he must have found out how much Steve was going
to pay him.

The scene was set in the same dining room Bobby
had supposedly jumped into earlier. Chesty was
playing the sister of the deceased girl, and Bobby
was now supposed to be after her, which was another
reason the father was so angry. The man had a silver
candlestick and was just poised to pretend to club
Bobby to death when there was a crashing in the
background. Someone had knocked over one of the
rear lights.

"Damn it, what's going on back there?" Steve said.
The pace of filming was wearing on him, too, and
he was not prepared to be nice to oafish crew
members.

Three men stepped out of the shadows, hands
hovering threateningly over their ribs. A fourth man
held back, lurking in the darkness.

"Greetings," the leader said.

They all looked kind of alike, tough-guy clones,
complete with dark jackets and stubble on their chins.
Steve stared at them in amazement.

"Look, tell Sal that I'll get his movie done and he'll

get his money," Steve said, with as angry a voice as he dared muster in armed company. "If he interferes with me, I won't be able to get it done and he can forget about that liver."

The men exchanged baffled looks.

"I don't know any Sals," the lead man said. "We're here for the Landon Institute. We hear you have another werewolf. We just want to borrow him for a little bit."

Steve glanced at Bobby and then back to the interloper.

"Look at him! Would we have to dress him up like that if he was a werewolf?"

Bobby smiled, displaying the plastic teeth. He pushed them out of his mouth with his tongue and then pulled them back in. The lead thug looked dismayed.

"You mean he's not a werewolf?"

Chesty reached over and pulled off his wig, displaying his spiky hair. Some of the glued-on facial hair went with it.

"Damn," the man muttered. His hand left the area of his ribs and dropped to his side. "Do you know where we can get one?"

Steve shook his head.

"Do you think I would work with this if I had more werewolves?"

The men turned to go, looking confused. Chesty dropped the wig back on Bobby's head. Steve, emboldened by his success, shouted at the retreating men.

"I thought you were done over there at the Landon Institute."

"Not quite," their leader called back.

The men were rounding behind the werewolf light, with various crewmembers stepping respectfully out of their way.

"Tell Cynthia and Carl I'm all out of werewolves," Steve called again.

The men stopped. Bobby frowned at Steve.

"Steve, they're dead. They got killed."

"They did?" Steve put his hands on his hips, looking genuinely surprised. "Huh. Was it on the news?"

Bobby nodded.

"I should watch the news once in a while, I guess."

The men started moving again, but then one of them tripped. Like the moon bursting from behind fast clouds, the blue light came on and caught Bobby full in its beam. He was sitting on the couch, his legs twisted underneath him like a pretzel. The thugs stared closely at him. He struggled to get up but his awkward pose had cut off the circulation to his legs, and when his feet hit the floor it felt like he had stepped on an electric wire. He giggled despite himself. The giggle dropped in volume until it became a growl.

"Well, well, well," the lead man said.

They had come back around the light, guns in hand. Three of them were aimed at Bobby, one at Chesty. She had been edging away from Bobby as he made the change, but stopped moving once one of the men had her in his sights. The rest of the crew saw they did not appear to be targets and took off, vanishing behind the equipment with surprising speed. Their fleeing footsteps echoed off the walls.

"I'll be damned," Steve sputtered as Bobby sprouted hair. "He *is* a werewolf."

"Better trank him quick," the lead man said, ignoring

Steve for the moment. "He'll be on us in another second or two."

One of the other men had pulled out a pistol with an oversized barrel. Bobby, as fully changed as the light would allow, snarled from the couch through two sets of teeth. His real fangs had apparently grown to fit the plastic ones. He poised to spring.

"I need him! You can't have him!" Steve shouted, but the man with the tranquilizer gun shoved him aside and lined up a clear shot.

He would have made it, too, were it not for the two-by-four that came down on his hands, knocking the gun away. The tranquilizer gun slid to Steve's feet, and he picked it up. The man turned to see who had attacked him, only to see the same two-by-four, this time up close. He crumpled just as the three others turned their pistols to their new attackers. They were two long-haired young men wielding boards from a nearby construction site, one of which had a wicked nail in it.

"Now would be a good time," said the one with a red Caesar's Palace baseball cap.

Steve, finally coming to life, obediently shot the lead man in the back with the tranquilizer gun, also sending him crumpling to the floor. One of the other men got off a shot, but the two young attackers had ducked behind the werewolf light and it went wide. Then the gunmen realized they had done the unthinkable—turned their backs on a werewolf. It was too late. The stage couch made an excellent launching pad, and Bobby was airborne. He came down on the nearest thug, who screamed as the claws dug into his back. The remaining man whirled to fire, but one of the long-haired attackers was quicker. The gunman took a two-by-four full in the face, staggering back into the werewolf light.

It creaked and swayed on its massive base. Steve dropped the tranquilizer gun and tried to steady the light, but he was too late. It was a relic, after all, dating back to the early years of the Second World War, and he really hadn't taken very good care of it. One side of the round base was rusted nearly through, and the staggering man had shoved it further in that direction. Despite the tug of Steve's desperate hands, the gigantic assembly gave a metallic groan and crashed to the concrete warehouse floor. Everyone present, even Bobby, clapped their hands over their ears to ward off the noise. The blue light winked off, forever.

Steve stood dazed before the expensive ruin. He had bought the light a decade before, at an illegal auction. It had cost him thousands, years of savings. For the first few months he had polished it frequently, replaced its frayed wiring, and dealt with the already-troublesome rust as best he could. Gradually he slacked off in his ministrations. The light resumed its slow decay, and now it was gone. The shock wore off quickly and pioneer tears came, charting courses down his cheeks.

"My light," he said, just above a whisper.

Bobby stopped shredding the gunman's jacket. The light hadn't been on him long enough to render him completely brainless, and its noisy demise brought some sense back to him. His tufts of gray hair were disappearing, and he spat out the plastic fangs. They were probably the only things that had saved his victim's life. He had tried to bite the man in the back of the neck, but the cheap plastic wasn't tough enough

to break the skin. He had succeeded only at bloodying
the man's jacket and scaring him into unconsciousness,
a state shared by all of his compatriots. Or so it
seemed. The lead man, the trank dart still jammed
in his back, suddenly swiveled his pistol arm. He tried
to aim at Bobby but was apparently having some
trouble functioning. He did manage to get a bead
on the weeping Steve, who presented a wobbling but
relatively easy target. Bobby growled a warning, but
it was too late. The man fired, catching Steve square
in his narrow chest. The wiry director fell back on
the tangled mess of the ruined light, gasping. Then
the gunman passed out, denying the two long-haired
young men the guilty pleasure of striking him.

"Who are you guys?" Chesty shouted.

The stage was both cluttered and elevated on risers,
making it difficult for her to reach the floor. She took
a moment in her descent to unscrew a small light from
its base, hefting it like a small baseball bat. She didn't
know who these new people were, and after last night
she wasn't taking chances.

"Jean Grenier Society," the one with the red cap
said, sounding a little out of breath. "My name is
Talbot."

"I'm Eric," said the other one. He wore a plain white
T-shirt with blue jean cut-offs. The Jean Grenier Society
had apparently abandoned its dress code in a big way.

"Forget them!" Bobby called. "They're always outside
with their picket signs."

He hunched over Steve, whose eyes were half-open,
staring at nothing.

"Steve . . . hold on, Steve."

Steve trembled. His eyes opened a little wider. He
was not doing well. A red flower of blood bloomed

on his chest, its center a black hole going deep inside.

"I'm stuck on a piece of metal," he gasped. "Move me over."

Bobby lifted him slightly, with Chesty's help, and slid him over two inches. It seemed to help. The Society members stared over their shoulders.

"Steve, can you hold on?" Bobby asked.

Steve, not lying for once, shook his head.

"That man . . . that man said the Landon doctors were murdered," Steve sputtered. Bobby nodded. "They used to come in here. I loaned them werewolves for their tests. Some of them came back, some didn't. I wouldn't let them take you, Bobby. They wanted to. You were too good."

Bobby closed his eyes. He replayed the pictures from the TV screen in his mind. So that was where he had seen them.

"I wouldn't let them take you. The man . . . Carl . . . gave me a package once. It had some videotapes. I think of the tests. And some other stuff. I didn't watch them. I think something is wrong over there, maybe. I think he wanted them for blackmail."

Steve uttered a hacking cough. His body trembled slightly.

"Where did he put them? The videos?" Talbot asked.

"Steve, where did you put the videos?" Bobby asked, as if he was now the only one the director could hear.

Steve's eyes flew open wide, and then shut halfway down again.

"It's in . . . in . . ."

His hands struggled weakly, trying to point. They wavered like butterflies.

"I'm on some metal again," he said.

"Sorry," Bobby said.

They tried to move him again. It seemed harder this time. Talbot tapped Bobby on the shoulder, and Bobby looked down. Steve was dead.

"Well," Bobby said.

He and Chesty let go and Steve sagged in the metal frame of his greatest possession. The four stood around, saying nothing, until they heard the police siren. The gunshots shouldn't have carried far in this neighborhood. One of the crew members must have overcome the usual distaste for the police and called 911.

"Come with us," Eric said.

"Where?" Chesty asked.

"We can take you to Paul Moreau."

"No, we can't," Talbot interjected.

"I thought he was in jail," Bobby said.

"He isn't. And, yes, we can take you to him."

"Since when?" Talbot asked.

"I know where his hideout is," Eric said. "I had to give him a ride once when his truck broke down. He told me not to tell."

"Aren't *you* special," Talbot sneered, but Eric ignored him.

The sirens sounded closer. One of the thugs on the floor began to stir, fingers groping automatically for a pistol. Talbot and Eric took a moment to round up all the weaponry from the floor and from the drugged fingers of the downed gunmen. It made a nice little collection.

"What about the videos?" Chesty asked.

Bobby wrapped an arm around her as they ran towards the side door, behind the clanking Jean Grenier Society members.

"I don't think this is a good time."

They piled into a ratty Chevrolet that Eric claimed
as his. On the way out they drove by the front of the
warehouse where the two guards sat, headphones on,
camouflaged legs splayed comfortably, oblivious to the
world. The guards smiled and waved as Eric peeled
out and blasted the Chevy down the road.

FOURTEEN

Despite his coating of hair, Bobby Chaney shivered under the moonlight. It felt as cold as the moon looked.

"Concentrate," said the gravelly voice in his ear. "She's right over there, on the cactus. Concentrate on her."

Bobby put the cold out of his mind and concentrated. His werewolf eyes pierced the night in a way he hadn't known was possible. The owl appeared to swoop closer, but she hadn't moved; his perception of her had improved, had stretched to take in every feather, every curve of her talons. He could see the tiny insects that burrowed under the feathers and over the talons, watched them stream around each other like pedestrians viewed from a skyscraper. The dark shape of the cactus faded away, leaving only the owl and its parasites, only the pulsing animal life. He concentrated, taking a breath in deep past his sharp teeth. He could see everything about the owl, but he could not see through its eyes.

"It's not working," he reported. "I feel something but it's not like what you said."

"Maybe I should up the dosage," the voice said.

Paul Moreau stepped around from behind him, holding the giant needle that sloshed with blue fluid. Chesty, Talbot and Eric stood around in a ragged semicircle, watching.

"Are you sure that's safe?" Chesty asked tentatively.

Moreau seemed to know what he was doing, but he had already given Bobby two fat needles full.

"I think so," Moreau answered, even as he was rooting around under the hair for a vein. "I used to get shot up with it a lot, lots more than this."

Eric and Talbot traded glances. They had heard this story before.

"In the Army," Talbot whispered almost inaudibly to Eric. Eric didn't smile.

Moreau had a little of the moon drug out here, stored in a gallon-sized glass bottle with a cork stopper. The stuff only filled it halfway. It looked like a jug of Ty-D-Bol, or some exotic fruity drink. He said the moon drug would have a more intense werewolf effect than did the light at the warehouse, and that seemed to be true. The hair had started sprouting from Bobby even before the needle had cleared the vein the first time. It grew out longer and thicker than it ever had in the warehouse. Steve would have been jealous. Bobby felt a warm rush as the fluid streamed into his body again. He shivered involuntarily and waited.

They were at Moreau's secret hideaway, which, despite Talbot's predictions, turned out to be nothing fancy. In fact, it made the Jean Grenier Society's Vegas apartment look positively luxurious by comparison. It

was two old silver Airstream trailers, their sides
inexpertly welded together to form one larger unit.
The interior walls had been cut away so roughly that
the Airstreams seemed to have merged through some
kind of horrible highway accident, and there were bits
of hair caught on the ragged metal where Moreau had
failed to duck his towering head adequately. Desolation
stretched around the monstrous Airstreams on all sides,
a desert moonscape complete with something that
looked like a rough sketch for an Apollo lander.

"I think," Bobby said, and Moreau and the others
watched him expectantly. "I think it's—"

He saw them staring back at him, Chesty, Eric,
Talbot, Moreau and a werewolf he didn't know. The
werewolf was short and thin, wearing only a ratty pair
of jeans, the gray hair of its chest ruffling softly in
the night breeze. Its eyes were fixed eerily on him,
glowing like buttons in the moonlight. He tightened
his claws on the cactus as he realized that the werewolf
was him. He was outside himself. Paul Moreau was
right. It was working. He felt his heart hammering
away in his chest. He rotated his head around to peer
into the night behind him, then brought it back
around. The world rotated neatly on its axis to
accommodate his new eyes. He extended a wing to
them in greeting, then folded it back against his chest.
Chesty brought her hands to her mouth, her face
unreadable. Talbot and Eric gaped in open surprise.
Moreau just smiled.

He caught sight of a desert rat scuttling along
beneath scrub grass. It was nothing more than the
vaguest shimmer of movement, but his owl brain
knew what it was. He opened his wings and took to
the air, as silent and deadly as a hurled knife. The

rat paused to sniff a pebble, its eyes and attention turned in completely the wrong direction. Bobby snatched it off the ground and delivered it to the afterlife in an instant, one sharp claw piercing its tiny heart. The earth receded below him as he climbed, and then rose to greet him again as he banked into a turn and dropped the dead rat at Moreau's feet.

He opened his eyes again and the moon hung before him. He had fallen onto his back. Chesty hovered over him, a look of concern on her face. On the periphery of his vision he saw the baffled owl alighting back on the cactus arm, unaware of having left. Moreau and Chesty helped Bobby to his feet. He thought he might stumble, but he didn't. He didn't feel disoriented at all, but instead seemed even more in control of his own body. The change had gone, taking with it the hair and fangs. Chesty brushed desert remnants from his back, her caresses a little softer than what was actually required to remove the dirt.

"That was great," Bobby said.

He wanted to say something more profound, but couldn't think of the words. Talbot and Eric peppered him with questions, their jealousy apparent. The group headed back for the composite Airstreams. Once they had walked a suitable distance, the owl pounced again on the dead rat, taking it this time for a meal rather than a trophy.

"Can I try that?" Talbot asked. He walked backwards in front of Moreau, his face pleading.

"Yes," Moreau said. "But not now. You have to make the change hundreds of times before the fluid will take you to the next level. I got it thanks to the Army. I know you think my stories are old and boring, but it's true."

A quick blush darkened Talbot's cheeks.

"I have good ears, you know," Moreau continued. "Bobby was ready because he has apparently made a lot of changes as an actor. Later, I'll work with you to make it happen for you. And you, too, Eric. Unless—"

"Unless the cure goes through," Chesty finished for him. "Then you're sunk."

"Yes, then we're sunk."

"We just need to find those videos, those things that man at the warehouse told us about," Chesty said.

"That's right," Moreau said. He paused and looked at Chesty. "You certainly seem to be on our side of things."

She shrugged.

"I'm tired of getting pushed around." She rubbed a hand across Bobby's bare shoulders. "I'm tired of seeing him get pushed around, too."

"Thank you," Bobby said quietly. He still felt a bit like he was up in the air, in the owl.

"What we need to do, then, is find those videotapes. You said that this Steve said he had been given the tapes by Carl Johnson. Would Steve have kept them at home?"

"I doubt it," Bobby said. "He sort of lived at the warehouse."

"So they're there."

"Probably. But there are thousands of videos there. Everything is shot on video. Steve said he couldn't afford film."

They had reached the Airstreams. Moreau gestured

towards the jug of blue fluid, which was plopped in the dust like a bottle of moonshine outside a distillery.

"Take some of the moon drug with you. Get into the warehouse. You still have keys?"

Bobby nodded.

"Okay. Get in, go where the tapes are. Use just a little bit of the drug—I'll show you how much—and then use your sense of smell."

Bobby grabbed a sweatshirt that Moreau had loaned him, pulling it over his head. It made him look like a little kid dressing up in his father's clothes.

"I never noticed having a better sense of smell before."

"That's because you were under that light. The light was one of the first ways the military tried to turn werewolves into soldiers, but it was too crude. It just turned them into beasts. The military sold them off and they ended up on the black market, which is probably how your director got his. But this stuff was synthesized later. It amplifies the change without completely shutting off the higher parts of your brain. If you concentrate on your nose this time instead of your eyes, it might work."

"But—how will smelling better help me find the tape?" Bobby asked.

Moreau rested one large hand on his shoulder.

"I'll explain it before you go. Let's just say that you'll need to fully explore your new sensory powers."

"Oh."

"It will be difficult." He checked his watch. "God, it's past three. You all must be tired."

"I sure am," Bobby said.

"I apologize for getting you started tonight, but we don't have much time left and I needed to know if the moon drug would work. It does, so we can relax for just a bit. Let's all get some sleep and we'll do more exercises tomorrow. You'll go in tomorrow night."

"Okay."

Moreau smiled, extending his hand for a shake.

"Congratulations. You're finally becoming an animal."

FIFTEEN

Bobby peered around the yellow Buick, eyes open wide in a look of anticipation that would have suited Don Knotts.

"Guards are gone around back," he whispered.

Chesty's head appeared atop his, nearly resting on his right cheek.

"Let's go."

The warehouse had new guards who actually seemed to take an interest in their job. They were bigger, beefier guys than the last ones, and looked more ex-military than ex-biker gang. The two Schwarzeneggers kept a regular beat, clomping back and forth out front for a bit and then working their way down the sides and around the back. Sometimes one was in front while the other was in back, which made things difficult for Bobby and Chesty. Once in a while, though, they would walk around together, muttering in voices that seemed to vibrate right at the low edge of the audible spectrum.

Bobby and Chesty edged around the car and darted for the building, aiming for the porno mill side. Too much had gone on in the part devoted to werewolfery, and the guards seemed to be focusing their attentions there. Fortunately for Bobby, his old key worked for either door. Or so he thought. He jammed it in the lock and pushed with as much force as he dared, but it wouldn't turn. The old lock had wiggled and bucked as if it was trying to impale itself on the key and end it all. This one felt new and impregnable.

"They changed the lock," he whispered frantically.

He was a little surprised, given the expense, but apparently the film crews inside were tired of killer werewolves and teams of assassins running amok in their workplace.

"I don't blame them," Chesty whispered back. "Stand aside."

She gave him a firm push on his shoulder, moving him before he had time to respond. She pulled a thin strip of metal out of her left boot and deftly inserted it into the lock. After a few seconds she grunted and gave the strip a twist. The door creaked open.

"Where did you learn to do that?" he whispered as she pushed past him and went into the dark warehouse. Once safely inside, with the door shut behind them, she answered in nearly a normal voice.

"Old boyfriend."

"Stoke?"

"Stoke is dead."

He couldn't see her in the dark, but he felt her hands lightly brushing him, working their way across his shoulders, behind his neck. An electric tingle went through his legs when he thought she might be kissing him, but he couldn't tell if her lips were really that soft or if she was merely breathing hard across his mouth. Then her arms pulled him closer and his eyes closed despite the darkness and he knew for a fact that she was kissing him. He smiled even as he kissed her back, although she couldn't see it.

"You're brave, Bobby," she whispered when they parted, and he merely swallowed hard and leaned against her soft but sturdy chest. He lowered his head onto her shoulder and she brushed his chin with her lips. They heard one of the guards crunching past outside. There was silence for a moment and then she whispered, "We'd better get started."

Bobby fished around in his pocket and pulled out a tiny flashlight, shining it around the room. He had never explored the porno side of the warehouse much. He was usually far too tired, and the porno actors generally appeared more appalling than alluring. For their part, they did not welcome a sharp-clawed werewolf in their midst, especially since they were naked much of the time. Now that he was here looking around, Bobby saw that he had not been missing much. The porno mill had not set up even the meager niceties Steve had paid for; they did not share the outer reception room, and used this door as the only entrance. It was not impressive, had not so much as a welcoming fern. There was a water fountain in one corner, but the rest of it looked more like a storage area. Dozens of fleshy-looking appendages dangled from the walls or peeked out from stacks of boxes. There was also an odd assortment of whips, chains, shiny rings of various sizes and even a dusty motorcycle, a boxy old German rattletrap with a sidecar. Bobby remembered when they had filmed some spectacular porno scenes in that. The idiot who rode it in forgot to shut it off for a few minutes and nearly asphyxiated the werewolf crew.

"Come on," he said, leading Chesty to the room's only other door. They could tell when they stepped out into the main area of the warehouse. The air seemed different, their footsteps magnified. Chesty nearly tripped over a mattress laid out on the floor, for one of the shoots that couldn't even be bothered with scenery. She felt something round and rubbery under her feet and kicked it away in disgust.

They passed the looming, useless hulk of the blue light. Bobby splayed the light around its carcass, which had been taped with an evidence tag but had not been moved. There was no trace of Steve, no strip of fabric or smears of blood. Bobby thought there would be something, some kind of evidence Steve had died there. There was none. The light was just old ex-military junk, not a monument to Steve.

"I asked you before, but you wouldn't tell me," Chesty said as she gazed at the ruined light. "How did you get into this stuff?"

Bobby was only fifteen years old, but he had already packed a lot into that time—mostly bad things. How could he tell Chesty that he considered the werewolf movies a step up? Living with his mother, a failed showgirl, in a series of apartments as her work took her from big casinos to small casinos to truck stops to private parties; finally striking out on his own, running away to sleep on the floors of friends he didn't really know very well, and who ended up seeming like only young versions of his mother. And then, one night, one of the other people crashing at an apartment turned into a hairy beast and bit him. The other kids knocked out the werewolf with an empty Boone's Farm bottle, but it was too late. The bite was deep, and Bobby had the bug. It was hard for him to make friends after that, after everyone knew what he carried inside. One night he bumped into the kid who had bitten him. The kid apologized and said there was a place he could go if he wanted to make some money with his new affliction. Bobby did.

"I was kind of homeless, and I heard there were guys looking for werewolves to make movies. I was pretty good at it, they said. I've been doing it for a year. A year is a long time."

"So it's showbiz, huh?" Chesty said.

He thought of the dubbed voices, the shifting lighting behind scenes, the scripts that changed from day to day and sometimes hour to hour.

"Not really."

"It's all showbiz." She felt her way over to him and took his arm. "You and I are showbiz veterans together. You know, I made a movie once."

"Really? What was it?"

"Don't get excited. It wasn't a real movie. It was one of those over there."

She grabbed his arm and aimed the flashlight at the porno side of the warehouse, but its beam was too weak to travel that far.

"Oh. What was it like?"

She paused, as if not wanting to discuss it. She sucked in a breath.

"Interesting. I got really drunk beforehand. It's not really romantic. You're lying there with some guy's thing in your mouth and his belly's pooching out and two other guys are aiming cameras and lights at you. But you know how that is."

He nodded but she couldn't see him.

"Are you disgusted I told you that?"

"No."

She brushed his cheek with her hand.

"Stoke was. For a drug dealer he was pretty moralistic. It happened before I met him, but he threw me into a wall anyway. When I told him."

"I'm sorry."

They kissed again, both feeling at home in the dark warehouse, surrounded by the ghosts of their pasts. After a moment they remembered they still had work to do in the present. They walked to the far side of the warehouse, to a set of three doors. One led to the outer office, Bobby knew, and one led to Steve's office. The tapes were stored behind the third one. Steve had been fanatical about keeping everyone out of there, and Bobby had no key for it. Chesty picked it, too.

"Voy-la," she said as the door swung open, exposing its contents to the flashlight beam.

It opened to a long hallway that in turn opened to another room. It was chillier than the rest of the place. Steve had always bought cheap videotapes, but he thought keeping them cool would make them last longer. Bobby aimed the flashlight and they looked around with sinking hope. What they discovered were videotapes arranged in towering racks, making the room look like a scale model of a big city. A video editing booth was set up in one corner of the room, complete with a nineteen-inch monitor and knobs and switches for playback and editing. The tapes were in clear cases with strips of white tape along their spines, which bore neatly typed titles like "Claws of Death" and "Fangs Again." Bobby had hoped that the tapes they needed would be strewn about the editing booth, out of their cases, with big lettering like RECENT LANDON INSTITUTE TAPES or INCRIMINATING

EVIDENCE scrawled on them, but that wasn't the case. He would have to do as instructed and use the moon juice again.

Bobby put the flashlight on the floor, facing up, and dug around into a pocket. He tried to look nonchalant as he pulled out a rubber tube and wrapped it around his left bicep. The liquid in the syringe looked orange in the flashlight beam, and rolled back and forth in the clear tube like a small ocean.

"I don't want to do all of this at once. I'll take a really, really small hit."

Chesty watched him closely. Most people would think twice about being in a small room with a person preparing to turn themselves into a werewolf, but she didn't flinch or step back.

"You really seem more alive since we met Moreau. You used to be such a slug. You watched TV more than me. He's made you feel better about being a werewolf, hasn't he?"

Bobby tugged on the tube with his teeth, pulling it into a knot. He clenched and released his fingers several times, his left fist beating like a heart. A wormlike vein surfaced in the crook of his elbow.

"That stuff with the owl last night was amazing. I wish you could have shared it."

She stroked his arm, feeling the swelled vein.

"I wish I could, too."

He readied the needle.

"You may not want to watch this," he said softly.

"I'm not a Girl Scout, I've seen this before," Chesty said. "I want to make sure you do it right."

His thumb twitched on the plunger. A half shot, nothing more, but Bobby paused for a moment as if stunned. Chesty watched as short, soft gray hairs began

to form on his face. They were much shorter than the
ones that had come last night. He looked more like a
big, poorly-groomed cat than a werewolf. He raised
his nose higher and sniffed a few times. He picked
the flashlight up and waved the beam around, as if it
could help corral the scents in the house.

"What do you smell?"

"You," he said, pointing the beam at her and looking
serious for a second, until a shy smile spread across
his face. His teeth were slightly pointed, his voice
deeper and rougher than usual. "You smell good."

"You get to work, you goof," Chesty shot back, but
she was smiling, too.

He walked around for what seemed like hours,
sniffing like he was coming down with a serious cold.

"There were a lot of people in here," he said at one
point.

He walked around so long that Chesty started to
worry.

"Are you getting anything?"

"I think so. There's one smell that's dominant, sort
of seeped into everything. Like it's old, it's been here
a while. Mr. Moreau said that's how the dominant smell
would feel. I think it's Steve. It's sweaty. Sometimes
having a better sense of smell isn't so good."

"So how can you find the tapes that we need?"

He directed her to bring the rolling chair from the
video booth.

"I need to get higher and sniff the tapes. I'm getting
too much scent down here."

"I think you're a really good bloodhound," Chesty
said, rubbing one furry arm to give him encouragement.

Chesty helped roll the chair around, one arm
wrapped around his skinny knees to brace him as he

stood and inhaled. She had nuzzled his legs with her face at first, until he laughed and told her it was pleasant, but a distraction. Then he let his cold, black nose get to work.

"You getting anything?" Chesty asked. She had stopped looking up because it was putting a crick in her neck.

"I think so. Most of the tapes smell like just Steve. Steve smelled like cheese nachos."

Steve's scent was weaker at the top of the stacks, which made him unhappy because the stacks were eight feet tall and he was getting dizzy. But there at the top the tapes started to give off a different odor. They smelled more like shoe leather. He sniffed some more. There was a row of tapes on the very top that smelled like they had barely been touched by Steve at all. Chesty handed him the flashlight and he beamed it along the row. These tapes were edged with white strips like all the others, but didn't display movie titles, just cryptic markings: 312/16/DW/0001-0239 said the one closest to him. The one next to it was 312/13/IJ/0001-0456, and he couldn't read any beyond that.

"I think these may be them, but I'm not sure."

Bobby handed down the tapes and wiped his facial fur, which was sweaty with the effort. He looked at his arm. Almost all the hair was gone. The shot was wearing off, and the thought of another depressed him.

"I can't deal with changing anymore," he said, his voice now close to a whimper, a sound not befitting a werewolf. "I hope these are the tapes. I can't look anymore."

Chesty gave him a quick hug and he felt better.

"You've done good," she whispered, nuzzling his ear. "Let's go."

They rolled the chair back to the editing console and staggered down the hall, juggling the tapes.

"Bobby!" Chesty said. "Moreau said he doesn't have a VCR out there. See if you can find one. I'll wait."

He left her standing in darkness at the end of the hall and clumped back to the room. Two VCRs were attached to the editing console. He grabbed the wires on one and yanked. Theft required more exercise than he had thought, and this was turning into a heavy haul. It was hard to aim the flashlight so he could see where he was going and hold the loot at the same time. They had almost made it back to the warehouse's side door when Chesty gave a little whoop and fell. Bobby tripped immediately after, visions of a shattered VCR and an angry Moreau dancing in his head. Then Chesty laughed.

"We tripped on the porno mattress," she said, whispering.

Bobby laughed too, and started to get up, when suddenly he felt arms around him, dragging him back down. He met Chesty's lips again, felt her rubbery breasts pushing into his chest. She slid her hands across his back, lifting up his shirt.

"Aw, too bad, you're not hairy anymore," she whispered. "That would be fun."

"Uh, Chesty, what are you doing?"

"We're already on a mattress." She nibbled on his earlobe and he shivered. "We might as well make use of it."

"We don't have much time," Bobby replied.

Chesty ignored him. She rolled him over and unzipped his pants, reaching in to a place no one had ever reached before, although he wasn't going to tell her that.

"If you're like a lot of guys, we won't need much time," Chesty whispered, laughing.

He felt the rhythmic action of her fist, and felt a sensation flowing through him that wasn't too different from the way the werewolf light used to feel when it hit him full in the face. He rubbed his hands up and down her sides, her breasts, letting his fingers make the first forays below the waist of her jeans. She stretched and writhed like a cat.

"You never told me," Bobby managed to say between gasped breaths. "What's your real name?"

She sighed as he slid her jeans down her legs.

"You know, Stoke never asked me that."

"He didn't?"

"No."

He felt something wet on his cheek and pulled back to look at her. A lone tear streaked down her face.

"I'm sorry," he whispered.

"Don't be. It's sweet. My name is—"

They heard a creaking sound, and not one they were making. They stopped still and then heard the side door open. Bobby cursed inwardly. Maybe the porno people were going to work day and night now that the werewolf operation was gone. He rolled off of Chesty and they tried to button and zip themselves up without making any noise. They didn't succeed.

"Hey!" said a voice. A beam of white light played over their faces. "Freeze!"

It was one of the guards, advancing on them rapidly, gun drawn. Bobby closed his eyes. He heard a cracking noise, but not the one he expected. He opened his eyes to find the guard prone on the cold concrete floor, unconscious in the illumination of his own dropped flashlight.

"What did you do?" Bobby hissed.

"I didn't do anything. He stepped on this."

Chesty held something ugly and alien up to the light. It was round, pink and squishy, inhumanly sized. He remembered it being used in one of the porn flicks once. The girls had nicknamed it Kong. The sight of Kong made Bobby feel a little amorous again, but he had his scare for the night. They needed to get out now, before the other guard showed up. Bobby clicked off the prone guard's flashlight and pocketed his pistol, just in case.

"I want to finish what we started," he said quietly as they picked up the videotapes by feel. "But I want to do it back at the trailer."

He heard Chesty blow him a kiss.

"Until then."

SIXTEEN

It was after midnight when she got back to her hotel, and the arid desert had sucked out whatever remained of the day's warmth. Ashly Durban shivered in her blazer and made a mental note to stick her overcoat in the trunk of the rental Grand Am so she would always have it ready. Of course, then she would probably forget it and it would end up in the possession of someone else.

Her latest show had gone pretty well, considering she had no actual guests to talk to. Moreau had escaped, the police were very busy trying to find him, Allen was occupied with telethon details, and members of the public were annoyed at having a killer man-beast on the loose just when they were considering digging into their pockets to get rid of man-beasts. Her segment on tonight's *Live Entertainment* had concerned another protest in front of the Universal Monster Grand, this one even bigger than the last, and more furious. This one was also a little more focused than the previous shoutfest. There were no vampires around, no

disagreements about intrawerewolf policy. It was anti-
werewolf in general, anti-Moreau in particular. People
from all over had come to rally against werewolves,
and to excoriate the police for their butter-fingered
handling of Moreau.

This segment of "Living with Lycanthropy" had
consisted entirely of angry voices from the protest,
people shouting into the camera, occasionally depositing
spittle on the lens, which upset Savik to no end. Durban
felt about a good half step below Geraldo, and she
didn't like it. For now, she just wanted to watch
something mindless on TV for a few minutes and then
go to sleep. She was tired of hearing the shouts of
angry people, no matter how justified their anger. Their
raving had given her a headache, and she had little
hope for the immediate future. The week was only
going to get worse.

Her steps echoed down the walkway which threaded
around the building. The Hoover Arms Hotel complex
was a monument to 1970s style, with a fancy concrete
wall that stretched the length of the sidewalk, making
the guests feel like they were slipping into a tunnel
every time they returned to their home away from
home. Durban had taken five steps into the shadowed
walkway when she heard a rustling in the bushes on
the other side. Probably just some birds in there, rooting
around, trying to stay warm, she thought. She took a
few more steps and heard it again. Sucking in her
breath, she walked on until she saw movement out of
the corner of her eye. She gave an involuntary squeal,
but it was just a Siamese cat, hopping to the top of
the concrete wall and balancing itself on the flat top.
Guests of the Hoover Arms weren't supposed to have
pets, but that apparently didn't stop all of them.

"Hi, kitty kitty," Durban cooed.

The cat looked down at her in the typical superior feline way. There was more rustling and then another cat appeared, this one a splotched brown tabby. She didn't call to it, but it looked straight at her, ignoring the other cat. Maybe they were just having a lover's spat and she had interrupted. She moved on down the sidewalk, a little faster now, until she heard still more rustling. She looked up, expecting the cats to have followed her, but now she was greeted by the sight of a small dog, a chihuahua, and another cat, its fluffy fur making it look like a huge ball of cotton. They were looking straight at her. She gulped. More animals were appearing on either side of the wall, their heads popping up quickly out of the bushes, their eyes turning towards her, catching the reflections of the streetlamps behind her, shining like tiny bright moons. She had seen a lot of trained animals, had even seen comedian Tom Serbini's controversial camel show at the Luxor once, but she had never seen anything like this. There couldn't be that many pets in the place—it would be a zoo. They must have come from the apartment complexes across the road to see what was in those fascinating bushes of the Hoover Arms.

Squinting down the line, she thought she even saw an iguana peeking out at her, seemingly happy despite the cold. The animals didn't seem antagonistic and were all small enough that she could have probably fought them off should they attack, but she didn't want to try. The day had been eventful enough without having to end it by killing or maiming a slew of pets. Durban sucked in a chilly lungful of air and ran down the sidewalk in a blind sprint for her room. She didn't look to verify it, but she could feel every eye on the wall following her.

She fumbled with her key until the tumblers clicked and then gave the knob a violent twist and kicked the door open with such force that her big toe throbbed. She slammed the door back in case the animals tried to get in, and stood leaning against it, taking in the warm hotel air in big gasps that made her frozen lungs hurt.

"Honey, what's the matter?" a voice said, and she let out a yelp.

A man rose quickly from the couch, dropping a magazine to the floor.

"What's wrong?"

She looked at him as if he were one of the animals on the wall.

"What the hell are you doing here? Who let you in?"

The man put a hand on her arm, but she shoved it away. Too many things were happening today.

"I used to be your husband, remember?"

"So? Who gave you a key to my room?"

"I have my sources."

"I'll kill your sources."

"Go ahead. I'll just get new ones. And don't think I haven't noticed your recent meteoric rise to the top of the local ratings heap. I just wanted to stop by and congratulate you on your latest scoops. Even though you work for a sleazy, trashy show, you've had us beat for the past several nights. All week, really."

"Thank you, John," she said, too quickly.

"And now you come back to your room like this. What's going on? You came storming in here like someone's after you."

"There are animals out there," she said slowly, her breathing settling down to almost its normal pace.

His soft patch of thinning brown hair was neatly combed to the left side, as always, and he was wearing the light cream sweater she had ordered for him from L.L. Bean three Christmases ago. John Robinson, former golden boy television reporter. He looked so caring and nurturing that she almost wanted to get a quick hug. She waited a fraction of a second, and the feeling passed.

"Animals? What sort of animals?"

"Little ones. Furry ones. Pets."

He frowned and tilted his head slightly sideways like a dog trying to figure something out. He took a slug of beer to help the cognitive process along. While he pondered her statement she pushed herself off the door and walked quickly to the small table by the bed to check her messages. There was only one. The machine's red light blinked ominously.

"Are you speaking symbolically? Do you want to get a dog or a cat? Is that what this is about?" Robinson asked, but she waved him to silence.

"No, no. John, I don't want anything from you anymore. I haven't wanted anything from you in years. I want you to leave."

He crossed his arms and tried to look stern, but it only made him look like he was hugging himself.

"Look, Ashly, I think something is going on. You almost drank yourself out of a job at Channel 12 back when you lived here, and suddenly you're the hotshot flying in from Hollywood back to little old Vegas to do your little show *and* to do the news. Who are you sleeping with out there in La-la land?"

She had once read a science fiction story about a

woman who had laser beams for eyes, which she used to melt the skin of those who angered her. Durban wished for a pair.

"My sleeping habits are the last thing you're going to hear about. And you're certainly one to talk about drinking. *Your* career has hardly been helped by it. I have stopped."

"Oh, yeah? I had a look at your minibar. It appears to have been decimated. You've gone through enough of those midget drink bottles to last through an airplane ride around the planet. I certainly hope *Live Entertainment* is picking up your booze tab."

"You shut up," she said, her voice dropping into that low register she had perfected in so many of their fights.

It was a shame things had come to this. They had been such a fun couple once, back when they were young broadcasters in love. They worked hard all day at rival stations, then spent their nights together. The problem was they spent a lot of them in bars, before and after the wedding, even during a significant portion of the honeymoon. After a while it seemed that Ashly was the only one who wanted to rise above their life of bottom-level jobs and top-shelf liquor. They got a divorce and Ashly began a series of efforts to dry out, one of which involved moving to Los Angeles and climbing up the ranks there. She was actually capable of going days on end without alcohol, something John had probably not tried in years.

"I've been working hard, John, believe it or not. You should be glad for me."

"I am. I *am* pleased to see you're making progress. But I want you to do it the right way. Come on. Who are you sleeping with at the network these days?"

If she wasn't so tired she would have walked over and smacked him.

"I'm not sleeping with anyone, John, and I like it that way. I *prefer* it to having you around, as a matter of fact. Now why don't you get the hell out of here. I want to see who cared enough to call me."

The network had set her up with various means of communication, including a beeper, a cellular telephone and a fancy answering machine that the hotel had agreed to let her use. The latter's small red light was blinking. She pushed the round blue PLAY button on the machine and held the handset to her ear. Robinson frowned and, before she could stop him, flicked out a hand and hit the button that activated the speaker phone.

"Damn you, John," she said, but was silenced by a burst of static that was itself sliced by a clear baritone voice.

"Ashly Durban, this is Paul Moreau. Long time no see. I was told I could reach you here. I know something about the murders of those people. I didn't do them. I have something you need to see, and we need to talk. You have to come to me. Alone. It will be a good story, I guarantee you. Please go out to your car and follow instructions. Ignore my little friends. They won't hurt you, they're just keeping an eye on you. I look forward to seeing you. Thank you."

John's mouth fell open.

"Paul Moreau? *The* Paul Moreau? The werewolf guy? You have an escaped murderer calling you up? What the hell is this all about, Ashly?"

"I don't know." She bit her lip and stared at the light, which had resumed blinking as if it still had something to tell her. "There is some weird stuff going on around here this week."

"I'll say. You can't go with him alone. You have to let me come. I'm your goddamn husband, you know."

"Ex husband. *Way* ex-husband."

"Whatever. I have to come. We'll do a joint news story, show some cross-network collaboration. It'll be just like old times."

"I don't think so. I'm sleeping my way up, remember?"

"Look, I didn't mean that stuff, Ashly, I was just a little jealous and you know that—"

He tried to stand between her and the door, but she did a quick spin and evaded him. John had taught her that particular spin years ago when they used to play touch football with their neighbors. Now he would regret it. She beat him to the door and sprinted out, realizing immediately that she had once again forgotten her coat. She could hear John's footfalls behind her; she couldn't go back for it.

The animals were gone from the wall as she dashed down the sidewalk, emerging from the end of the enclosure and shooting out into the parking lot. She fairly vaulted into the Grand Am's driver seat, but didn't get the door shut quickly enough. Robinson got both hands on the window sill and pried it back open like an oyster. Once he had it open he wedged a hip and a leg into the door and grabbed her with both hands.

"This is crazy! You'll get hurt," he gasped as he tried to hold onto his wriggling ex-wife.

Suddenly he yelped in pain and let go of her. Ashly looked down. The chihuahua from the wall had appeared and fastened its teeth around his ankle. Robinson kicked, sending the little dog hurtling through near space. He didn't have much time to recover, however, because suddenly three cats were on him, claws ripping through his pants legs. A tabby vaulted onto his back, getting its claws into the sweater. Robinson had nearly gotten his hands on that cat when suddenly the iguana flashed from the car's roof onto his face, knocking him so off balance that he whirled around and fell flat on his back, nearly mashing the tabby cat beneath him. Ashly slammed the door and started the engine with one hand while rolling the window down in three brisk turns of the handle with the other.

"You animals don't hurt him!" she shouted, and the cats backed off in surprise.

The iguana sat motionless on Robinson's chest. It was bigger than it had looked before, nearly three feet long, and Robinson grunted with exertion as he lifted it off and chucked it on top of one of the cats, which yowled in indignation.

"Wait!" John shouted, but Ashly stomped the gas and the car squealed away. She was almost out of the parking lot when she realized that she didn't know where she was going. It was then that a figure sat up in the back seat.

"Is he gone?" the figure said. Ashly screamed and hit the brakes, causing the figure to bounce off the back of the seat with a thump.

"Who are you?"

The figure crawled back into the seat and turned out to be a boy who couldn't have been more than fifteen years old.

"Bobby Chaney, ma'am. I'm with Mr. Moreau. He told me to take you to him."

Ashly gasped for breath for what seemed like the fifteenth time that evening.

"I'm glad Mr. Moreau selected a relatively youthful reporter like myself to tell all his secrets, because if I were old and out of shape I would have a HEART ATTACK with all these SURPRISES and ANIMALS!" Durban screamed. The boy looked like he was trying to push himself into the trunk through the back seat.

"I'm sorry," he said, so quietly she could barely hear him.

"You said your name is Bobby Chaney? I thought you were dead!"

"You can't believe everything you see on TV, ma'am." He raised up slightly and peered out the back window. "You better hurry. I think your husband's catching up."

"Ex-husband," Durban said, and saw that the boy was right. She peeled out again, this time putting the car out on the road.

"I better get a good story out of this," she said through clenched teeth. "All right, young man. Take me to your leader."

SEVENTEEN

"When did you first become interested in helping werewolves, Mr. Allen?"

The great man casually stroked his chin, as if, two days before the much-advertised Lycanthropy Telethon, it was a query that was unexpected.

"Actually, back in the Sixties, when I first started making movies. That's when Hollywood was still exploiting werewolf myths and people with lycanthropy. You remember that one, *Canis Summer*? That piece of trash, starring Andrew Harris? He suffered from lycanthropy, but he was a damn good actor, too. They just cast him in that movie because everyone knew he was a werewolf. He acted his heart out in that movie, and the studio treated him like dirt. All they wanted was the publicity about his disease."

Monty Allen was leading a thick knot of print and broadcast reporters through the hallways behind the Universal Monster Grand's telethon stage, pointing out various items of interest for use in the feature stories that would appear in newspapers and on television on the day before Halloween. Good publicity. The group moved through the narrow passages like a big hair clump working its way through a drain. The walls had pretty good paint jobs, but the cameras were scuffing them up.

"I don't think I did enough for Andrew Harris," Allen continued, pausing for a moment to lean on a huge box of confetti, which would be tossed around the stage at some point in the proceedings.

Allen himself had a small part in *Canis Summer*, a movie more famous for the Harris scandal than for its quality. He played a caddy who tried to convince the Harris character, a pro golfer, to get help for his lycanthropy, which he contracted after a round of night golf played too near a wolf den. Harris' character had walked out to retrieve a ball from the rough and was bitten. The other players on the tour began disappearing shortly thereafter. The movie ended with Allen's caddy character beating Harris' character to death with the same silver golf club that was supposed to be presented to the winner of the tour. Movie reviewers gave the film a similar beating, praising only the special effects. Ironically, it was Allen himself who later rose to stardom by portraying werewolves.

"That movie really sapped Andrew's spirit. He started to think that he couldn't act, that he was just some kind of beast. Things went bad for him after that. And then he killed his sister, Patricia, of course. The studio didn't encourage him to get help, and they had a tragedy on their hands."

"And then he killed himself," one of the reporters said, a sharp-faced young woman who appeared on a tabloid TV show every night and was not famous for her tact.

There was a moment of silence. Dozens of microphones hovered like puffy round insects, but Allen looked down at his feet and furrowed his brow. The Harris scandal itself was old news. A good bloody affair like that was bound to be featured in all the trashy books about the lives of the stars, and it was. The house where the murder/suicide occurred was a staple of the Hollywood scandal tours, and daring Bel Air kids always tried to break in on Halloween. Even Allen's mention of the case as a catalyst for his activism was hardly new; it was usually the focal point of any interview he gave, and was mentioned in all the press releases his office sent around. Still, having him personally rehash it three days before the telethon was good television.

"I know," Allen replied. "That's when I decided that no one else should have to suffer like that."

"But you kept on making werewolf movies of your own," the sharp-faced reporter chimed in.

"Yes. Yes, I did. But from then on I took care to add a human dimension to my werewolf characters, one that had been largely missing until then. That's also when I decided that if there was ever anything I could do to help werewolves, I would do it."

He seemed to be wiping away a tear. Then, as if on cue, he brought his big face back up and smiled.

"Hey! This is no time to be down. This, good people of the Fourth Estate, is the eve of destruction for the disease of lycanthropy."

He opened a door to the hallway that connected to the main stage and then quickly shut it against the noise. A local punk band was grinding their way through a practice version of "Bad Moon Rising," and apparently they were having some trouble with the sound system.

"In there, a lot of talented people who really care are going to help us raise money to beat this thing," Allen said, slamming the door back against the squealing sounds that echoed down the hall.

Just then a rising young movie actress who could also sing a little bit passed by, eyeing the cameras enviously. She wore a tight-fitting black sheath dress complete with the same light gray lycanthropy awareness ribbon everyone else in the casino was wearing. Allen grabbed her by the shoulders and gave her a massive hug before presenting her to the cameras. The presence of reporters seemed to please her immensely.

"Here's one of those people now! Folks, you all know Alicia Gonzalez. You've seen her serving up the laughs on NBC's *Different Times* on Thursday nights. Soon you'll be finding out that she's got the good pipes, too. Ain't that right, Alicia?"

"Well, I used to be in *Up with People*," Alicia said, twirling a lock of her long brown hair as if suddenly shy.

"Alicia wants to help us beat this thing, too, don't you?"

She also frowned and looked at her feet. That seemed to be the proper pose for answering serious lycanthropic questions.

"Yes, Monty, I do. My uncle was a werewolf. He took his medicine but he still had trouble. He killed himself."

There was a quick pause, and then the tabloid reporter shoved forth her microphone and barked, "How'd he do it?"

Alicia looked horrified, and even the affable Monty Allen lost his cool for a second.

"Who the hell cares? Don't ask questions like that." He paused, as if waiting for an apology, but none was forthcoming. He gave Alicia Gonzalez another hug and sent her on her way, waving to the cameras as she passed. "Come on, then, kids," he said, his anger passing as quickly as a western rainstorm. "We've done this place up pretty nicely."

The casino had been given an overhaul. All the animatronic statues inside had been fixed up and polished, and a new monster-movie roller coaster ride now wended its way through the east side of the building, carrying screaming children past lumbering mockups of the Frankenstein monster and the Gill Man, along with licensed versions of non-Universal creatures like Godzilla and King Kong. A Dracula was also there, although various vampire groups had been protesting for its removal. The werewolf was originally supposed to have been there, too, but in deference to the telethon was never put in place. Instead, a small room at the end of the ride had been set aside to educate children about lycanthropy and its victims.

The interior of the front gaming rooms had also seen some revision. Enormous movie screens now graced its walls, looming over the assembled gamblers, showing non-stop werewolf movies.

"We put on everything decent that we could find, even some Spanish-language stuff," Allen told the reporters. "Some of my own films, of course, because it's part of what's out there and, with all modesty, they're some of the best. We're showing everything but the exploitation movies. And *Canis Summer*."

The movies had drawn some criticism in the days preceding the telethon. Some gamblers said they were disturbing and distracted from the immediate business at hand in Las Vegas.

"My wife and I are thinking of going over to Luxor or the Taj Mahal," one man had told Channel 9's John Robinson the day before. "These damn werewolf movies are scaring her to death."

Members of the suddenly notorious Jean Grenier Society were also complaining about the showing of the werewolf films. They noted that for sensitivity reasons some of them had been outlawed from regular theaters and television, and therefore shouldn't be shown at the telethon site.

"He doesn't care about werewolves," a Jean Grenier member from New York said on the *Montel Williams* show. "He's exploited us every step of the way. He made a fortune by living off the image of werewolves, and now he's going to wipe us out."

The Society's voice wasn't traveling very far, however, as its leader was a wanted man, pursued by the police on murder charges.

When asked about the movies, Allen shrugged. "I know that some people don't like them. I know that stuff like *The Wolf Man* is wrong in many of its details about lycanthropy and is generally inflammatory. But they're not all wrong. The movies do show what a destructive disease lycanthropy is. I want to show people what the disease does. It turns people into killers. This is what we're up against. This is what we're going to end."

The final stop on the media tour was outside the Universal Monster Grand, where workers were winching a new werewolf in place to replace the comparatively stubby and inactive old one. The new lycanthrope was 120 feet high, as tall as the Dracula and Frankenstein figures combined. Its eyes were as bright as beacons and its teeth gleamed menacingly against the neon background of Las Vegas. It wasn't hunched over like the old one, which had been sold to a Shoney's Big Boy restaurant in Kentucky, but stood straight and tall and would have seemed almost noble if it didn't look so fierce. It had also drawn a crowd of protesters, but the casino security guards kept them well away from the action while the news cameras were filming.

"Why are you putting up a new werewolf right before you cure their disease?" the tabloid reporter shouted over the grinding sound of the crane that was lifting the enormous beast in place.

Monty Allen was staring up at the creature, hands on hips, and for a second it was as if he hadn't heard her. Then he turned and flashed his famous smile at the cameras.

"Something to remember them by," he said, shouting over the noise and giving a thumbs-up sign.

He turned back to the figure and muttered to himself.

"This one's for you, Andrew."

EIGHTEEN

"I'm sorry about all the theatrics. I think they were necessary," Paul Moreau said.

He looked a little scruffier than the last time she had seen him, less like an aging matinee idol and more like an aging leftist radical hiding out from the Man.

"Two days ago only you and CBS would air my debate, and CBS still bumped me from *Good Morning America*. Now I understand I am a very popular and sought-after man in Las Vegas. I thought it would be better to bring you here."

"I'm glad you picked me and not CBS," Durban replied nervously.

She took a quick sip of the water that the boy from the backseat brought her. Her voice had wobbled when she spoke, and she didn't want to seem too scared. Could werewolves sense fear, like dogs? Despite herself, she made a face when she swallowed the water. It wasn't bottled, and brought with it the sharp tang of rusty pipes.

"That's what I like to see, loyalty," he said with a laugh.

She gave a quiet laugh of her own, to humor him. Maybe that was some kind of threat.

He smiled and sipped his own water from a mottled clay mug that matched hers. Its taste didn't seem to bother him. Couldn't be too picky when you're a fugitive, she thought.

"Well, you're here now, aren't you? Trust me, this is an exclusive."

That didn't make her feel much better. She was tired from the trip and was having a little trouble focusing her thoughts. She had expected a quick jaunt to some exotic, scruffy locale in the city, but instead had been told to drive to the airport and abandon the Grand Am. Then she and the boy were met by a busty girl who looked like a Pahrump hooker and who drove a heavily modified four-wheel drive Jeep Wagoneer that could nearly qualify for skyscraper status. The girl kissed the boy, nodded to Ashly and then hightailed it out of town, veering off at one point to drive them straight into the desert at nearly the same speed she had used on the road. The ensuing bumping and bashing had left little room for conversation, and Durban found herself inordinately proud of the fact that she hadn't thrown up all over the back of the Jeep.

"Nice place," she muttered when she saw the melded Airstreams.

Moreau received his dusty, battered visitor inside the trailers, in what could pass for a small living room if it had decent furnishings. The room was in the middle of the outer trailer; small hallways, their destinations blocked by dangling strips of cloth, led off in three directions. Moreau balanced his towering frame on a tiny stool, motioned for her to sit on the only upholstered chair and politely asked the boy to bring them water. She sat as near to the edge of the chair as she could without looking strange. She wanted to be able to run if she had to, but didn't want him to notice how precariously she was perched there. Moonlight streamed through a small round window in the door and was assisted by the yellowish glow from a small plastic table lamp, which had no table and so was forced to squat on the floor.

"So what is it you're doing out here? Did you kill those people?"

"I have not killed anyone. I haven't broken any laws at all. I haven't even kidnapped you, you came of your own free will."

"So why are you hiding out here? All your Society members were in town."

"Well, I brought Bobby and Chesty out here because their lives were in danger. I'm here now because I do not feel like being incarcerated."

"And why did you have this trailer out here in the first place if you weren't up to something?"

He looked uncomfortable. Bobby passed through the room, and Moreau waited until he was gone before answering.

"I'm a little paranoid by nature, so I like to keep by myself as much as I can. And to be honest, Ms. Durban, most of my adherents these days are young men. They can get very noisy sometimes, and I'm not as young as I used to be. It's hard to sleep while they're playing Nine Inch Nails at two in the morning."

Durban took a big glug of the water before remembering she didn't like it.

"Oh."

"I can see you find that suspicious."

"No, it's just that the water is—"

"Another thing is that I fear I'm losing control over them sometimes. These young people are so . . . well, young. Did you know that the Jean Grenier Society was about to have a schism because some of the members wanted to stop shaving? Some said it represented wild nature better, while others thought it was just a sign of laziness. All the things going on with our issues, and they were prepared to split up the group over that. And they may still do it. Isn't that something?"

He rested his sizable jaw on his fist and looked into the distance, pondering the divisive power of facial hair.

Dreading the thought of another sip of the rancid water, Durban dug around in her bag to produce the little jewel she had found on the drive out, by accident, while she was rooting around for a weapon. It wasn't a weapon, but something equally welcome under the circumstances. She had forgotten she had squirreled it away, but was glad to see it resurface just the same. It was a tiny bottle of Tanqueray, just big enough for one good, stiff drink.

"No offense to your water, but this stuff is better," Durban said, pouring it into the mug at an enthusiastic angle.

She took a sip, closed her eyes, and said, "Aaaah. You want some?"

She offered the mug to Moreau, who eyed it indecisively for a moment and then accepted it. He held it to his mouth, but then seemed to lose his balance. The cup fell and the gin darkened the carpet.

Durban didn't know she had enough energy to jump out of her seat, but she did.

"Hey! You did that on purpose!"

"I'm sorry," Moreau said, regaining his perch. "But you didn't really need that drink."

Durban's fists balled and released. Should she hit him? No, probably not.

"That was not *nice*," she finally said. "I wanted that drink."

Moreau appraised her coldly.

"I see that you did, and pretty badly, too. Maybe you should think about that."

She was so annoyed she could feel the blood pumping in her head.

"It seems that a man who advocates turning into wild animals should go a little easy when it comes to telling others what they can drink and what they can't."

"Mrs. Durban, despite all your reporting on the subject, you still don't seem to understand lycanthropy very well. There's more to it than you think. You have just seen the chrysalis. You have not seen the butterfly."

"It's *Ms.* Durban. I don't know what butterflies have to do with this. Don't tell me werewolves aren't wild animals."

"I won't."

"Then why are you so sanctimonious? Why can't I have my drink? I want to get a little bit wild, too. I think I've earned it."

He laughed.

"You have. But non-lycanthropic humans attach the oddest meanings to the word wild. Getting snockered isn't getting wild. Now that young man in there, Bobby—" he gestured to the trailer "—can get wild."

"He's a werewolf?"

Moreau nodded.

"Two days ago he was just a miserable creature making movies, living by his wits. He reminded me of myself when I was his age, and I didn't like that. I'm glad I found him. Now he's becoming proud of his gifts and learning how to use them. He was the one who did the tricks with the animals at your hotel. I thought he might be able to handle two or three animals at once, but I understand he did more than that. He may be better at that sort of thing than I am. You've got to admit it got your attention, huh?"

They were silent for a moment. Ashly looked mournfully at the gin stain on the carpet, then decided that it was gone. It wasn't like she was willing to lick the wet fibers, not just yet. She sat back down.

"Mr. Moreau, I know your take on things, I mean about having lycanthropy, and all. I read that *People* magazine interview with you from last year. I even applaud you for refusing to be a whining victim. But I can assure you that lycanthropy is a disease, and one that's about to be cured. I fail to see what you're trying to prove here. If you didn't kill those people, give yourself up."

His laugh was flinty and short-lived, more like a bark. Very fitting, Durban thought.

"That's impossible. The people who trumped up the charges against me did a good job. I could very well be convicted. After all, my hair was reportedly all over those two sites, and maybe some of the others, too, who knows. And I certainly have a motive."

"You're the *only* person with a motive, I think," Durban corrected. "You are the only person who stands to lose if lycanthropy is cured. If there's no disease, there's no need for a Jean Grenier Society to represent its victims."

"That's certainly the conventional wisdom. You have interviewed people who have said as much. And John

Robinson, in fact, articulated that very point in an editorial on his station last night. Channel nine, I believe."

Durban frowned, and Moreau caught her eye and smiled.

"Don't worry, I watched your report before I switched over to him. Your channel is clearly ahead of the game."

"Thank you."

"But your conventional wisdom is wrong. I'm not in this to preserve lycanthropy as a disease because I no longer believe it is, or rather that's not all it is. You heard what I said at the debate before I was arrested."

"Yes."

"I know it sounds unbelievable, but it's true. You saw evidence of it tonight, at your very own hotel."

It's important to agree with nut cases, isn't it? Durban thought. With considerable effort, she managed eye contact.

"Okay."

"If people would just listen to me, we could reorder our whole society to reflect our place within nature, not just on top of nature. I can imagine that more people will *want* to become werewolves, not be cured of it. They will *beg* to be bitten and *given* lycanthropy."

"Well. I can't imagine why *Good Morning America* turned you down."

He missed her sarcasm completely.

"I can't either."

He downed his water in a long gulp and frowned at the empty mug.

"But all this talking will not do any good. I can't fight against circumstantial evidence without some real ammunition. Come here with me," he said, rising. "Now that you've had a chance to rest, I have something to show you that should change your mind."

She warily stood up and followed him further into the trailer, through one of the doorways. This is it, she thought. He's going to kill me. But why would he bring me all the way out here and protest his innocence? He's going to kill me. She cast a glance behind her. Moreau was now three feet ahead, in the darkened hallway. She could run back through the room and out the door, and then out into the desert. Not sure what she would do then, but it would beat following a wanted killer into a dimly-lit trailer.

She nearly jumped when she saw a mass of blonde hair floating in the air like a spectral mop head. Then she realized it was attached to a girl, the busty girl who had driven the Jeep. She was standing in the doorway of the other hallway, watching her. The girl was smiling, but the weird light combination in the room made her smile look ghastly and threatening. What did he say her name was? Chesty? How fitting. Chesty and Bobby seemed to be the only other people in the Airstreams. Ashly didn't know if that was good or bad. At any rate, that escape route was blocked. Time for another tack.

"Uh, do you have a lady's room around here?" Durban asked. "It was kind of a bumpy ride."

Moreau's face adopted a politely attentive look again, as if pleasantness was a mask to be popped back into place.

"I'm so sorry. A few hours out in this dump and I lose all my manners. Chesty, would you show Ms. Durban to the restroom?"

Chesty led her down a short hallway that stretched out from behind her chair. They passed a room that boasted a huge leather recliner and an enormous television with four-foot aerials extended like stick arms on a fat man. The boy, Bobby, was fooling around in the wiring.

"Just leave a quarter on the counter when you're done," Chesty said, and Ashly thought she was serious until she smiled.

Once inside, Ashly turned on the tap and pulled her tiny cellular phone out of her purse. It probably wouldn't work from out here, but it was worth a shot. Things were getting a little too creepy. She had to admit that coming out to visit an accused serial killer without Bob Savik and his camera had not been the best idea she'd had lately. She hit the numbers, leaning over the phone to drown out the sound, wishing she had spent the extra money to get one that had an adjustable beep volume.

She heard what she thought was a voice, and started whispering violently into the phone.

"*Bob*! Bob! I need your help! You've got to—"

A rapid series of knocks on the door interrupted her.

"Mrs. Durban, we don't have much water out here!" Chesty shouted. "Can you turn off the sink?"

"Sure. Sure."

She turned it off and waited a few seconds before putting the phone back up to her ear. Judging from the sounds coming from the earpiece, she had either gotten a very groggy Savik or a drunken space alien.

"Bob! This is Ashly! Get your gun and drive out Fifteen North. When you come to—"

Chesty didn't knock this time. She kicked the door in with such force that Ashly nearly lost her balance and got dunked in the toilet. The poor phone wasn't so lucky, and hit the drink with a wet beep. Ashly looked behind her. The bathroom had a small window, and she wasn't at all sure she could fit through it, but decided she would rather try than stick around here and see what punishment would be meted out for her treachery. She gave the already unbalanced Chesty a shove that sent her sprawling into the hallway, and then jumped on the toilet lid and slid the window open. She managed to slip through with an acceptable amount of grace, although she lost her shoes in the process. Once on level ground, she took off running, heading out into the desert toward what she hoped was the distant highway.

It took nearly a minute before she realized that the quiet night around her had erupted into long, chilling howls, inchoate moans that finally grew to the point that they overwhelmed the sound of her own gasps. She expected that at any moment she would catch her foot on a patch of scrub and pitch headfirst to the ground, but her years of running track in high school had paid off. Her feet seemed able to find solid patches of ground, even at top speed. In another minute, she realized speed would not be enough. She saw something looming out of the darkness, something all red and black and white, an approaching meteor.

Durban managed to change direction faster than she would have thought possible, skidding briefly on her left leg in a smooth ski slide before shooting off to her right, away from the approaching creature. She had gone only a few yards before she saw another attacker nearing her. She didn't have a chance to change directions again. The shades were upon her. She was surprised that her lungs had the air to spare, but somehow managed a scream and fell, skidding, to the

ground. Her only wish was to breathe in as much air
as she could before being torn to shreds. She closed
her eyes and squeezed out hot tears. Nothing happened.

"All right, back off! Back off!" a harsh voice said, a
voice that sounded as winded as her own.

She opened her eyes. Chesty stood over her, gasping
as if to mimic her own breath spasms, frowning at her
shadowy pursuers. They were fully transformed
werewolves, their long dark hair not quite able to hide
the sinewy muscles underneath. Their teeth gleamed
white in the night. One of them wore a red Caesar's
Palace baseball cap, the brim flipped around to the
back. She expected that they would be staring down
at her, slavering, ravenous, but instead they stood
upright, looking curiously at Chesty, their doglike front
paws crossed awkwardly in front of them.

"Good job!" she shouted. "Good work! Now back
off!"

The werewolves apparently did not like her tone of
voice. They snarled in unison, displaying the white
flowers of their teeth. Their front paws extended,
looking less like paws now and more like gnarled fingers
tipped with inch-long, curving claws.

"Back off, I said!"

Just when Ashly thought they were going to attack,
a sharp yipping bark erupted from the desert.
Everyone, including Ashly and the werewolves, turned
to look behind Chesty. A white dog bounded out of
the night, its long hair bobbing royally as it ran. Ashly
gave a little moan of recognition. It looked like the
same dog she had seen outside the Jean Grenier
Society apartment. The dog trotted up behind Chesty
and then stopped so suddenly that its snowlike paws
sent small dust clouds into the night air. In one smooth,

quick motion it turned into a naked man. It turned into Paul Moreau.

Ashly had read somewhere that werewolf shape-changing was not the elongated, painful process that the movies had always made it out to be, but she didn't expect it to be so beautiful. For all her recent reporting on the subject of lycanthropy, she had never actually seen the change done. Moreau made it look as easy and graceful as a dive into smooth water. It was as if the dog had merely arisen on its hind legs, and, having done so, discovered itself to be human.

"They're not *deaf*, Chesty," Moreau said. "Just look at those ears. You don't have to yell at them."

The werewolves had dropped their aggressive attitude, now appearing as genial as puppies. Had they had tails, they would have wagged them.

"Good work, boys. You can go back to the perimeter now. We'll take things from here."

The werewolves shuffled their feet in the dirt, gave what seemed to be slight Japanese bows, and began trotting off in opposite directions.

"Talbot!" Moreau shouted after one. "Take that damned hat off! It ruins the effect!"

He looked after the offending employee for a few seconds, and then turned his attention back to Durban, who gazed up at him with a blank stare. Moreau was naked, and appeared unashamed of that. Given the wondrous transformation that had just occurred, his nakedness seemed to be inconsequential, a petty detail, although Durban did notice reflexively that Moreau was in pretty good shape.

"Well, now that we've all had a bit of exercise, shall we go back inside?" he asked, and smiled.

Durban gave a weak smile back, and extended an

arm to be helped off the cold desert ground. Chesty
heaved out a few more gasps and spat on the ground.

"I broke a nail running after you."

"I'm glad it was you that caught me, not them."

Moreau shook his head and frowned.

"Oh, now. They wouldn't have hurt you. Chesty, you
just have to be a bit more gentle with them."

Chesty looked abashed and sullen, and kicked absent-
mindedly at a clump of scrub grass.

"Gentle with *werewolves*?" Ashly asked, and Moreau
nodded.

"These aren't your ordinary werewolves. I injected
them with a fluid that lets them make the change
without getting overly violent."

"Oh."

"And anyway, werewolves are people most of the
time, don't forget. They just look fierce when they're
after you. Part of their training."

"And who trains them?"

"Me."

"What do you teach them?"

"To be better werewolves, of course. Ms. Durban,
I'm sorry if I've been beating around the bush. I didn't
realize you were in such a hurry to leave. The main
reason I brought you here is because the breakthrough
drug to cure lycanthropy doesn't work. Once the
telethon is finished, two hundred thousand werewolves
in this country will be given bad drugs. We can't allow
that to happen."

Durban coughed. She was out in the desert with a
madman. Not just a madman, but a madman capable
of turning into a dog; Sam and Son of Sam all rolled
into one. She was exhausted and covered with dirt.
But she was still a reporter.

"How is it that you turn into a dog and they turn into big wolflike things? Did you get some kind of upgrade?"

"No. I told you, the gift of lycanthropy changes over time. After thousands of transformations, the werewolf shape becomes more doglike, more fully animal. I also can make the change without any drugs at all now. I don't know why. It's part of what I want to continue researching, and why I oppose this disastrous cure."

"Okay. So who do you think is behind this impending disaster?"

"I'm not sure."

"How much evidence do you have?"

"Enough. I think. Come back and I'll show you."

She had little choice but to agree. Moreau shifted back into dog form and trotted eagerly ahead.

NINETEEN

"How does it feel?" asked the off-camera female voice.

"Not too bad," said the werewolf in the chair.

The creature looked limp and wet, having hardly even the energy necessary to move its snout and laboriously form the words, but it was nonetheless strapped firmly to the big white chair.

"You don't have much energy?" asked the voice, and suddenly the blue light that bathed the creature grew brighter and sharper.

"Pause it, please," Paul Moreau said. "It's that red button." Bobby, lying stretched out on the ratty carpet, reached over to Steve's purloined VCR and complied.

"You see that light? The blue one?" Moreau asked, looking at Ashly Durban. She nodded. It was hard to miss.

"That's a light like they use in the werewolf movies that Bobby used to make. It can turn you into a werewolf at any time, you don't need the moon at all. It was developed by the Pentagon and mimics the effect of moonlight. There is a liquid drug, administered intravenously, that accomplishes the same thing, but does a better job. There's an illegal trade in all this stuff. I'm a little surprised that the Landon Institute is using a light, but maybe they have a more powerful one than the kind that's on the black market."

Durban nodded solemnly, not quite taking it all in. She had helped hook the VCR to the TV, after Bobby had made a botch of it. He had reversed the video in and out connections, giving them nothing but snow. She had never seen a teenager who didn't know how to work electronic equipment, but apparently Bobby was one of the rare few. When she had finished correcting his mistakes, Moreau had rounded up mismatched furniture for them to sit on, except for Bobby, who chose to sprawl on the floor.

"Let's hope it isn't a porno tape," Chesty had said when she popped it in the camera's side slot.

It wasn't. It was a tape monitoring the progress of an experiment, and tiny numbers shining in the lower left corner of the screen showed it to have been made the night before Cynthia Wardoe died.

"Hit it," Moreau said, and Bobby, after a tentative examination of the VCR's front panel, clicked the pause button off.

The light was at full blast in the video now, so that the listless werewolf resembled a light blue stuffed animal. Its eyes stared blankly at the camera.

"Still no energy?" asked the voice, and the werewolf now didn't even nod, didn't twitch a finger. "Let the records show that test subject 16 required three injections of batch number 312 to lose his aggressiveness under the change. However, he's obviously still a werewolf."

"That's Danny Wexler," Bobby said, so quietly that the others almost didn't hear him. "He's not subject 16. He's Danny Wexler. He was funny. He was in this movie I was in one time, but then he just seemed to disappear."

A blonde woman with red plastic glasses walked into camera range, stopping next to the oblivious Danny Wexler. She rubbed one hand along his arm, ruffling his fur, almost as if she was petting a cat. Then the picture dissolved into black and white static for two seconds. When the picture reappeared, Danny Wexler wasn't quite as hairy, and was even more motionless, if such a thing was possible. As the tape progressed, each experiment separated by a woman speaking comments to the camera, he became more docile. By the time the end of the tape neared, Danny Wexler wasn't a werewolf at all. He was just a chubby teenager, staring listlessly at the camera, occasionally twitching his fingers.

"Look at his eyes," Bobby said, scooting across the floor and planting a finger on Danny's videotaped face.

Danny seemed to return his gaze with a bovine stare, his eyes devoid of any spark or life. A thin trickle of drool coursed down one rounded cheek.

"He looks like a zombie, not a werewolf," Durban said.

Dr. Wardoe had left the camera range but her voice was back, sounding grave.

"Subject 16 cannot become a werewolf now, so there's progress on that end," she said nervously. "Unfortunately, his cognitive processes and motor control skills are severely impaired, just like some of the others."

Moreau held up the copy of the video case so Durban

could read the script printed on the outside of the tape case: 312/16.

"She said batch 312, and 16 subjects. There are other batch numbers on these other tapes. That means 16 subjects on this batch alone. There could be more."

Durban nodded. She looked at Moreau. Maybe he wasn't crazy after all. There seemed to be something here.

"Carl and I have changed the formula again, because we think we know which receptors are being adversely affected. It's still hit and miss. All of them show an increase in size of the *guorguol* region of their brains, which we expect with advanced lycanthropy, but they don't all respond uniformly. We think the drug abuse evidenced by some of these patients may have blocked up some of their ability to react to treatment, but on others we just can't tell. Dr. Stumpf isn't doing so well and he's not any help. We need more time. We can go ahead and hold the telethon, but the cure won't be ready this year."

The tape cut off into snowy static, and Durban sat stunned before it.

"Dr. Stumpf? Who the hell is Dr. Stumpf?"

Moreau stood up and clicked the tape off for good.

"I'll tell you in a minute. Now, Ms. Durban, you're the professional here. Do we have suitable evidence to show that something is wrong?"

Durban stood, too, and started pacing like a lawyer in a TV crime show.

"This is amazing. So Wardoe and Johnson knew this wasn't working, but they also knew Monty Allen was saying it would work. So Johnson decided to do some blackmail."

"Only somebody got to him first."

"But who was he blackmailing? Monty Allen or this Stumpf?"

"Maybe both. I really don't know."

Durban clapped her hands joylessly, her forehead stern.

"Why don't we just turn the tape over to the police and be done with it?"

"There's more stuff tucked away in those video cases. Apparently somebody was paying off the police to make sure the warehouse never got bothered, so the Landon Institute could have its research fodder. That's why the doctors resorted to blackmail. But I can't tell who's in on it and who isn't."

Durban sighed in frustration. It had all seemed so clear just moments before.

"Who is this Dr. Stumpf, anyway?"

"There's something else," Moreau said.

He held up the videocassette box and a small card fell out. It was Carl Johnson's, but there was writing on the back. BREEZY PINES NURSING HOME, the card said, blue ink making the name look inviting.

"I think he's there. Stumpf. I think he's been working with the Landon Institute. I need to talk to him. We need to find out how deep this thing goes. You stay here. When I come back, we'll figure out how to proceed."

"But you can't go into town," Durban said. "The police will be all over you. They're ready to make you their recaptured crook poster boy."

"I know. But there is a way. They'll be looking for *me*, not a nice white dog. Maybe it's time that Dr. Stumpf's long-lost granddaughter pays him a visit."

"But how do you know he has a long-lost grand-daughter?" Durban asked.

"I don't." Moreau looked at Chesty. Her eyes slowly opened wide. "But we'll give him one."

"You still haven't told me who this guy is!" Durban wailed. "Explain! Who is he?"

"Remember how I told you I was kidnapped by the Army?" Moreau asked.

She nodded vigorously. Everyone knew that story by now.

"He was there. He was in charge."

TWENTY

When Moreau next became aware of anything, he was lying naked in a small, filthy park, his body stuffed halfway under a park bench. A pigeon was pecking at some bread crumbs that were placed perilously near his eye. He must have blacked out. He tried to remember if the huge dark man on the horse had conked him on the head, or the horse had kicked him, but he couldn't be sure. He had apparently just lost time. Some bum had tossed a tattered blue tarpaulin over him, but he still shivered in the morning cold. A man with white broomstraw for hair and a nose like a rotten cherry saw he was awake, tugged him out from under the bench and leaned over him.

"Didn't take your medicine, huh?" the old man said, his every word preceded by a blast of sour mash. "Came staggering in here, blood all over your face, whimpering like a damn puppy. I just hope you didn't kill nobody."

Moreau had an awful taste in his mouth, and his muscles ached. He was wishing he could at least have held onto the wolf skin to keep him warm.

"Where am I?"

"I ax myself that same question a lot," the old man said. "Come on, let's get you down to the shelter. They'll give you your medicine and help you figure out what you did last night. I wouldna thought there would be any of you out last night. Wasn't no moon."

Memories began creeping back into Paul Moreau's mind. Suddenly he felt scared. The first thing he wanted to get was a fresh suit of clothes, but that wasn't as easy as he had thought. He wasn't exactly sure where he was, and the bum who found him insisted on taking him in person to the clinic. This was not out of altruism, as the bum carefully explained, but rather from a desire not to have ravenous creatures stalking his home, the great outdoors, at night. The bum had clothes stashed away that he swore up and down were clean, so Moreau relented and put them on. The jeans looked okay but the thin T-shirt appeared to have been on the losing end of a food fight. The bum explained that the stains were baked-in grease that wouldn't come out no matter what, and Moreau's head hurt far too much to protest too much.

He had expected, indeed, the bum had led him to believe, that he would get the usual indigent treatment at the clinic—long lines, a stash of tranquilizers and a pamphlet on how to use them for something other than entertainment, maybe a half-hearted lecture, and then he'd be back on the street by the afternoon. It didn't quite turn out that way.

"What was your illness again?" the large, unsmiling woman at the desk asked him. She hunched over her government forms like a prisoner protecting a good meal.

"I don't know what the technical term for it is,"
Moreau said. His head was pounding and his hands
shook.

"He came into the park all hairy," the bum told the
woman. "He was a werewolf."

She looked at Moreau with newfound respect, stood
up quickly and backed away a few steps toward the
door that led into the inner labyrinth of the shelter.

"That's really not my department. I do alcohol and
drugs. Please hold on one second."

The bum smiled and patted him on the shoulder.
Moreau smiled back weakly, and wondered if he
smelled as bad as the bum did, or if he was even worse.

"You'll be fine," the bum said. "Now if you'll excuse
me, I have errands to run."

Moreau wanted him to stay, but the old man was
not to be delayed, saying it took him a while to get
enough for the first bottle and he was already behind.
Moreau waited there for quite a while, shaking in
his ratty, borrowed clothes. There were clumps of
paper in the pockets of the jeans but he didn't really
want to know what they were so he rested his hands
on his knees instead. When the door opened again,
it wasn't the severe woman, but a thin man with close-
cropped hair. He walked around the counter as if to
shake Moreau's hand, and even made a game attempt
at a smile. Moreau tottered to his feet and extended
a hand, but the man quickly dropped his smile and
grabbed Moreau's arm. Before he could move, the
man produced a needle and jammed it expertly into
a vein. Stunned, Moreau plopped back into his seat
and felt cold all over, inside and out.

"What did you do?" he asked, his youthful bravado
replaced with fear.

"I'm sorry. You'll be okay," the man said, but Moreau was out cold by the time he finished talking.

When he woke up, he didn't seem to be in the clinic anymore. He was in what looked like a padded fishbowl—four gray walls and a soft tan floor, capped with a clear ceiling. He at first thought he was wearing only floppy white cotton pants, but a cursory examination revealed clean white boxers underneath. The self-examination was curtailed when he remembered that the ceiling was transparent. He also discovered that several white-clad men, looking like refugee scientists from a Timex commercial, were perched on a catwalk arrayed around the ceiling and were peering intently down at him. He wasn't sure what to do, but it was clear that he didn't have the upper hand in this situation so he just waved shyly. One or two of them waved back.

"Don't be afraid," one of them said, a stocky man with virtually no hair and thick black glasses. His voice was piped in from somewhere in the walls. "We won't hurt you."

"Where am I? What time is it? Who are you?" Moreau shouted, but the people didn't seem to hear him.

The stocky man gave a vague smile and walked off, as did the others. They didn't come back for a long time. Occasionally Moreau would catch a glimpse of one of them passing overhead like a ghost, but the visions were few and far between and he quickly grew bored and stretched on the padding. Whoever the men in white were, they had cleaned him up nicely. His hair felt like it had been trimmed to a manageable length, and he smelled better than he had in a long time. His head didn't hurt anymore. He wished they had given him something to read, and then he fell asleep again.

When he awoke again he was bathed in a blue light harsher than anything he had seen before. It seemed to force its way past his eyelids and into his brain. He felt strangely peaceful, like the light was a drug. He faded away again. When he came to, he was standing and felt hot. The light kept coming, beaming down from the ceiling. He thought he saw a few round heads poking up behind it, but wasn't sure. He held a forearm over his brow to block the light, and discovered that he seemed to be wearing some sort of fur coat. Thick brown hair jutted from his arm, which was a lot more muscular than he remembered it being. Somehow, this made him mad. For the second time in as many minutes, his consciousness faded again, drowned out this time by a blinding rage. He opened his mouth to shout and discovered that it was easier to howl instead. Moreau howled as loud as he could and proceeded to try to destroy the room.

The padding proved to be more resilient than it looked; it resisted the claws that had suddenly appeared on the ends of his fingers, and this made him madder than ever. He could hear words coming from the ceiling, words as faint and ghostly as the people who spoke them.

"*. . . maybe too strong, cut it down. . . .*"

He decided to try for them. On the first jump he miscalculated and slammed his head hard against the clear ceiling, leaving a sudden bright bloodstain, which looked black against the unforgiving blue light. Black or red, it allowed him to gauge the distance the next time, and he hit the glass with his fists, his hairy legs propelling him upwards as fast as he could go. The ceiling erupted in a spiderweb of cracks, and he caught an image of a lot of round heads moving backwards quickly. Even the relentless blue light wavered a bit. The voices grew more animated after that.

"Hit the gas!"

Suddenly the room was cloudy, but he could still see his bloody mark. He went for it again, and could have sworn that the tip of his snout made it through, drew in fresh air. He could smell fear and he wanted so desperately to be there where it lived. One more time and he'd be through, he knew it. Moreau dropped back to the cushions and tensed his muscles for the final ascent, but something was wrong. He wavered. He growled and fell face forward on the soft yet indestructible floor, oblivious to the world once again.

When he woke up this time, he was in what looked like the waiting room for an unsuccessful doctor. There was a small round table with an ugly lamp and two large green chairs, but little else except for an innocuous landscape painting on the wall that could have been lifted from a cheap hotel. He would have felt more comfortable if he hadn't found himself strapped to one of the chairs so tightly that he could barely wriggle. The door opened. The doctor would see him now. A stocky man with very short hair and thick black glasses walked in and smiled, and Moreau recognized him instantly. He didn't smile back.

"I have some apologies to make, young man," the man said.

His voice was a southern drawl, although certain words carried remnants of a hard-edged German accent: molasses spiked with razor blades.

"We really should have debriefed you earlier, but . . . well, there's no excuse, really. I'm very sorry."

The man pulled up the other chair, not too close, and plopped himself down. He looked to be in his mid-forties, maybe a youthful early fifties. Met under different circumstances, he probably would have seemed quite pleasant.

"My name is George Stumpf. I'm a chemist with the Army, specializing in biological agents. For the past fifteen years, I've been doing some work in a particular illness which you seem to suffer from."

Moreau exhaled noisily. His head was hurting again, and they hadn't fed him.

"I'm a werewolf."

"You suffer from lycanthropy. But don't let it get you down."

"Where am I?"

"In a place owned by the Army. In Maryland."

"Maryland? What part?"

Stumpf gave a sad smile and shook his head, as if he wasn't quite sure himself.

"Maryland," Moreau repeated. He had always wanted to visit the South, but not quite this way.

"Yes. We're sorry to have, uh, used your services without permission, and spirited you away from New York, but—"

"You kidnapped me."

Stumpf frowned, as if Moreau's reasoning wasn't quite right.

"Whatever. The point is that you are doing a patriotic duty for your country. We need research subjects to delve into the mysteries of lycanthropy, and as you can imagine they aren't all that easy to come by these days."

Moreau squirmed some more, even though he knew he wasn't going anywhere.

"Why am I in this chair?"

"We're redecorating your room. It really wasn't designed for its current purpose, and after our earlier tests we decided to make a few revisions."

"How long will I be held here?"

"We really wish you'd try to look at this experience in a positive light. You will have a chance to learn some new things about yourself and your illness."

"Great."

"And you will be doing a great service for your country."

"How long will I be held here, you NAZI!" Moreau shouted, and then grew quickly embarrassed when his voice cracked at the very peak of his anger. He wanted to sound threatening, but instead had come across as just being a peeved teenager.

Stumpf frowned furiously and was silent for a few seconds, time in which Moreau was apparently supposed to suffer from guilt feelings for having impugned the doctor's Germanic background. It didn't work.

"Now, you listen," Moreau started when he thought his voice was more stable.

"No, you listen, you little punk," Stumpf said. His voice was no longer even patronizingly polite, and his big eyes were cold behind their lenses. "You're right. I used to work for the Nazis. We used to do experiments to try to make werewolves into soldiers. We would take people at random, kidnap them and turn them into werewolves whether they wanted to be or not. If they got out of control we killed them and threw them in unmarked graves and nobody ever heard of them again. And then we'd go get someone else."

Stumpf was right up in his face now, fairly spitting out the words. Despite himself, Moreau was suddenly afraid.

"But none of it worked. Then I came over here and now I work for the Army. And we're trying to make werewolves into soldiers, too."

He leaned back in his chair, although none of the fury left his voice.

"So that's where we are. If we succeed, we'll have werewolf soldiers fighting communism, and that's a good thing. I truly regret working for the Nazis, I really do. But it's too bad we couldn't have procured a little punk like you back under that system. You'd be dead now, my friend, in a pit somewhere, not sitting here in this chair talking back to the very man trying to save your country."

Moreau fumed but said nothing. Stumpf fumed right back, but after a moment his demeanor softened.

"Now then. Excuse me, I got a little carried away. I will tell you that we've had an interesting side effect that may interest you. We've been working with another young man, a Negro. He has responded to our regimen in a strange way."

"So? What does that have to do with me?"

Stumpf seemed annoyed that Moreau was not more appreciative of the advances he had made here in Maryland for the Army.

"We dosed him with some of the same stuff we're using on you. Oddly enough, it burned the lycanthropy right out of him. He's cured. If you're lucky, maybe we'll accidentally cure you, too."

"Like I said. So?"

"So we plan to keep you here until it either cures you or makes you a damn fine werewolf."

Moreau wanted to jump up and strangle Stumpf, which was probably exactly the wrong response.

"Now just a minute—"

Just then he heard a faint mewling sound and a tiny cat padded into the room, making a beeline for Stumpf's left leg. Stumpf's face lost its nearly permanent frown as he picked up the cat with one arm and held it under his fleshy chin.

"Please, we'll discuss this later," Stumpf said, cutting Moreau off in mid-complaint. "I'm sorry that you are being so unreasonable. I don't want you to upset Tuffy here."

"Hello, *Tuffy*," Moreau said in as threatening a voice as possible. He expected to be ignored, and was moderately surprised when the cat swiveled its tiny head around to look at him.

"Oh, Tuffy *likes* you," Stumpf said as he stood and walked from the room.

Later still, he woke up again to find himself back in the padded room. The ceiling had been raised by six or seven feet, which didn't surprise him. Large portholes had been placed in three of the walls, and the fourth wall was replaced by some kind of clear plastic. The better to see me with, Moreau thought. The fishbowl effect of the room was now complete. With the ceiling raised, it was harder to see the round heads of the scientists, but he began to see a lot of Tuffy. The tiny cat appeared to know that the clear wall was unbreachable, so it would sit for hours and watch him. When the light hit him and he turned into a werewolf the little cat would back away and look nervous when he snarled and raved at it, but it never left the hallway completely.

Indeed, having the kitten around seemed to be part

of the experiments. Occasionally while making threatening jaw gestures at the cat he would spot one of the round heads watching him and jotting things down in a notebook. He would then lunge at the round head, who, unlike the cat, would quickly disappear.

Uncountable days passed and the scientists started using the light more than ever, sometimes turning it so high that it seemed like he was underwater. They attached electrodes to certain spots on his body but he almost always managed to rip them off and sometimes eat them. During the day, he noticed that the food they slid through the wall to him tasted funny, almost metallic. He decided they must be increasing the dosage of whatever they were giving him. It was probably still better than prison food.

The round heads started to engage in experiments whose scientific purpose seemed dubious at best. Once he awoke to find himself sharing the room with a human-shaped dummy, complete with a fake wig and reading glasses. It was dressed up to resemble a helpless old lady. He looked at it but ignored it while in human form, so the scientists hit him with the blue light. He ripped the dummy to shreds in no time, and even tried to swallow the glasses.

Then he started noticing that he was changing. He no longer woke up on the floor, wondering where he was; he could remember. Eventually, after what seemed like weeks, he was conscious all the time, even while he raved at the cat. He could relax, in his mind. He could think. One day they beamed the light at him at a record level of intensity, and about midway through the day he grew tired of stomping around and sat down to rest like a regular human being, with his knees folded up and his chin on his hands. This posture and his relaxed state caused several new heads to appear on the other side of the portholes, but he ignored them. His head was amazingly clear and he wanted to enjoy it. Even Tuffy came closer and sat just on the other side of the transparent wall. The next day they tossed the dummy in again and hit the light. Instead of ripping it to bits, he gave it a low bow and then slowly, gently, started to waltz around the room with it.

He had hoped that by displaying nonviolent behavior he could win an early release from the experiments. If the scientists figured he was being cured, they would let him go. Only they didn't. The tests continued, as nonsensically as before. Now they were putting crockery in the room with him along with the dummy, to see if he would smash it. Sometimes he did, out of frustration. Once he did it as a human, just to annoy them and screw up their results.

He decided they were never going to let him go. Stumpf had never said that they had let their celebrated Negro patient go, after all. Moreau decided that he needed to escape, and he needed a plan. One night, nearly two months into his captivity, it came to him. Or, rather, Tuffy came to him.

He was lying on the floor after a particularly grueling session with the blue light. They had also shot him up with a blue liquid he had never seen before, and he was despairing; the combination of the two had made him lose his mind again, made him fly off into a lycanthropic rage. He was lying on the floor, picking at the padding, wanting out, when he noticed Tuffy had plopped herself down on the other side of the clear wall. She looked like a stuffed animal, only less animated. Moreau sighed and rolled over on his back, looking straight up at the clear ceiling. His head was hurting again, and it hadn't done that in a long time. Tuffy was so darned cute she made it hurt worse.

Then he began to hallucinate. He suddenly felt as though he were walking down one of the hallways, but everything looked strange. The hallways were huge, and the ceiling was so far away it might have been the Milky Way. He was bopping along, his eyes bouncing up and down. Even the doorways looked enormous. Moreau put his hands down flat on the padded floor to try to stabilize himself. He felt he would be sick, and throwing up while on his back was probably not a good idea. That made him feel better for a second, but the images didn't stop.

He was outside now, loose in this same nightmare world. It was like something out of an *Amazing Stories* book he had read once: an astronaut had been reduced to the size of a mouse, and had proceeded to have colorful adventures in the big city. Moreau's hallucinations were a bit more prosaic, unfortunately. He was walking down the hallway, and then he found an open door and went outside. He padded along in his strange new gait until he came to an enormous flat saucer, several times bigger than his whole head. Before he could stop himself he had shoved his whole mouth into it. And he didn't even like milk.

Then it struck him what was happening, and he rolled over onto his stomach and peered at Tuffy. He wasn't hallucinating at all. He was reliving Tuffy's morning. Two things suddenly occurred to him. Tuffy had an even less complicated life than he had suspected, and he could read her mind. He smiled.

"Tell me more, kitty, kitty, kitty," he said.

She did. Over the next few days, Tuffy regaled him with the memories of her life, which culminated in being chased across the complex yard by a dog that was the mascot for one of the other buildings. Tuffy did not like to be chased. As boring as the memories were—and at times Moreau felt like he was being forced to watch someone else's home movies of their vacation—they did serve a purpose. He got a sense of the layout of the buildings. It turned out that he was housed in the building at the farthest edge of a smallish complex. To one side were other buildings, and guards. To the other side was a small parking lot and woods. The building itself was divided into several rooms like the one where he was confined, with a network of laboratories and observation rooms strung above them.

He was also finally able to figure out how to formulate his thoughts so Tuffy could read them. It was not easy, but it could be done. With his newfound skills, the cat could serve as his small, furry secret agent. As he requested, Tuffy took to resting on some of the scientists' notes, which were scattered on a desk in the room above his head. If he concentrated, he could see through Tuffy's eyes in real time, in addition to sharing memories. This was haphazard at best because Tuffy tended to fall asleep, giving him a nice vision of the inside of her eyelids.

What he did see was not heartening. Stumpf and his roundheads had figured out that lycanthropy affected a part of the brain they called the *guorguol* region, as near as he could make out. As the condition progressed, that part of the brain would get bigger. Moreau's guorguol was "seven times the normal size," according to the jottings of one of the scientists. "Rather than curing him, we appear to be making him worse."

That was enough for him. A few days later he asked

Tuffy for a big favor. The next time the Roundheads turned on the blue light, they were in for a surprise. He had not eaten his food, so whatever they were putting in there to send him over the edge didn't have a chance to do its work. He was just a clear-headed werewolf with a set of keys in his hand. The keys had been heavy, but Tuffy had managed to get her teeth around them and drag them down the hall. He made a big show of holding them up, just for a few seconds, just long enough for the roundheads to realize what they were. He saw a few mouths widen into startled Os, and would have barked out a laugh if he had time. Alarm klaxons were sounding by the time one of his furry feet touched the hallway floor, but Tuffy had shown him that the guards were all in the next building because this one was apparently considered secure. It would take them a few seconds to get here, and that was all he needed.

Tuffy was waiting outside the door nearest the parking lot when he burst out into the night, free for the first time in months. Her little mouth was working furiously to produce loud meows, and her mind beamed out only one thought: Me too. Me too. He didn't even break stride to pick her up, and then wolfman and cat took to the trees. Tuffy didn't know what was on the other side of the woods, but Moreau was willing to find out.

TWENTY ONE

"Are you sure this will work?" Chesty asked Moreau, but he couldn't answer.

He tugged on his makeshift harness and led her closer to the door of the Breezy Pines Nursing Home, a large facility that was not at all breezy and that boasted not a single pine tree, only a few stunted palms transplanted from California. Chesty followed behind him, trying to look as if she couldn't see where she was going. She had borrowed dark sunglasses from Ashly Durban, along with her blouse, which looked a little less conspicuous than her pirate shirt. She still looked a little like a stripper, but at least now she looked like a blind stripper who was all dressed up to visit her long-lost grandfather.

"Oh, we don't allow pets in here," the woman at the front desk said, but then she noticed Chesty's sunglasses and blushed. "I'm so sorry. I didn't realize you had a seeing-eye dog. Can we help you?"

"Yes," Chesty said, thumping her way to the desk, trying not to look directly at the woman. "I'm here to visit my grandfather, Mr. Stumpf."

"I'm new here so I haven't learned everybody," the woman said, leafing through a registry book. "Let me seeeee," she started to say, then looked up at Chesty in alarm, remembering her apparent blindness. "Oh, I'm sorry. I mean, I'll *look*—oh, God, I'm so sorry—"

"It's okay," Chesty said with a vacant smile. "It doesn't offend me."

"Here he is," the flustered woman said. "Room G-5. Right down the hall. I truly am sorry."

"Don't be," Chesty said. Moreau was already underway, leading her down the hall.

"That's a beautiful dog," the woman said as they passed.

They passed through the building's cavernous main room, where several elderly women gathered around a large color television to watch Vanna White turn letters. No one paid them any attention. They padded down the hall to G-5 and entered slowly. Chesty shut the door behind them. A very pale old man was lying on his back on a plain bed that was far too neat and clean to be homey and comfortable, a bed that would almost certainly be the last one this man would ever know. The small room smelled of age and chemicals and contained only a table next to the bed, a TV with no antenna or cable, and a cream-colored chair full of lumpy pillows. They approached the bed slowly, as if walking up on a slumbering lion. The man was so pale it was hard to tell where the thin sheets left off and his skin began. He appeared to be dozing.

"Is that him?" Chesty asked.

The man awoke with a flinch and stared at her. He then looked down and saw the white guide dog, which did a curious thing; it stood up and turned into a naked man wearing a harness. Moreau had assembled the harness out of canvas straps from an old travel bag, to make it look like he was really a leader dog. The straps were still looped around his chest after the change. Chesty unzipped the backpack and handed Moreau his sweatshirt and jeans, which he put on without underwear. The old man closed his eyes and swallowed hard.

"Hello, Dr. Stumpf," Moreau said once he was dressed.

He stood above the old man and peered down at his head, which sported only a few ghostly wisps of hair above the ears. His head hovered only a foot above the old man's, and he moved it slowly back and forth, side to side, before bringing his nose down close to the old man's mouth as if he were trying to steal what little breath remained. The old man's eyelids reopened slowly, revealing watery blue eyes. The corners of his mouth slowly turned up into a vague semblance of a smile.

"I knew you'd find me again some day," he said in a voice that fought its way above a whisper. "Thank God. Will you make him go away?"

Moreau frowned in incomprehension. He exchanged a curious glance with Chesty, who was still wearing her sunglasses.

"What? Who?"

"He's here every night. He's going to kill me. I knew you'd come back. You can make him go away."

"Who's here every night?"

"Him. You *know* him. The man on the horse. A big man. Ask him to leave me alone."

Moreau's eyes flared wide for a fraction of a second.

"He's connected to lycanthropy, isn't he?" Stumpf asked.

Moreau nodded.

"That's why we could never figure this out. It's not just a disease. I suspected as much. I don't know what he'll do to me. I see his eyes and no one here believes me, no one sees the horse. Can you make him go away?"

Moreau grabbed his shoulders, none too gently, and dragged him to a sitting position. Stumpf drooped even when sitting upright. He slowly reached over to the table and retrieved his glasses. They looked like the same bulky plastic frames he had worn in the Sixties, although they held thicker glass. Stumpf's hand shook violently, but Moreau made no move to help him.

"I need your help first. Does the cure work?"

"The cure? I'm not sure you could call it a cure. It's more like an eradication. Mr. Moreau, I've made a terrible mistake. That's why he's here. The man. That's why he—"

The old man was sliding back down the bed in his agitation. He attempted to hold his position, but his stick arms weren't up to the task, and Moreau was obviously not going to help. Chesty grabbed two pillows off the chair and stuffed them under the fragile head to catch him when he fell back.

"Thank you, dear."

"You never stopped your research, did you, Dr. Stumpf?" Moreau asked. "The Landon Institute didn't come up with this on its own."

The skeletal arms twitched in an attempt at a shrug.

"What could I do? The Army cut off my funding

years ago. They said it wasn't doing any good and they cut it off."

"Do you think it's doing any good now?"

The watercolor blue eyes opened and closed with fatigue.

"What happened to Tuffy?"

"She died a long time ago. I learned a lot from her. I miss her. Do you think your work is doing any good now, Doctor?"

The old man was silent for a long time.

"No. And it's darker than you think. I've watched you over the years, talking on TV. You've talked about why werewolves exist, what good they can do. But you don't really understand."

Moreau was not used to being on this side of a werewolf argument.

"I don't? What don't I understand?"

Stumpf's eyes sought his, showed a little fire underneath the water.

"Tell me, Mr. Moreau. Do you have nightmares?"

Moreau nodded.

"Let me guess. Tornadoes? Earthquakes? Snow ten feet deep? Fires?"

Moreau leaned back, obviously startled. Chesty gave him a questioning look.

"Forest fires," Moreau answered. "Always fires. The animals are running out of the woods but there's nowhere to go."

Stumpf smiled.

"All werewolves have them. Did you know that? Did you ever ask your followers?"

"Some of the Jean Grenier Society members have mentioned them to me," Moreau admitted. "I didn't know what to tell them. Just nightmares, I said."

"You can think up preposterous theories about discussing zoning laws with animals but you thought those were just nightmares?" Stumpf asked, his voice carrying a good dose of the didactic tone Moreau remembered from the Maryland lab. "I'm surprised you've made it this far."

"So what do the dreams mean?" Chesty asked.

Stumpf gave her a weak smile.

"They're the means of saving the planet, I think. Did that ever occur to you, Mr. Moreau?"

Moreau shook his head slowly.

"Well, it should have. I think that's what the dreams are. They're sort of a genetic memory, but they're the memory of something that hasn't happened yet, that may not happen for a long time."

"What?" Chesty asked.

"Sometime in the future, my dear, there will just be too many people on the planet, spewing too much gunk in the air. Global warming, you know. Maybe we'll have some nuclear explosions here and there. We'll cut down too many rainforests and new viruses will keep appearing. And those may just be for starters."

"Oh," Chesty said.

Moreau just glared.

"The dreams are a warning," Stumpf continued. "Mother nature sees her own death—hundreds of years from now, thousands, tens of thousands, I don't know—and so she creates a defense. A hybrid. We all know that animals are more attuned to the environment than we are. Cows can sense rainstorms, and things like that. Didn't you ever think that might be useful? Maybe mother nature has decided it's time to use it. Maybe she created something to be a mediator between mankind and nature. Something that can sense what's going on in the environment and figure out how to solve it."

"My God," Moreau said.

"Exactly. Better than what you thought of, isn't it?" Stumpf asked. He crossed his bony arms and looked pleased with himself. "The planet creates its own defense, lets it develop over hundreds of thousands of years. When the crunch starts, people won't be riding along on top of nature, sticking sensors in the ground and wondering what the hell is going on. They'll have a way to understand the world better. They'll have go-betweens that combine our brains and the sense of animals. Werewolves. What we see today is just the early version, maybe."

"So eventually, we might start turning into other things, right?" Moreau asked. "Like fish or birds."

"Maybe. I don't know. But you've already changed from other werewolves in just the space of one lifetime. Who knows what's next?"

Moreau leaned his face in close.

"There's just one little problem. Your cure will get rid of us, won't it?"

Stumpf's face seemed to fall, his chin nearly disappearing into the wattles under his neck.

"I'm afraid so."

"So why didn't you stop? Why is the telethon going ahead with it?"

"I didn't know these things until too late. I just worked on my research. Who would have thought getting rid of werewolves was a bad thing? But after I come here, the man on the horse appears. He shows me visions. My God, Mr. Moreau, they are horrible."

Stumpf started shaking, nearly falling off the pillows until Chesty steadied him.

"Thank you. They're terrible. But I didn't know until too late."

"Did you have Cynthia Wardoe and Carl Johnson killed?" Moreau asked.

Stumpf closed his eyes, wreathing himself in silence, not even breathing.

"Tell me or I'll have the man on a horse in here."

The eyes opened a crack, just enough to let some fear slip through.

"Yes."

"Why?"

"They got greedy. I worked with them until I broke my hip, then they were on their own. But they couldn't get the tests to go like they wanted. They didn't like the fact that the cure turned some people into vegetables, so they tried to blame me. They said they would throw me out of here and expose me, and they wanted their money back. I need that money. This place is expensive, believe it or not."

"So you hired a killer who's also a werewolf, to get the public even more behind the idea of a cure."

"No, that was just an added bonus. There is an outfit out of Rhode Island that specializes in werewolf contract killings. I learned of them during my Army days. They were easy enough to find. The killer took care of Dr. Wardoe and Dr. Johnson and then found a list Johnson was trying to fax to someone, probably the police. He tried to go after the people on the list, but someone shot him up. I understand he's in intensive care somewhere in town. I haven't even had to pay him yet."

"*I* shot him up," Chesty said. "So that's why he came after Bobby. Too bad he made it through."

Stumpf looked at Chesty with newfound respect.

"What about Monty Allen?" Moreau said. "What does he know about all this? Does he know?"

"He does not know."

"He doesn't know? Are you sure?"

"He does not want to know."

"What do you mean?"

"He believes the cure works. He has seen some evidence to the contrary but he chooses not to believe it. He believes it will work."

Moreau stood up and stomped around the room in impotent disgust.

"Why is Monty Allen in such a rush? What's the hurry?"

"Look at the financial records of the last several Werewolf Telethons. The numbers go down, not up. People have compassion fatigue, they don't give as much after a while unless they see results. If he doesn't do it this year, he won't have enough money to do it next year. It will be just another one of those charities that limps along and does nothing."

Moreau sat back on the bed.

"Dr. Stumpf, have you told Monty Allen your new theories?"

"I have tried. He won't see anybody anymore. He is busy with the telethon. I broke my hip six months ago and have been in here ever since. I have not seen him. I have left seven answering machine messages for him. Nothing. He doesn't even like *your* theories. Imagine what he must think about mine."

"What about video proof? I have Carl Johnson's videos. They show what the cure really does to some people. What will happen if I show them to Monty Allen?"

"Nothing. You won't get near him."

"What if I showed the video to the police?"

Stumpf smiled, as if he enjoyed the thought.

"He has them in his pocket. They would throw you in jail, maybe shoot you."

"But what if I did get to him?"

"Still nothing. I told you. He believes. He knows, deep in his heart, that something, somewhere, is wrong, but he believes. He will not change his mind."

Chesty walked up beside the bed and stared down at the doctor.

"Why does he care so much?" she asked.

"Who are you, anyway?" Stumpf asked, but Chesty just glared at him, waiting for an answer.

"He does not want to be remembered only for having made bad werewolf movies," Stumpf said when he realized he was far too old and weak to be able to stare her down.

"You two are quite the humanitarians," Moreau muttered. "But thanks for the information. You've told me something I didn't know. Come on, Chesty, let's go."

He pulled off his jeans and handed them to Chesty. The old man reached out for him, his arm trembling, his fingers shaking uselessly.

"No!" the old man said, straining forward. "Make him go away! Help me. Make him go away. Please. I'm sorry."

"He does what he wants. I doubt you've seen the last of him. He's probably very angry about what you've done."

Moreau gave the doctor a slight smile and then his face fell towards the floor, only to melt into the false grin of a large white dog.

"Goodbye," Chesty said.

The girl and the dog hurried down the hall, eager to escape before the nurses could hear the high-pitched wailing from the old man's room, a siren that grew louder with each step they took.

TWENTY TWO

And so Halloween dawned and the show began, carried live on every broadcast network but Fox, a point which had not escaped the late-night talk show comics.

"Do you know why Fox won't carry the Werewolf Telethon?" Jay Leno asked on his Thursday night show. "They said they couldn't guarantee there wouldn't be a dogfight."

The crowd groaned, and Leno made a face to indicate he knew it was a bad joke.

The throng around the front doors of the Universal Monster Grand the next day, however, was considerably more enthusiastic despite the fact that many of them appeared to have been up the entire night. Crowd members watched as Monty Allen hopped out of his enormous black limousine and trotted through the casino's main hall through a hail of flashbulbs, waving and smiling all the while. He was followed in short order by a bevy of unidentified starlets, and then by some of the talent that would be making up the morning portion of the show. The lobby was thick with media; anyone who stopped moving was fair game for an interview, even if they had little connection to the event. Once they had been questioned by a camera-wielding reporter, tourists would crush around them and take pictures, thinking they were perhaps famous. One of the more handsome doormen at the casino was rapidly becoming a celebrity.

Allen had lined up a decent early morning roster to appeal to people who might otherwise seek out syndicated talk shows on cable, or hope for blood and guts or sex (or all three) on Fox. There were a couple of fairly famous bands, mixed in with good but obscure groups such as the Gospel Five, topped with a smattering of local comedians and Marko the Ventriloquist, who had a couple of David Letterman appearances to his credit. The real heavy hitters would come in the evening, but all in all the morning wasn't bad. There was even a magician who used a couple of the scantily clad starlets in his act, and Allen made sure that he got a good spot.

Media and performers alike mashed into the main ballroom, which had been decorated with red, white and blue bunting and stars, making the temple of Mammon suddenly resemble a political rally. There was much waving and smiling and the cameras flashed like strobe lights. As Monty Allen took the stage to wild cheering, it looked for a second like the great man was going to run for president.

"Hello, America, and Happy Halloween!" he shouted, loud enough to overpower the microphones closest to him. "Are you ready to have a good day today doing good?"

None of the assembled journalists said anything, but

the group of Allen supporters who had been crammed near the stage yelled their heads off.

"That's what I like to hear!" Allen shouted. "My good people, you are witness to history today. You have read about how smallpox was cured and how tuberculosis was cured and how . . ."

And here he faltered a bit, suddenly unable to remember another disease that had been mastered in the recent past. The pause was only for the blink of an eye, however, and he continued at full volume.

". . . how heart disease was lessened as a threat through the advice of doctors that we should all eat right and exercise. And today, ladies and gentlemen, is a day more spectacular than any of those. By the time the next twelve hours are over, you will have given from your hearts and we will stand ready to cure thousands of ailing Americans of a disease that brings nothing but pain and anguish."

One of the cameras zoomed in tight on Allen's face, and he made his moustache do its trademark wiggle.

"And in the meantime, we'll have a little fun."

TWENTY THREE

Ashly Durban's reappearance in Las Vegas, on the very day of the Werewolf Telethon, was a small sensation in a day full of big sensations. *Live Entertainment* had hyped her disappearance on the Thursday night show, running an especially flattering picture of her behind the substitute anchor's head. They had even put together an ad hoc biography, detailing her birth in Kentucky to alcoholic parents and her subsequent escape from home to the big city of Las Vegas, where she clawed her way up the television ladder until she made the jump to L.A. and the big time. *Live Entertainment* obviously considered itself to be the epitome of the big time. The docudrama hinted at her own battle with the bottle—it said her success meant overcoming her "personal demons"—but never put it in plain words, never showed any of the old Channel 12 footage of her drunk at the Christmas party, which was notorious in local broadcasting circles. It was a nice little show. Durban watched it herself at Paul Moreau's trailer, and made a mental note to get herself a copy. It would come

213

in handy for future job interviews. The substitute anchor, who was the weekend weatherman for Channel 12, even solemnly intoned, "Ashly Durban, missing . . . Day One."

The other channels in Las Vegas also ran their own grudging tally. Channel 12's main competitor, Channel 9, had a unique take on the situation: An ashen John Robinson faced the camera and begged the Jean Grenier Society to bring his wife back. He even squeezed out a tear or two. The local newspapers had even managed to get in on the act. The *Review Journal* ran a long, tear-jerking interview with Robinson. He showed old pictures of himself and Ashly and reminisced about their early years together as hungry young journalists in the City of Sin, conveniently leaving out the parts about their weekly boozy brawls. The *Sun* even ran a version of the story, after it had been chopped down to size by the Associated Press.

And then, suddenly, the center of this attention ruined it all by coming back, only one day later. *Live Entertainment* would never be able to say, "Ashly Durban missing . . . Day Two." At six A.M. on Friday she suddenly appeared on the Strip, near the Flamingo, at just the hour when the only people around were either broke, depressed, drunk, or all three. Her clothes were dirty, and she held her head with one hand as she staggered around, muttering, "I'm Ashly Durban, I escaped from my kidnappers. Can you help me?" Most people passed her off as a drunk—one guy even gave her fifty cents and two gaming tokens—but not the morning manager of the Flamingo, who recognized her from a favorable story she had done on him years ago, and who also wasn't averse to a little good publicity for having "saved" the missing newswoman.

Durban was taken to the police. They had her examined by a doctor, who said that she appeared to be in very good shape for a kidnapping victim. Durban got on the phone and promised the Channel 12 station manager an exclusive interview about her ordeal, which they began advertising every half hour during their news updates, but she had to talk to the police first. The cops let her clean up and change clothes. They took her dirty clothes away in an evidence bag and gave her thick black coffee and doughnuts that gleamed with sugar.

As it turned out, they gave her more than she gave them. Durban told them she couldn't remember much, that she spent most of the four days in a drug-induced haze, that she wasn't sure where she had been taken. She said she had been kidnapped by Paul Moreau and that he and dozens or even hundreds of followers had been camped out in what looked like an abandoned restaurant north of town.

"You sure it was Paul Moreau?" asked one of the detectives interviewing her. He was a clean-shaven man who looked much too young to have such a position of authority.

"I'm sure," she said. The coffee they gave her was not very good. Paul Moreau had given her bad water, and now she had bad coffee. She was not sure which was preferable. "It was Paul Moreau. *The* Paul Moreau. He said the police were after him."

"Ma'am, did he happen to say anything about killing some people here in town? You know, those murders? I think you had some stories on them."

She shook her head and frowned as if trying hard to remember.

"No, he didn't say. I was kind of woozy most of the

time, when I wasn't scared out of my mind. They said they were going to kill me, so I didn't latch on to a lot of the specifics. I don't remember."

"They were going to kill you?"

The young detective stopped taking notes for a moment and frowned. The other detective, an older, more rumpled man, took the news in stride, but the young one appeared to take it personally that someone wanted to kill her. She thought that was sweet.

"They are *werewolves*. Yes. I remember them saying they were going to kill me because I had done stories about them. They didn't like the stories. They wanted to prove some kind of point."

"How did you get away from them, if there were so many?"

Durban took a deep breath and closed her eyes for a long moment.

"They were planning something last night, there were a lot of them milling around, and they forgot to give me whatever it was they had been giving me. They were off doing something else. I got untied and then snuck off out the back way. I got to a road—I'm not sure what road it was, it was out north of town, I think— and this guy gave me a ride. He was a young guy but I don't know what he looked like."

"This was the man who dropped you off in front of the Flamingo? Why didn't he stop? Isn't your station offering some kind of reward?"

She brightened at that.

"Are they? How much?"

The older detective shrugged his shoulders and waited for her answer.

"Oh well. No, he said he'd had trouble with the law before, and didn't want to get involved. I didn't tell him that a bunch of werewolves were after me. I didn't think he'd like that. I just told him to drop me off."

"Do you remember anything about the car? Anything at all?"

"It was yellow. That's all."

"Big? Small?"

"Yellow. Smallish, I think. Maybe a Toyota."

The young detective was still looking at Durban's face earnestly, but the older one shoved his hands in the pockets of his ill-fitting gray pants and shrugged his shoulders again.

"Ahhh, we're through. Miss Durban, I trust you'll be available should we wish to talk with you further."

"Of course."

"Okay. Moreau and his gang were north of town, you say?"

She nodded.

"I'm sorry I can't be more specific."

"That's perfectly understandable. You get yourself some rest. Everybody we got who's available will be out there looking for your furry friends."

TWENTY FOUR

Ashly Durban leaned on the wall and got her breath, seizing it in quick little gulps that gradually lengthened and deepened. She had met with several advisors of Monty Allen, told them of her purpose, and, little by little, had been allowed deeper into the inner sanctum like a speck of sand permitted to drift through the chambered shell of a Nautilus.

The noisy telethon was proceeding down the hall, up on the new, expensive Universal Monster Grand stage. So far, $3.5 million had been raised, a fair sum, if somewhat below expectations for the hour. It was nearly 3 P.M. and Monty Allen had only cried four times. He probably had plenty of emotion left for the big 8 P.M. finale. Bands and comedians were still trooping on and off the stage regularly, interspersed with video tributes from movie stars and rock bands urging viewers to get off their duffs and send in their checks.

Durban had shown up at the casino hours before. She had been mobbed when she first arrived, despite an attempt at disguise using an old scarf wrapped around her hair. It didn't work. She had to smile and dance around questions for a while; she couldn't look too desperate. Eventually she had managed to catch the eye of one of Monty Allen's low-level managers. He was a dapper man paid to keep people away from higher-level managers, who were in turn paid to keep people away from the big man himself. She pulled him aside and whispered in his ear. After that it was merely a matter of waiting, as she began climbing the access ladder that would eventually, over the course of hours, lead to Allen. With each step higher on the ladder she was pulled deeper into the Universal Monster Grand.

She thought her jitters might have been quelled by the time she reached the inner sanctum, defeated by sheer time and boredom, but it was not so. Her heart thumped as she leaned on the side of a room that bore the sign DO NOT DISTURB. No performers loitered here. There was only a small hallway that led from the stage to this room, and a couple of bodyguards near the stage to keep anyone other than Monty Allen off of it. But she had made the cut, had made her way here. The bodyguards, two large men in dark suits, probably thought she was merely nervous at the thought of meeting the great man. That was not true. Monty Allen was old hat for her. Had the bodyguards been able to read her mind and figure out what she was really worried about, they probably would have shot her. She was nervous at the thought that what she soon hoped to accomplish might be terribly, terribly wrong. Had the videotape she saw in Paul Moreau's trailer really shown what it seemed to show? What if it were an old tape, from last year's show? What if Allen had seen it and fired a crazed, lying Stumpf and agreed to a year's delay, and now everything was hunky dory?

She closed her eyes and replayed the tape in her head as best she could. No, it seemed pretty damning. If she was wrong she faced a nice, fat libel suit, but maybe she'd get a good book deal out of the notoriety that would help pay the bills. At any rate, she'd at least be even more famous, and that couldn't hurt. If she didn't act, and the tape showed what it seemed to show, then other people would suffer. She opened her eyes again and felt a tremor from within the dressing room. The big man was walking to the door.

"Let's do it," she said, under her breath.

The door behind her opened and he stood there, looking as quiet and peaceful as if he had just been quietly reading all day, rather than shepherding a nationwide telethon. He wore a suit that was fancy without seeming formal, the kind of offhand elegance that only a great deal of money could buy. He had been sweating and crying profusely on stage all day, she knew, but now he looked as dry and powdered as a wax figure in a museum. The room itself was not a model of elegance. It looked like the model for a No-Tell Motel honeymoon special—big bed, big orange couch, one ratty blue chair, one tiny table that might, just might, be able to support the weight of a magazine or two, no TV, no telephone.

"Miss Durban?" he asked quietly, and she nodded, walking into the room and extending a hand for him to shake. He looked as if he was going to kiss it for a second, but then thought better of it and gave it a shy couple of pumps.

"It's nice to see you again, Mr. Allen."

His famous grin looked just as inviting up close as it did from across a darkened movie theater.

"And it's nice to see *you* again. Your news coverage is unusually good. I am pleased to speak to you whenever I can. You do a good job. Please, sit down."

She plopped gratefully onto the couch and he dragged up the ratty chair.

"Are you okay? I heard all about you getting kidnapped by Paul Moreau. Is everything all right? You weren't hurt?"

"No, I'm fine. I was a little scared—well, a *lot* scared—but I got out and I'm okay. I was just lucky that I could get away."

"I heard about that, too. I happened to catch the news during a break. What a daring escape. You are a very brave lady. What happened out there?"

"Paul Moreau told me he has a plan to get his Jean Grenier Society members to bite as many people as they can, to spread lycanthropy anywhere they can spread it. He was scary. He talked like a madman. He said werewolves will take over the world."

Allen grunted and shook his head in disgust. There was an awkward silence for a second or two while he considered her words.

"I guess you're wondering why I showed up here," she said.

"I assume you have a good reason, or you probably wouldn't have made it through my entourage out there."

"They were pretty tough, but once they heard what I had to say they agreed to let me through. Mr. Allen—"

"Monty."

"—Monty, I came because I think I'm in a position to help you with the telethon. It's going well, isn't it?"

He rubbed his forehead with fingers as thick as cigars.

"To be honest, it could be a lot better."

"I think I can help. You've had some problems with Moreau and his society, haven't you?"

He blew out his cheeks like Dizzy Gillespie and exhaled loudly.

"*Have* I. Those guys are a pain. Half the people in the media—no offense—seem to think that they're the good guys, them and their criminal boss. I can't believe the good press they've managed to attract. And did you see that writeup in *The Village Voice* last week on Paul Moreau, blaming society for his crimes? Incredible. And now you're telling me this."

He shook his head, and then seemed to remember who he was talking with.

"And *you've* certainly had a time with Moreau and his boys, haven't you?" he said, raising his famous left eyebrow. He looked at her with new understanding. "You got kidnapped by their leader, didn't you? You've seen them up close and personal, haven't you? You've seen how ugly their philosophy is, haven't you?"

The quicker he spoke, the more quickly and vigorously Ashly Durban nodded her head.

"And you're a newsperson, and you're used to being in front of the camera . . ."

She looked to the ceiling and held her tiny round chin in her fingers, making a *hmmm*ing sound as she pretended to struggle to follow his train of thought.

"You could tell everyone what a bunch of scumbags those guys are firsthand, couldn't you? You could give us the real story on Paul Moreau, couldn't you?" Allen continued, getting so excited that he started rocking back and forth on the edge of the chair. "You could go on our little show and be interviewed and tell us all about your experience. Or you could just get up there and talk. Or you could get up there and sing! Can you sing?"

She dropped her chin and laughed and shook her head.

"Yes! We could put you on tonight! We could move some of the bands up and get them out of the way. The Lemonheads wouldn't mind going on a little early, and the network shouldn't mind a surprise guest . . ."

Without stopping his monologue, Allen dropped to the floor on one knee, took Ashly Durban's left hand in his and looked up into her face.

"Ashly Durban, would you go on the telethon and help us cure all the werewolves?"

She bent down in her chair and caressed the back of his huge hand, which was softer than she had expected.

"Mr. Allen, I thought you'd never ask."

TWENTY FIVE

Bob Savik stood in with a crowd of tourists in a hallway at the Montage Casino, where the white Siberian tiger of the "Mandunk and the Amazing World of Animals" show were on display. The tiger was very energetic in the actual Mandunk performances, but right now it was so motionless it appeared to be waiting for the taxidermist. It was sprawled out full length on a fake Arctic tableau behind a thick twenty-foot-high glass wall, eyes only tight little slits, dead to the world. Even in deep slumber the tiger was an impressive animal to the tourists, who *oohed* and *aahed* at every rise and fall of its ribcage. Now and then the beast would emit a tiny snort or flick a paw, drawing squeals of delight from the kids that were watching.

Savik stood to one side, off by himself, trying to look casual, a large thirty-five-year-old man in a sweatshirt and jean jacket who just had an inordinate interest in a sleeping white tiger. He wandered to the edge of the hall, whistled a devil-may-care tune and checked his watch again. He didn't want to hang out here all night, but the regularly scheduled tiger feeding was apparently running late, not that the tiger seemed to mind. He would have gone to look at something else but unfortunately there was nothing to see in the hall but the tourists and the tiger, and he had seen plenty of both of them. Soon his casualness would be stripped away, revealed for the skulking criminal behavior that it actually was. He resumed his limp tune and hoped that Ashly Durban hadn't gone around the bend.

First she had disappeared without so much as a word on Wednesday night, becoming the subject of all that fawning crap on the news on Thursday. He even had to sit through the excruciating agony of watching John Robinson read a love poem to his ex-wife right there in the middle of the newscast; Ashly definitely owed him a nice dinner at Spago's for that. Then she had awakened him with a frantic phone call early this morning, spilling out a crazy story and involving him with an enterprise that definitely did not seem on the level. She assured him that the resulting notoriety would only enhance his name, and probably attract the attention of the *Cops* producers. That had hooked him, as she knew it would. He inwardly cursed himself for being a man of such simple needs.

"It's a nice kitty, ain't it?" a voice said suddenly from behind his left shoulder.

Savik nearly jumped out of his skin, but managed to hide his fear and turn around slowly. A small white man wearing a green John Deere cap stood behind him, his hands jammed down into the pockets of his jeans.

"Yeah," Savik said. "It's very nice."

"That it is," the man said in his reedy voice. "Looks plumb tuckered out, too."

Savik was annoyed. It was bad enough to be lurking around the tiger cage, but infinitely worse to be seen doing it. He turned his head away from the man, which did nothing to dampen his conversational tendencies.

"The wife and daughter are in the casino blowin' my money," the man said, with a sharp laugh. "I told them they can waste it all, but I won't help. I thought I'd look at this fancy kitty here. We don't have them around home."

This was obviously bait for Savik to ask where home was, but he didn't take it. Fate interceded before the little man could set out another chatty trap.

"Oh, look there," the man said. "Here comes that fella to feed him."

Sure enough, a long-haired man was approaching the back door to the cage, which was off to the left, nearly hidden behind styrofoam carved to resemble a snowy crag.

"Excuse me," Savik said.

He had been waiting for this, and had almost missed it. He gave up any pretense of being a cool observer, and ran to the the glass wall on the other side of the door.

"You must be pretty hungry yourself," the man shouted after him.

Savik made it to the edge of the glass just as the man started punching the entrance code into the lock on the other side. Savik had scoped this out earlier, and hoped it would work. There was no way for him to get to the other side of the cage, to the actual door, so this would have to do. He slapped his hands against

the glass, even though a sign specifically told him
not to, and stared at the lower right corner of the
huge glass wall. The Montage used mirror-like glass
on virtually every flat surface, including the wall on
the other side of the door to the tiger cage. Savik
had noticed earlier that the electronic code lock on
the door reflected back onto the outer glass wall of
the tiger cage with a minimum of distortion. The man
coming to feed the slack tiger was intent on his job
and hadn't yet noticed Savik. He punched in the code,
and the red light above the lock turned green. Savik
saw the whole thing reversed in the glass, and repeated
the number to himself: 364. 364. Reversed is 463.
463. He would have to write this down or he would
scramble it. Urgent hands tapped down his pockets;
he had a pen, but no paper. No problem. He scrawled
the numbers into his left palm in blue ink, so hard it
hurt.

A man and woman standing nearby eyed him
uncertainly. The father rested one hand on the
shoulder of their knee-high son and started to back
away slowly from Savik. They couldn't see the lock's
reflection and couldn't tell what he was up to. They
had merely witnessed a man dash over to the glass
wall, stare at the man bringing in a bucket of tiger
food, and then apparently stab himself in the hand
with a pen. That was not necessarily unusual
behavior in Las Vegas, but it seemed weird enough
for them. Maybe they could go chat with the man
in the John Deere cap; Savik's apparent insanity
would make a good ice breaker. Savik didn't care.
He had his code number. He didn't know why Ashly
Durban wanted it, wasn't sure he even wanted to
know, but he had it. He stuck his pen back in his

pocket, glad to be done with this chore at last. He walked quickly past the tiger cage. The tourists had turned their attention back to the tiger, which, with great effort, had managed to lift its lazy head at the thought of food.

TWENTY SIX

The breeze felt good blowing through his fur. He was glad it wasn't blowing any harder, or it might take him right off the side of the building.

"Do you see him?" Chesty called from down below.

"I think so," Bobby said around his fangs.

He clawed up another foot or two, his fingers tenuously jammed into the spackle between the bricks. His knuckles would ache later. Now, he had a mission. He peered inside, his wolf eyes able to probe deeper into the darkened room. A young man was there, a boy, really, just about his age. The boy's face was a round, empty mask. His mouth hung open and his eyes stared at a point somewhere above and beyond Bobby's hairy head.

"It's him," Bobby said to Chesty, as quietly as he could. "It's Danny Wexler."

Carl Johnson's trove of blackmail items had included a list of addresses. A little cross-referencing with the telephone book showed some of them to be hospitals, and one to be a nursing home that catered to children.

Danny Wexler was listed at the latter address. Bobby and Chesty had gone out to find him and as many of the others as he could. Bobby checked his watch: five o'clock. He was supposed to be in place in another hour and a half, at the latest, and Danny was the first person on the list he had found. The nursing home was now closed to visitors, but Bobby crawled around in the bushes to see if Wexler was in a room with an outside window. A search on the first floor didn't turn him up, so Bobby decided to use a dose of the blue fluid to see if he was on a higher floor. He kicked off his shoes and socks, shot up, and started climbing.

Wexler did have a room with a window. Unfortunately, it was on the fifth floor. As long as the wind didn't pick up, Bobby could hang on. The nursing home backed up against an office building, and everybody there seemed to have cleared out a little early on this particular Friday, probably to head off to Halloween parties. The arrival of the holiday meant that Bobby could turn into a werewolf with relative impunity. There were lots of costumed people already on the streets, clowns and hoboes and aliens of all stripes, starting the night's bar-hopping.

"Danny," Bobby said, as loud as he dared.

Wexler continued staring, sitting motionless in his wheelchair. He had never needed a wheelchair at the warehouse.

"Danny, can you unlock the window?"

Wexler didn't respond. The lights in his room were off, and so were the lights of his mind. He looked empty, like a rubber mannequin with glass orbs for eyes. Bobby wasn't sure how he would get Danny out, but maybe he could sneak him down the stairs and out the back door. First he would have to get the window open, and Danny gave no indication of being able to cooperate in that.

Bobby remembered his crash training with Paul Moreau in the desert. The mental control had worked with an owl, and with the small animals outside Ashly Durban's apartment building. Could it work with Danny Wexler? Right now it looked as if the owl would be harder. Bobby dug his fingers and toes in between the bricks as far as he could and concentrated. He stared deep into the lost eyes of Danny Wexler.

As quick as a thought, he was staring at himself as he hung outside the window, his blue rugby shirt and gray hair ruffling in the wind. Bobby took one pudgy hand and rolled the chair forward. The chair creaked slowly across the floor. His werewolf eyes looked green and ghostly; he tried to avoid looking at them, and concentrated on the window latch. It was on a high sill, probably to keep Danny away from it. Bobby reached Danny's chubby arm towards the sill, but it was too far. He would have to use the legs, if that were possible. He dug himself deeper into Danny's mind and pulled, and Danny rose from the chair. So the legs still worked. Danny just didn't know how to use them anymore. That was really some werewolf cure the Landon Institute had cooked up. Danny's fingers fumbled against the metal latch. His digits were weak, but the latch turned. Bobby heard a click as it opened all the way. He broke the mental connection, and Wexler fell back into the wheelchair with a muffled thump. Bobby was alarmed to find himself at arm's length from the wall; apparently his arm muscles had relaxed as he guided Wexler to the window. He quickly pulled himself inside Wexler's room and then leaned out again and waved at Chesty, who was pacing down below.

Danny Wexler betrayed no fear or curiosity about the werewolf who had just come through his window. Bobby hunched in front of him and smiled as best he could with a mouthful of sharp teeth. Wexler's glassy eyes stared straight ahead, as unseeing as marbles. He wore a thin hospital gown that gapped at the thighs, revealing milky white flesh. Bobby tugged on the gown, covering Danny as well as the hospital garb would allow. Bobby walked around behind him and rolled the wheelchair towards the door. The change was fading now, which was good. He could pass for a Halloween partygoer outside on the city sidewalks, but it would be harder to do in the nursing home. Once all the hair had faded, maybe he could just pass as a teen who had come to visit his ailing buddy.

They had almost made it to the door when Danny Wexler spoke.

"He's coming," he said, in a gurgling voice.

Bobby spun the wheelchair around and crouched in front of Wexler.

"Danny! What did you say?"

He thought the eyes might be more alive, but they weren't. Only speech had come back to Danny, and not much of that.

"He's coming," Wexler said again. His marble eyes still stared into space. "He's coming."

"Who's coming, Danny? Who?"

Wexler was gone again. Bobby hunched in front of him for a minute more, occasionally waving a palm before his face, but no more words came. The messenger had spoken, and had said all he was going to say.

TWENTY SEVEN

It was nearing 8 P.M., Pacific time, and all eyes that weren't watching cable were on Ashly Durban as she extended a dainty hand so that Monty Allen could help her onto the Universal Monster Grand stage. She looked smashing, even if a tiny bit prim. Unlike the starlets that had flitted across the stage from time to time during the course of the day, she was clad in a fairly businesslike red dress that revealed little cleavage but nevertheless showed her body off to good advantage. Her blonde hair was sculpted, her rouged cheekbones no less so. She thought she had dressed well for her impromptu meeting with Monty Allen, but after he decided to put her in the show his crew had rousted up a really nice dress and had turned a nice-looking woman into a tasteful knockout.

Allen led her to a single microphone and handed her a remote control, which she was supposed to use to pretend to queue up video segments for her talk. A technician stationed offstage would do all the real work; all Ashly had to do was hold up the remote and pretend to click the button while giving her talk. She had run through the drill a few times for Allen's staff during the late afternoon and had hit her spots with ease.

Allen's crew had gone all out for her presentation, despite having to cobble something together in record time. They had obtained decade-old video footage of Paul Moreau on a talk show, when he got so angry at another guest that he had nearly attacked them before he was hauled off the stage. They had spliced in graphic Army footage of a werewolf in full rave mode, slashing at a dummy. And for no real reason, other than titillation, they had also included footage of a gray wolf pursuing and devouring a rabbit. They had even written her script for her, taking the few facts she had presented about her abduction and punching them up a little to underscore that werewolves were treacherous and dangerous indeed if not cured. She had to admit these guys were good, even if their views were slanted. Monty Allen had to be paying them pretty well to keep them away from the networks.

"Ladies and gentlemen, in our audience and at home," Allen began, smile beaming. "I really don't have to introduce our next and final guest to you, or at least to those of you who appreciate fine broadcast journalism. The woman I have here is a very special person to all of us who have been in the trenches fighting the evil that is lycanthropy, because she has helped put a human face on this tragedy. Her reporting for NBC's *Live Entertainment* has given us joy for years, and her recent news reporting here in Las Vegas has helped people in this city realize that lycanthropy is not just something out of an old monster movie, it is a disease that can strike people just like you and me. She is Ashly Durban, a beautiful and talented young woman with a big heart."

Allen gave her a long bow, bending over so far that she could see the back of his head. The audience clapped their heads off and she smiled at them and waved, a little stiffly, a Queen of England sort of greeting. She started to reach for the microphone, but Allen quickly straightened up and resumed speaking.

"What most of you already know is that Ms. Durban was kidnapped just two nights ago by wanted felon Paul Moreau, who has taken it upon himself to try to perpetuate lycanthropy in the general population."

A brief, but loud, booing emanated from the floor. Allen had his crowd packed well with professional responders.

"Yes, yes. Her heroism enabled things to turn out for the best, however. She gathered her courage and intelligence and escaped from his clutches. Had she not done that she would no doubt be the latest victim of a man who has killed several innocent warriors in the fight for good health."

More boos.

"Yes, he's still on the loose, so watch your backs tonight. Anyway, Ashly Durban is here tonight in an exclusive appearance to tell us a little bit about her experiences, and to show once again how dangerous lycanthropy can be. Ms. Durban, take it away. And, you viewers, don't forget to phone in those pledges. We're still a little shy of $10 million, which is where we need to be. The number is 1-800-NO-WOLFS. Don't forget!"

He gave her upper arm a little squeeze as he left the stage. And then she was alone up there, the eyes of an estimated sixty million people coast-to-coast upon her. The crowd below rustled quietly in anticipation. She cleared her throat.

"Good evening, ladies and gentlemen. I'm here to describe my experiences to you, and to perhaps help change some preconceptions you might have about lycanthropy."

Offstage, Monty Allen winked and gave her a thumbs-up sign.

"For the past several hours you have been told that lycanthropy is a disease that can be very destructive. And that's true."

Allen was still smiling. Ashly Durban took a big breath; it was now or never. There would be no going back. She only hoped that Bob Savik and Paul Moreau had everything in place, otherwise this would be the most spectacular career suicide in history.

"You have also been told that it's a disease that can and should be cured as soon as possible. I'm afraid that I'm here to tell you that's not really the case."

There was a collective gasp from the crowd. Even the professional responders were stunned by her statement. Offstage, Monty Allen was instantly livid. He gestured frantically at a large, beefy man who stood near the stage door.

"You have been told that a cure is ready for lycanthropy. You have sent in donations on that premise. I have uncovered evidence that clearly shows this is false. I'm sorry to have to report to you that it's just not true."

"Stan!" Allen shouted to the large man, one of the bodyguards who protected his dressing room. "Get ready to drag her off that stage!"

The man named Stan nodded and touched something in his jacket pocket. He looked somber enough to attend a funeral.

"I ask you to stop calling in donations immediately.
The cure is a fake. Please stop calling."

"Go!" Allen shouted to Stan, even though Stan was
only two feet away. The large man lumbered out onto
the stage, Frankenstein-monster style.

There was a flurry from one of the camera crews
covering the event. One of the reporters from Channel
9 clambered up the tripod and used the video camera
as a launching pad, planting one wingtip right on the
expensive lens and hurling himself onto the stage right
in the man's path.

"Stop right there!" John Robinson shouted.

Stan gave him a nasty look and reached inside his
jacket pocket menacingly.

"John!" Ashly shouted from behind him. "What are
you doing?"

He didn't turn around to look at her.

"I don't know what *you're* doing, but just do it!" he
shouted. "I trust you!"

"How sweet," Stan said, taking another step forward.
"Why don't you blow the lady a kiss and then get back
down there and play with your little reporter friends,
Clark Kent?"

Robinson reached inside his jacket pocket, too.
Channel 9, which didn't quite have the ratings of the
other network affiliates in town, had always bought
the cheapest equipment it could get. It bought him a
cellular phone long after everybody else already had
one, and then the one it got was an old, heavy one, so
bulky he could barely stuff it in his jacket. Just this
one time, he was glad he had it. It had a solid metallic
heft, like a high-tech brick. With a banzai shout he
dashed at Stan, the Motorola held out like a sword.
Stan struggled in his pocket, but couldn't quite get

his weapon drawn in time. Robinson brought the phone across in an arc, connecting with an electronic beep to Stan's temple. The big man went down. When he hit the stage his fingers finally found what they were looking for. A gunshot rang out, fired from his inner jacket pocket to the upper reaches of the Universal Monster Grand theater. The crowd let out a cacophony of shrieks and shouts and took gunplay as their cue to leave.

Monty Allen issued a quick stream of curses and stalked onstage himself, his muscles alive with pulsing veins. He'd have to persuade Ms. Durban to leave the stage in person. He grabbed John Robinson, who was still dazed by his success, and tossed him out into the crowd by his lapels. The crowd held him aloft, like he was a kid at a rock concert.

"Turn the channel, NOW, all of you!" Durban was screaming at the cameras. She grasped the microphone stand like it was an oak that would save her from a gale. "Turn to FOX! Fox, RIGHT NOW, if you want to know the truth about lycanthropy and Monty Allen!"

Just as Monty Allen closed within three feet of her she picked up the heavy stand and, with surprising strength borne of fear, tossed it into his face. He staggered back and Durban ran toward the other wing of the stage, only to see three new bodyguards shoving *Hard Copy* cameramen out of the way, waiting for her.

Monty Allen stabilized the microphone and shouted, "Ladies and gentlemen, allow me to apologize for Ms. Durban! I will return in one moment!"

The crowd didn't seem to want to stick around. Its members were beating a hasty retreat from the stage, or trying to—the small doors of the Monster Grand were slowing things down considerably. A couple of young men bucked the tide to go the other way. They wore gray suits, and their long hair streamed across their shoulders.

"Durban!" shouted the one who was also wearing a red Caesar's Palace baseball cap. She didn't hear. Talbot Braudaway cursed. This kind of action was only slightly better than being a perimeter guard at Monty Allen's hideaway. He shoved his way onto the stage and grabbed her around the waist, causing her to yelp.

"I'm on *your* side," he shouted in her ear, before leaping back into the crowd, knocking aside a young woman, who fell on her back and glared up at them.

"I'm sorry," Durban said, making an apologetic face.

"No time to be polite," Talbot said. "We're supposed to follow your orders. I suggest you think of something quick."

Durban glanced across the stage at Talbot's compatriot, a Jean Grenier Society member who had also hopped up on the stage and was holding a big pistol on Monty Allen, keeping him from going any further. Allen fairly pulsed with rage, and screamed obscenities at them, despite the presence of the cameras. Apparently he would worry about the public relations problem later. Allen was temporarily at bay, so they couldn't go in his direction, and the other side of the stage wings were now clogged with excited camera crews who were sending out the chaos live to the television sets of America. The only way out was with the crowd, which was slowly, very slowly, squeezing itself through the back doors, and making a lot of noise in the process.

"I hate to say it, but I suggest we go out those back doors," Durban shouted into Talbot's ear, pointing above the molasses-slow crowd.

"No problem."

He reached in his jacket pocket and pulled out a gun he had swiped from one of the thugs the Landon Institute had dispatched to the warehouse. He knew it would come in handy. Ashly Durban stuck her fingers in her ears and Talbot fired the pistol three times in the air. It cleared a path through the crowd very nicely.

TWENTY EIGHT

Henry Hull smiled at the camera nervously and took a big sip of what the studio audience hopefully assumed was water. He had long since learned how to drink straight gin and make it look innocent. The booze helped a little, but he still drummed his fingertops along his desk nervously. He had already mangled several jokes in the opening monologue, and the audience had barely roused itself to clap politely. He sneaked a glance at his watch: almost time. Tonight was the night. Tonight would make him or break him, or possibly even both at once.

Fox had been flailing in the late-night network wars for some time now, and he was partly to blame. The timing had seemed perfect. He was just coming off a much-beloved sitcom on another network, where he had played a wisecracking talk-show host. When Fox offered him the job for real, he bucked NBC and made the jump, hoping to pull in the young, hip crowd that had gradually turned against Letterman and Leno. That's when he discovered that the young, hip crowd wouldn't necessarily turn to him, not if they had cable. He also learned that being a real-life talk show host was very different from just pretending to be one. On the sitcom, he was onscreen for maybe ten minutes a show, at most. Now he had an entire hour to kill.

Vegas was his last hope. The network was opening its Fox Family Casino, a nice G-rated endeavor on the other side of the Strip from the Montage and the Universal Monster Grand. The casino was a huge yellowish crescent, its top wall shaped like Bart Simpson's spiky hair, surrounding a large front courtyard which boasted as a centerpiece a giant silver-covered statue—a cartoon fox. Not the best color combination, but one considered appropriate for Las Vegas.

Fox offered to let him host his show live from Las Vegas for a week, to tie into the casino's grand debut. The shows would be time delayed on the west coast but live on the east. Given his miserable ratings and fire-breathing reviews ("he's looking kind of fat and he's not funny without a script," Tom Shales had ranted in the *Washington Post*), he had little choice. In truth, this was a much harder job than even he had made it out to be on the sitcom. He had joked in the press that taking on the show would be a walk in the park, but it had turned out to be a run through a critical minefield. His show had trouble booking guests, and at one point the lead singer of an obscure punk band had actually vomited during their song, sending their album sales through the roof but setting off a deluge of angry calls to the Fox switchboard. The camera had cut to him after the incident, and he knew that some funny, offhand response was called for, but he had simply sat there, frozen, holding his unsharpened pencil and staring back at his dwindling TV audience.

The Fox offer to do a week's worth of absolutely live broadcasts had seemed a godsend. For one, he got to go to Las Vegas, a town he liked very much because one could obtain cheap drinks and food at all hours. At least the people he knew in Las Vegas and L.A. didn't have to watch him fumble around live like the unfortunate residents of the east coast. He could do a show and still be done by 9 P.M., plenty of time to tie one on and try to forget everything. Two, it boosted his ratings. Fox had hyped the live aspect of the show in magazine and billboard ads with a sly campaign that hinted at the furor the queasy punk band had caused.

"Catch Henry live in Las Vegas . . . or you may be *sick* to find out what you missed," the ads said, showing a picture of a smiling, cocky-looking Henry Hull, a genial pasty-faced man who was, in truth, getting a little chunky, just like Shales had said.

Fox also hyped the fact that it was providing alternative programming to the other three networks, who were glued to the Werewolf Telethon until roughly 12:30 A.M., eastern time.

"Give generously to help stop lycanthropy . . . then do yourself a favor and watch Henry live from Las Vegas at 11:30," the east coast ads said.

His ratings had gone up for the first couple of days, but unfortunately nothing particularly interesting happened during the live week. The guests his bookers managed to pull in were some of the lamest wheezers ever to gasp out an old song in a second-rate casino, and there was no way in hell he was going to attract the youth audience with them. None of the Vegas legends would appear on the show because they didn't want to seem to be going up against Monty Allen and his great work.

And so, in his last, desperate hour, Henry Hull was flopping like a fish in a hot pan, to the extent that the only way he could keep cold sweat from breaking out on his forehead the minute the lights went on was to switch his water with gin. It didn't make him any funnier—he had watched the videotapes, and even he had to admit that—but at least it made him feel better. It was possibly a combination of the gin and the sinking feeling of failure that had made him agree to the absolutely suicidal proposition that the woman identifying herself as an NBC reporter had called him about. It seemed that someone was willing to highjack the viewers of the other networks at the very peak of the Werewolf Telethon and deliver those millions of peepers right into Hull's miserable little talk show. Hull had thought it over for a few seconds, but, heck, for a second time in recent days he didn't really have a choice. The woman said there was just one little catch. Something was going to happen on the show, she said, and she wanted Henry Hull to get the hell out of the way when it did.

Hull took another sip of gin and cracked a mild joke about his next guest, the star of a daytime soap who had just been killed off from the show and therefore faced uncertain prospects. The audience laughed a little at that one, which made Hull feel better. Maybe things would go okay tonight. Maybe he would stay onstage no matter what happened. It was still his show, after all.

TWENTY NINE

Ashly Durban, looking a bit sweatier and slightly less radiant than she had on the Werewolf Telethon, came dashing full speed onto the set of the Henry Hull show, Jean Grenier Society members in tow. Hull perked up at this. He was right in the middle of listening to the lousy former soap star explain about his recent discovery of the healing power of New Age crystals, and how placing one of them under his bed had cured his bad back. Hull bent over the edge of his guest's chair, not even caring if he was sending off toxic alcohol fumes.

"Get the hell off the stage," he whispered to the startled actor, loud enough for the mikes to pick up.

But he didn't care, and neither did anyone else, for the back of the room was filling up with guys who looked like extras for *Hair*. The soap star gave a feeble wave to the audience, which went completely ignored, and trotted ignominiously into the wings and deeper into showbiz obscurity. Durban dashed down the stage left aisle at a clip only slightly faster than that of a tall gray-haired man who was approaching down the stage right aisle. Hull usually liked for his guests to enter from behind the stage, but the audience was paying extremely close attention now, so he didn't care where they came from.

Durban vaulted to the stage, sped across the floor and handed Hull a blue note card. The gray-haired man lumbered up beside her, panting hard, sniffing the air suspiciously. Probably wanting the gin, Hull thought; he'd only get it if he was a good guest. Hull looked at them in confusion, not sure if he should try to maintain the typically friendly pattern of mindless chat and air-kissing. Durban solved the question for him.

"Read the damn card!" she shouted, before plopping down into one of the guest chairs and panting like a greyhound. The gray-haired man did the same, but kept eyeing the back of the desk.

"Is that gin I smell?" he said quietly.

Hull ignored him and faced the cameras. His director, in the booth, was shouting into the tiny mike in his ear, but Hull pretended not to notice.

"Ladies and gentlemen, I'm sorry that Mr. Larson of *General Hospital* was called away, but we have two very, very special guests here tonight. You may know Mrs.—" he glanced at the card—"Ashly Durban from her work on *Live Entertainment*. And you probably have heard of Mr. Paul Moreau, founder of the Jean Greenier Society—"

"Gren-YAY!" Moreau shouted.

"Some of whom are here with us now."

The long-haired youths raised their hands and smiled at the crowd, but got no applause.

"It also says here that Mr. Moreau is currently wanted by both the Las Vegas Police Department and the FBI. Well, now, isn't that nice."

His forehead was beading furiously now, the sweat forcing its way through his thick pancake makeup like lava inexorably driving through mud. Everything had been all right up until he read the card. If he must have mystery guests, he would prefer they not come with rap sheets. Hull glanced up into the control booth, gave a shrug and said, "I'm doing this for the ratings, Hal."

The audience laughed nervously, but then No. 1 Fugitive Paul Moreau stood up and grabbed Hull by the collar, shoving him back into his chair.

"I'll take over from here," he whispered furiously into Hull's ear.

He held up a videotape, which Hull accepted with a shaking hand.

"Can you play this right now?"

"I can get Hal to play it. D-does it have any nudity or nasty words on it?"

"NO! Play it now!" Moreau whisper-shouted.

The boom operator had gotten the mike in place, and it was picking all this up. The audience was on the edge of its seats, especially now that the half a dozen Jean Grenier Society members were nervously fingering unseen objects in their jacket pockets. Hull hit the button that made his forty-inch TV and built-in VCR pop up from behind the seats. That startled Ashly Durban, who emitted a little squeal, causing the boom operator to whip the microphone over her way.

"Ladies and gentlemen, and those of you who have just joined us, I have no idea about what we're going to see, but it better be good," Hull said, bringing his water glass to his lips.

Paul Moreau's eyes went wide at the sight of it, but he didn't say anything. He pointed to the monitor.

"Ladies and gentlemen, what you are about to witness

is a secret tape taken from the laboratory of the Landon Research Institute, the group that Monty Allen has hired to cure lycanthropy. Or so he says. I'm sorry that we had to bring your attention here from the telethon, but we need for people to see this. This tape will show what Monty Allen's cure actually does."

Hull pushed the tape in and hit play. Moreau turned to the monitor expectantly, but nothing happened. Hull looked nervously around, and Durban checked her watch. Suddenly a voice boomed out. It was Hal, in the control booth.

"Look, I don't know who you people are, but you can't do this. I've shut the VCR power off. I'm sorry. No tape for you."

A buzz went through the crowd. Henry Hull frowned up at the booth. In the rocky course of his talk show, he had put a live hamster down his pants and had engaged in the basest kind of sex talk imaginable with the most untalented B-movie stars ever to weave across a TV stage. And here was Hal getting ethics all of a sudden. He had visions of ratings plummeting once more, as his newfound viewers switched back to the telethon or to cable or VCR.

One of the Jean Grenier Society youths tried to solve his problem. The kid, who offset his nice suit with a red baseball cap, shoved his way past the cameras and the cue-card guy and whipped out a very nasty-looking gun. A shriek went up from the crowd but nobody moved.

"Hey, pops!" the youth shouted. "Show the damn tape!"

"Sorry, son," a voice came back. "Henry's been a little unstable for a while, so I took a few precautions. This is bulletproof glass. Take your best shot."

A rustling sound carried over the microphones from the booth, followed by a quick series of violent thumpings, and then a new voice came over the airwaves.

"This is associate producer Bob Savik, available for future work on the show *Cops* and any others. But first, *this* show must go on."

The monitor suddenly popped to life. Hull leaned back in his chair, indifferent to whoever was in the broadcast booth. He hoped Hal had a black eye. The video slot made a whirring noise. Nothing but black-and-white snow appeared on the screen. Muttering a curse, Hull lunged at the machine and ejected the cassette. It came out, with two feet of tangled tape trailing it like cheese from a pizza slice.

"Damn it!" Hull shouted. "Why won't Fox give me good equipment? This is the same thing that happened to Tom Selleck's movie preview!"

Ashly Durban leaped off the couch and ran off into the wings, abandoning Moreau to the couch and to Hull.

"I'm really sorry about that," Hull offered earnestly, but then noticed a bustling going on offstage. Ashly Durban reappeared with another young man, this one with only moderately long hair, and a woman with shocking blonde locks and a sizable chest. They were pushing three wheelchairs.

"We're sorry to have to do this, but we're desperate," Durban shouted to the audience.

The wheelchairs contained young boys, but apparently not healthy ones; they were hunched over like they had no spines, and one was drooling. The boys faced the audience but gave no sign that they even knew where they were.

"The young man in the middle is named Danny

Wexler. You would have seen him on the tape, had Mr. Hull's machine not screwed up," Durban said, speaking quickly. She shot a glance at Hull, but he just shrugged and gave a weak smile.

"All three of these young men have lycanthropy, and all three of them used to appear in illegal werewolf movies that were filmed right here in Las Vegas. Then they got suckered to be test subjects for the nonexistent lycanthropy cure, which has been funded by Monty Allen. Ladies and gentlemen, look at them now."

Hull glanced out at the crowd. It was working. Some of the women and even a man or two were sniffling softly. Ashly Durban had offered no proof, but in an age of Donahue and Oprah, none was needed. They believed her.

"We found them dumped in local hospitals and nursing homes, dropped there with false papers and identification," Durban continued. "We found them thanks to the aid of Dr. Carl Johnson, who was murdered because of what he knew."

The audience erupted into applause, which Hull noted was probably helped along by the Jean Grenier Society members in the aisles, who were urging the crowd to clap. The one in the red cap did so by waving his gun around. I'll have to try that sometime, Hull thought.

The clapping was quickly drowned out by the noise of splintering wood and the eerie sound of weapons being prepared for use. An angry Monty Allen stalked down the stage right aisle, flanked by dozens of policemen armed with nasty assault rifles. Ashly Durban looked offstage to where Bob Savik was crouched. She hadn't seem him come in, but he had apparently made it. He had a pistol in his hand but a sheepish look on his face. He shook his head. He apparently knew he was outgunned, but didn't know what was happening.

"We appear to have more unscheduled guests on this most interesting evening," Hull said, taking a quick slug of gin. It made him snort, but he no longer cared if the audience saw him.

Before he could react, Paul Moreau reached out a long arm and snatched the glass away.

"I knew that was gin," he said, tossing the glass on the stage behind him, where its precious contents poured out. "You don't need that."

"Oh, but I *do*," Hull complained, but it was too late.

"All right, everybody freeze!" one of the cops shouted. "Drop your guns!"

The long-haired youths did as they were told. Monty Allen stalked through the police and the Jean Grenier Society members, who were now reaching for the studio catwalks, police pistols shoved in their ribs. He stalked past the cameras and up onto the stage, which he had done a thousand times before on other, better, talk shows. He stalked right past Ashly Durban and the wheelchair-bound kids, pausing to give one of them a gentle pat on the knee, which made the kid moan quietly. Henry Hull rolled his chair away from the desk as Allen approached.

Allen spread his muscular arms on either side of Moreau's shaggy head, steadying himself with an enormous hand on the back of the guest couch and the other on Hull's desk. Camera 2 moved in for a closeup of the hand, and showed the veins twitching so fast that the blood seemed to be escaping. Allen waited until the boom mike was in position above his head.

"Your little game is over, Paul Moreau."

THIRTY

"Ladies and gentlemen, I must apologize for this travesty," Monty Allen said, his arms held up like a televangelist. "With every sin, there are some who claim it. With every disease, there are a sick few who revel in it and proclaim it to be normality."

He pointed a muscular finger at Paul Moreau, who sat rigidly on the couch, his face an expressionless mask.

"This man would have you believe that there is some benefit to being sick. That there is some benefit to losing control once a month, or even more. He purports to have wisdom, but he is nothing but a wanted criminal. He—"

Moreau stood up with such surprising force that even the far larger Allen backed away two steps.

"You shut up," he said, his own finger pointing back at Allen. "I know all about you. I talked to Dr. Stumpf, the man you illegally bought your research from. The Landon Institute work was a joke. I don't know how you got it past the FDA, but I'm sure someone will be looking into that."

"*All* our research was duplicated by FD—"

"I'm not so sure. Why don't you tell these good people why you're doing this? You don't want to be known just for your crappy movies. You want to go down in history as having cured werewolves, whether you really did or not. That's why you're doing this. And you're also doing it for love."

That charge stopped the argument cold and roused *oohs* and *aahs* from the crowd. Henry Hull sat back and looked on in amazement.

"What are you talking about?" Allen said.

"Carl Johnson managed to get hold of some items he planned to use for blackmail. He had a collection of receipts. For flowers. Roses. They went back for two decades. Every year, you sent roses to the grave of a woman. Patricia Harris."

There was some muttering in the crowd as they tried to remember the name.

"You mean the sister of Andrew Harris?" Hull asked tentatively.

That rang a bell. Many visitors to L.A. had taken the scandal tour, had gotten off at the infamous house where the troubled young werewolf actor killed his sister and himself.

"You loved her, didn't you?" Moreau asked. "But then Andrew Harris killed her. You never forgave him."

Monty Allen trembled with rage. His voiced quavered when he spoke.

"I did love her. After what Andrew did, I vowed to cure lycanthropy. It is a good thing to do."

"By any means necessary?"

Monty Allen looked angry enough to breathe fire. He shoved Moreau back onto the couch so hard it nearly tipped over.

"NO! Look at me! You're talking libel suit now, buddy. Yes, I'm doing this for Patricia. I'm also doing this because I feel sorry for all the poor bastards that are werewolves! I want to cure them!"

Moreau looked angrily at Allen, who looked even more angrily right back.

"You know the cure is unreliable," Moreau said, his voice starting quietly and building from there. "You know that some people will be ruined by this."

He turned to face the audience.

"You heard it here first, people. If this cure is introduced, some werewolves will be drained of their minds. They will be like vegetables. Mark my words."

"Damn you! Don't take away from my triumph!" Allen shouted. "That's just the disease speaking, people. It's just a disease trying to hold on to its existence."

They resumed their glaring match. The audience watched, quiet and enraptured.

"People with lycanthropy can do more than you let on," Moreau said finally, and Allen snorted with disgust.

"I tell you one thing, they won't be able to break out of a jail cell again," he said, and then looked offstage and snapped his finger at one of the police officers. "Quit lounging around down there! Come arrest this man!"

Moreau suddenly bent over on the couch and rested his head on his hands, his eyes closed. His jaw seemed to be moving, as if he was talking to himself. He was repeating a string of three numbers. Henry Hull leaned slightly toward him and tried to peer into his face.

"Are you feeling okay?"

"Arrest him!" Monty Allen shouted to the cop, who wasn't moving quickly enough to suit him.

Then he froze in place. A white Siberian tiger is

an awesome sight, but it's even more awesome to see one sailing through the air, a sleek muscular missile capped with several very sharp warheads. For a split second, Monty Allen's mouth hung open at the beauty of the creature in flight, its Arctic eyes shining like torches. Then it occurred to him that the tiger was vaulting over the guest couch, over the head of Paul Moreau, aiming its claws and milky white fangs straight at him. Henry Hull was so shocked to see the airborne tiger that he tumbled over backwards in his chair. Abandoning all hostly decorum and what little concern he had for Moreau's health, he screamed. Monty Allen screamed too, as did most of the audience. Moreau's face, when he brought it back up into view, held only an enigmatic little smile.

The tiger slammed Allen back across the floor, knocking him off the carpeted upper tier of the stage and skidding him across the slick lower floor. Ashly Durban and the two kids onstage scattered, although they maintained presence of mind enough to take the wheelchair-bound children with them. For just a second, all was silent in the theater. The cops froze; the Jean Grenier Society members were already frozen. All that could be heard was the tiger growling and Monty Allen sniffling quietly as the massive beast scraped its teeth across the fleshy part of his neck. Then the overhead mike swiveled back to Paul Moreau, who had hopped up from the couch and was peering intently at the tiger.

"Nobody move!" he shouted. "If anybody tries anything funny, the tiger will bite his head right off!"

Some of the cops in the aisles were having trouble figuring out what to do with their pistols. About half had now trained them on the tiger, and the other half had bowed to necessity and were using two pistols, one for whatever Society member was being detained and one for the snarling Siberian.

"As much as I hate to use these tactics, I'm afraid I must," Moreau said. "Mr. Allen, you have been saying for months that lycanthropy is a disease that's of no use to society. I'm proving the opposite right now."

There was a bustle behind the stage, and then Mandunk burst into view in full silver sequined costume, his bottle blonde pompadour trembling. A couple of the cops now trained guns on him. The rest had gotten used to the idea of having too many targets and too few guns.

"Vot are you doing with my tiker?" Mandunk shouted. "Elsa? Elsa, is he hurting you?"

"Shut up!" Moreau shouted, not turning his eyes away from the big cat, which still had Monty Allen's throat buried deep in its mouth. "I'm not hurting her. I'm communicating with her."

"Oh, *please*," said one of the cops near the stage. He had his gun trained on Moreau. "Give it up, mister, or you'll be combing brains out of your hair for a month."

"Yes," Mandunk said. "Only *I* can communicate with Elsa."

"I'll show you," Moreau said, his voice heavy with concentration. "Elsa will now use the claws of her right paw to remove Mr. Allen's wristwatch."

Nobody fired a shot. Everybody, Mandunk included, waited to see if he could pull it off. Elsa's right paw slowly reached into the air, forcing her to shift her considerable weight to her left front paw, which forced her to move her teeth around a little, which made Monty Allen grunt in fear. The paw extended and began moving in the area of his left wrist, which caused him to grunt more, and finally to speak in the clench-mouthed style common to bad ventriloquists.

"She's ripping off my fingers! She's cutting my wrist!" Allen spat out between taut lips.

"No, she's not," Moreau said in a voice that sounded like he was under hypnosis. "She's doing fine . . . come on, Elsa."

Suddenly Moreau paused, and leaned against the couch for support. Elsa let out a snarl, which prompted a new series of whimpers from his prone victim.

"What's wrong?" Ashly Durban shouted from offstage.

"I—I'm losing it—" Moreau sputtered. "It's too much."

A nervous clapping from the studio audience distracted him. There was a big shift in weight again and then Elsa's paw rose slowly into the air, one claw dangling a gleaming, blood-free Rolex.

"My Elsa, geared for a life of crime!" Mandunk shouted before saying quietly, "You *must* show me how you do that."

"I could show you," Moreau said. "But I'd have to bite you."

He stared wearily into the wings, saw the look of otherworldly concentration on Bobby Chaney's face. Chaney stood just offstage, his eyes far away, his hands slightly outstretched, as if Elsa the tiger was just a big marionette and he was the puppetmaster. The tiger was hard; the kid was good. Chaney had saved his bacon.

"Thank you," he whispered.

The cops muttered among themselves.

"They're going to shoot your tiger," he said matter-of-factly to Mandunk, who proceeded to rip a big chunk out of his pompadour in anger.

"Shoot my tiker?! No! I'll have your heads! Elsa cost more than all your salaries put together!"

"Sorry, sweetie," one of the cops said, taking careful aim with his pistol at Elsa's head. "Let's just hope her jaws don't clamp shut when we blow out her brains."

"*Whtttttt?*" Monty Allen hummed.

Then the policeman heard the clomping of what sounded like horse hooves on the stage, to the right, out of his field of vision.

"Aren't there enough animals onstage?" he muttered as he turned to look. What he saw made him drop his aim at Elsa, and almost made him drop his gun entirely. Striding onto the stage was a gigantic man in thick gray furs, riding a gigantic horse. Together they seemed to tower higher than most of the buildings on the Las Vegas strip.

Paul Moreau staggered back to the couch and dropped onto it in surprise, releasing his mental hold on Elsa, who slowly removed her mouth from around Monty Allen's neck. She gave him a giant lick across the cheek and then turned to face the newcomer, stretching out on her stomach towards him as if in supplication. Monty Allen propped himself up on his elbows. He was covered in tiger spittle and ready to complain.

"Gimme my watch back," he muttered at Elsa, and then noticed the new guest and fell silent in amazement.

The giant man and horse seemed to shimmer softly in the harsh studio lights, as if they were oddly-shaped thunderclouds come too close to the ground. Ashly Durban slowly emerged from backstage and crossed behind the guest couch, hunching down behind Paul Moreau, never taking her eyes from the massive figure.

"That's him, isn't it?"

She put one hand on his shoulder and was surprised to find that he was trembling slightly. He only nodded.

Henry Hull slipped out from underneath his desk and groaned when he saw the latest interloper on his show.

"Oh, God," he said, coming to a kneeling position beside his chair. The giant man swiveled his head to regard the talk show host, and the horse snorted at him dismissively.

"Welcome to the most consistently interesting talk show on the air," Hull said with fake bravado. "C-could you, uh, tell us who you are? Are you in that new Schwarzenegger movie? That's supposed to have good effects."

The man's voice was like frozen air.

"I am the Lord of the Forest. I am of the trees. I am of the soil. I am of the wilderness."

Hull looked blankly out at the audience, who were frozen in their seats. Even the cops weren't moving.

"So, what brings you to the city?" Hull asked, so weakly that his words almost didn't reach the dangling microphone.

The Lord of the Forest extended his index finger, which was as thick as Hull's wrist, and pointed right at the center of Monty Allen's forehead. Allen's elbows fell out from underneath him, and he gave a disgusted little chuckle.

"Oh. Great."

THIRTY ONE

"You think you can destroy what I have created," the Lord of the Forest said, his voice overpowering the microphones, making Savik in the booth squirm out of his headphones in a panic and clutch his ears. "You can't. But you could do harm to some of my children. I won't let that happen."

Allen slowly rose to his feet, flexing his muscles for effect even though it was evident that the monstrous man had him outclassed under all those furs.

"And what do you propose to do to me?"

The Lord of the Forest gave a monstrous smile, which shone through even the wreath of darkness that seemed to surround him.

"Here. Catch."

He moved surprisingly fast, tossing something through the air, something gray and hairy. Monty Allen collapsed from the weight of it and it seemed to expand to cover him. There came a thundering sound, and everyone in the audience and on the stage flinched,

260

except for the Lord of the Forest. One of the cops had shot him.

"You're attacking Mr. Allen!" the cop shouted to explain his action, once it became clear that his dead-on shot hadn't phased the giant man at all. The Lord of the Forest swiveled his head in the direction of the cop for just an instant, and the policeman fell backwards onto the floor, his eyes frozen open. The Jean Grenier Society member he had been guarding casually bent down and picked up the cop's gun, which caused the nearest audience members to look at him nervously.

"Don't shoot at me," the Lord of the Forest said as he turned his attention back to Monty Allen.

"Don't do this!" Allen screamed, but his voice was muffled and garbled, as if he was having trouble working his mouth.

The Lord of the Forest merely smiled, a gruesome maneuver that made light shine around his teeth from somewhere deep inside him. As Allen continued to struggle across the stage, sometimes thumping loudly down onto his knees and elbows, the gray hairy blanket seemed to insinuate itself to the curve of his body, turning his already muscular arms and legs into even larger and more muscular arms and legs. The blanket bunched up around his mouth and then stretched slowly out into a snarling snout, and his ears began stretching into conical shapes.

"Oh my God," Durban said quietly into Moreau's ear. "That's not what it's usually like, is it?"

Moreau hunched on the couch like a sports fan watching an unusually gripping football game.

"No. Not like that at all."

Monty Allen was clearly turning into a werewolf unlike anything anyone had ever seen. He was getting taller and bigger, and his new skin had long ago inched its way under his clothes and ripped them away like water pushing through foam. His eyes were wide open in surprise, as if he couldn't quite believe this was happening, but he made no other sounds aside from occasional grunts. Many members of the audience were on their feet now, the Henry Hull show having nearly proven entirely too engrossing, but none of them tried to leave just yet. The host himself was cowering behind two policemen who had come to the edge of the stage and were watching the proceedings with guns down and mouths open.

"He's even growing a tail," Moreau said. He slowly slid over the back of the guest couch until he was crouching next to Durban. "I've never seen that before."

Indeed he was. Allen was completely turned now into a gigantic, twisted parody of a dog, one capable of staggering before the screaming audience on its two hind legs. Standing up, he was taller than anyone in the theater except the Lord of the Forest, who was still sitting placidly atop his monstrous steed. The horse stomped the floor and snorted at the new incarnation of Monty Allen. He was looking very dangerous right about now. The policemen abandoned any effort to cover the long-haired youths of the Jean Grenier Society and instead aimed all their weapons at their newest enemy.

Allen scanned the crowd with his new beastly head, his eyes black and inscrutable, squinted nearly shut. His conical ears, which seemed to be a foot long each, twitched at the barrage of sounds which came from the screaming crowd, which *was* trying to leave now. Audience members were shoving police out of the aisles. The Lord of the Forest noted the movement, and responded with an almost unnoticeable flick of the hand. When the first members of the crowd finally made it to the double doors in back of the theater, they found them locked and pounded on them in frustration before turning back to watch the spectacle from which they could not escape.

Allen swiveled uncertainly on his massive, malformed legs and looked behind him, causing Durban and Moreau to duck behind the guest couch. Henry Hull had fainted dead away, and the policemen who had fired had propped him in a front row seat, where he was drooling on a lapel of his jacket. Monty Allen gave a couple of thumping strides and looked out the enormous picture window, as if enthralled with the blinking lights of Las Vegas. He glanced down into the courtyard, where the gigantic silver Fox network fox sat in puckish wait, its spiked ears mirroring his own. Then he turned around, took half a dozen lumbering strides toward the audience and jumped.

A blistering barrage of gunfire halted his progress, seeming to hold him in midair for a split second before knocking him to the stage. Stray bullets shattered the top part of the picture window, sending glass streaming down into the courtyard, tinkling off the giant fox. Police who were keeping pedestrians away from the casino looked up in alarm. The creature that was Monty Allen laid on its stomach for a few seconds but then struggled back onto its misshapen feet. He was getting the hang of his new body. The gunfire he had been hit with would have been enough to drop three elephants, but it appeared to have only made Monty Allen madder.

"There's no blood on him," one of the cops said, and it was true; his gray shaggy chest had no stain.

"Do we need silver bullets?" another asked, but several cops shook their heads.

"That's just a myth," one said, but it didn't make any of them feel better.

Monty Allen tottered back a dozen feet and then leaped again. The guns chattered and once again Allen hung in midair like a hairy angel before being knocked backwards, and this time it rolled him over a time or two until he nearly came to rest against what was left of the glass picture window. He was panting noisily, and didn't move for several seconds.

"What has that forest guy done to him?" Durban whispered to Moreau, who shook his head.

"I don't know. It seems like a weird kind of revenge, to make your enemy so powerful. That kind of shooting would kill a dozen ordinary werewolves, and it just slows him down a little."

The Lord of the Forest cleared his throat. Everyone, including Monty Allen, the police and the audience, looked his way.

"You're wasting your time shooting at him," the man said, and his horse snorted as if in assent. "It won't hurt him."

Monty Allen sat up at this news and cocked his head sideways in what would have been a cute gesture were he not so monstrous. Then the Lord of the Forest surprised everyone again by getting off his horse. The maneuver looked as monumental as a mountain getting off a plain. Neither he nor the horse lost any of their majestic gravity once separated; instead, their size seemed to double, as if two immeasurably dense worlds had been birthed from one. He strode across the stage, massive furs waving. The cops aimed their guns at him but their posture was slack because by now they knew it was just no use.

He clomped over to Monty Allen and jerked him

upright by the scruff of the neck as if he were a puppy. Monty Allen towered over anyone in the room, but the Lord of the Forest somehow made him look like a stray kitten. The wolf that was Allen looked humble before him. The Lord of the Forest released him to stand on his own and then walked a few steps away from him, facing the policemen, who then awkwardly pointed their guns away, not wanting to offend.

"This man has been turned into the sort of beast he imagines werewolves to be. I looked inside his mind; this is the image I saw, and this is what I made him. He is as powerful as he imagines werewolves to be. You cannot kill him. *I* cannot kill him."

"Oh, that's just *great*," Moreau muttered in Durban's ear.

The Lord of the Forest turned to face his creation. Monty Allen was paying keen attention to his every word, and apparently could still understand them.

"Mr. Allen, you despise werewolves in your heart, but now I have made you greater than any werewolf that has gone before. You are boundlessly powerful. You are immortal."

A low growling began to issue from Monty Allen's craggy mouth, and Paul Moreau did not like the sound of it.

"We should probably get out of here," he whispered to Ashly Durban, but she shook her head, not taking her eyes off the confrontation.

"Nothing doing. This is great television."

"There is just one catch, Mr. Allen. There is a price. That was my best skin that I gave you, and I can't change you back. You are a werewolf forever, frozen in this form, half beast, half man. Unless your cure works on you. That is the risk you take."

Allen rocked back on his shaggy heels. That didn't
seem to be what he wanted to hear. He tottered a few
feet to the side, then made a few quick steps to the
edge of the stage, looking out at the audience that
was standing in the aisles or hiding behind their seats,
watching him in terror. The police raised their weapons
again and faced him nervously. His days of adoring
audiences were gone. He turned on the Lord of the
Forest and starting ripping at the furs that surrounded
him, but a massive arm, as big as a tree trunk, knocked
him back.

"I said I couldn't kill you," the Lord said. "I could
probably hurt you."

Allen tried to speak, but the words were a whining
garble coming through his new mouth. His eyes, so
malevolent only moments before, now turned upward
at the edges in supplication, and he fell on his hairy
knees before his new god and tormentor, whining for
relief. The Lord of the Forest faced straight ahead,
not looking down. Allen howled in anguish, a sound
that made everyone in the audience shiver. Ashly
Durban looked at her arm; the hairs were standing
straight up.

Monty Allen raised himself up to his new full height
and lurched miserably towards the edge of the stage,
causing one of the cops to fire two shots into his chest,
which did nothing. Then he uttered another howl
and ran past the Lord of the Forest and the guest
couch, ran at full speed to the picture window that
looked out over the glittering candy store that was
Las Vegas. Without slowing down he hurled himself
into the night.

The police dashed to the stage, running up to where
the Lord of the Forest was peering out into the casino

courtyard. Monty Allen was hanging above the ground, speared neatly on one of the sharp ears of the giant silver fox. He wasn't moving, and his blood glistened darkly in the garish light beaming from the ground-level windows of the Fox Family Casino.

"I thought you said he couldn't die," one of the police officers said to the Lord of the Forest, momentarily forgetting his awe of the massive stranger.

"I said we couldn't kill him," the Lord of the Forest said, his voice quieter than before, but still as chilly. "I did not mention that he could die by his own hand. He deduced that himself."

Paul Moreau approached the window and peered down into the grisly scene. Moreau looked at the unmoving Allen, then peered up at the Lord of the Forest, trying to catch his eye. The massive man ignored him and continued staring out at his ruined creation.

"Why didn't you tell me all those things you told Stumpf?" Moreau asked. "Why not tell me our true purpose?"

"You know now."

Moreau had more questions for his maker, but the Lord of the Forest turned and crashed back across the stage. A policeman fell into step at his heels, jogging along behind like a puppy, taking two quick hops for each of the giant's strides.

"Listen, we, uh . . . would you mind coming downtown to answer a few questions?"

The Lord of the Forest stopped and drew up to his full height, a good two heads above any of the cops.

"Me?"

"Well," the policeman said, nervously running one hand through his sweaty hair. "Yeah, you know, if that's okay."

The booming laughter that came next answered his question. The Lord of the Forest continued on his way back across the stage and slowly remounted his horse, two worlds colliding once again. The horse snorted and cantered towards the edge of the stage, but the Lord of the Forest reined him in so he could look out over the still-cowering crowd. He scanned the auditorium slowly, and the people cowered behind their chairs or each other, as if fearing that laser beams would shoot from his eyes. Then he and the massive horse clattered off the stage, disappearing somewhere into the stage left wing.

Henry Hull, having been awakened from his faint just in time to witness Monty Allen's glassy demise, tottered back to his chair and flopped down. He still had guests—Paul Moreau and Ashly Durban were standing by the window with the cops, looking out— but they probably didn't want to talk, and he didn't really want to talk to them anymore.

"Let's hear it for the Lord of the Forest, ladies and gentlemen," Hull said, slapping his limp hands together like a seal, but only a couple of people joined in, and then not enthusiastically.

Then the horse hoofs came thumping out from offstage. The Lord of the Forest reappeared, and Henry Hull just put his head down on his desk and gave up. The horse and rider clomped out to center stage, and the Lord of the Forest held out both arms, his palms held upright. The crowd, which was now all packed in around the back of the theater, looked on nervously.

"I thought it might be nice for all of you to experience what it is like to be lycanthropic," he said, his voice even colder than before.

Ashly Durban, her attention having shifted from

Monty Allen back to the Lord of the Forest, grabbed Paul Moreau's arm.

"Did you hear what I heard?"

"I did," he said. "I better get some new membership slips for the Jean Grenier Society."

Someone in the crowd let out a shout of anger, but the Lord of the Forest drowned it out.

"Don't worry, all of you, it's just for tonight. It won't be permanent. I will also spare you the murderous urges that usually come with the first transformation. You can learn to be wild for a short time. You can talk to the animals. Enjoy."

THIRTY TWO

Chesty grabbed Bobby by the shoulder, turning his attention away from the Lord of the Forest.

"Bite me," she said.

"What?"

They had dragged Danny Wexler and the other lycanthropy cure victims into the wings, and stood behind them, watching the drama play out on the stage.

"He's going to turn everyone into werewolves," Chesty said, rushing her words to fit them between the silences left by the Lord of the Forest's booming voice. "I want my change to be for real. For good. I want you to bite me."

Only a few days ago, she had been willing to fall out a window to keep from being bitten. Now she was requesting it.

"I don't think that's a good idea," he said. "It's not something you ought to just do for the hell of it."

Chesty stuck her face right up in his. Her eyes were shining. He had never really looked at her face up

270

close before. The lines around her eyes testified to a hard life, but her cheeks were surprisingly smooth.

"I'm not doing this for the hell of it. Bobby, for the first time I feel at home. I want to be with you. I want to be with *him*."

She nodded her head in the direction of the stage, and he knew she meant Paul Moreau.

"I never felt at home in Kansas City and I never felt at home with Stoke. I feel at home with you. I like that feeling."

He smiled despite the fact that he was sternly trying to warn her off from being bitten. What else could he do but smile? No one had ever said anything like that to him.

"I can't do it until we start to change," he said. "Until I grow some fangs."

She shoved her right sleeve up her arm, bunching it around her bicep. Her white skin seemed to glow.

"When the time comes. Right here," she said, tapping the middle of her arm.

Then she brushed his hair away from his eyes and gave him a kiss. The Lord of the Forest was making some kind of noise, but they didn't hear him.

THIRTY THREE

The Lord of the Forest let out a low moaning sound, so low it seemed to come from everywhere. Moreau suddenly staggered, so that Durban had to hold him up.

"Oh, God," he said, falling to his knees. "It's coming on, but it's never felt like this before."

Everyone in the auditorium, including Henry Hull and the police officers, seemed to be sharing his feelings. They were sprawled out in their seats or on the floor like refugees from an ether party, thick tufts of hair already starting to show on their bodies. Paul Moreau was halfway into his white dog alter ego and his eyes had gone glassy and far away. Durban felt up and down her right arm with her left hand, pinching the skin, and then patted her face. There was no hair anywhere, except for her own golden locks.

"I don't feel anything. I feel fine," she said, but Moreau wasn't listening. He was mostly just a big dog now, and he was lying on his side, panting, looking up at the Lord of the Forest.

Durban stood up. She seemed to be the only complete human left in the entire auditorium. Even Savik, up the booth, had his big claws leaning against the window. She walked out onto the stage, where the Lord of the Forest sat on his horse. He had lowered his arms and was just watching his handiwork.

"What about me?" Durban asked, her voice sounding more quavery than she had intended.

The Lord of the Forest swiveled his massive head around. His eyes seemed to shine out from under a thick mat of hair, and she thought she detected a tiny ray of kindness there.

"Someone needs to tell the story."

She looked at the audience, which was now filled with lazy, sleeping werewolves.

"What's wrong with them?"

"I haven't given them the signal to wake up."

"How many . . . are like this?"

She thought she saw him smile, but wasn't sure. It was hard to see his face.

"Everyone in this town. Most everyone, rather."

"Everyone in Las Vegas?"

He nodded.

"*Everyone* in Las Vegas is a *werewolf*?"

"Most everyone."

"That should liven things up. Everyone in town is a werewolf but me."

"Most everyone but you. Tell me, where are the children? The ones you had here earlier?"

She looked around, then trotted backstage. Danny Wexler himself was still human, still drooling, and his companions were still human also, if one could call two motionless, soundless, empty-eyed children human. Durban knelt down beside Wexler for a second, but he betrayed no sense of her presence.

"So you're the other ones who aren't werewolves," she said quietly.

"Bring them to me," the Lord of the Forest boomed from the stage.

Ashly Durban hadn't been yelled at like that since she served John Robinson with divorce papers, but she decided not to complain. She rolled Danny Wexler slowly to the feet of the horse, which bent its head down to gently nudge the wheelchair even closer. Then she went back for the others while the motionless werewolves in the audience looked on silently. When all three of the damaged young men were arrayed before the giant horse and rider, the Lord of the Forest spoke again, his voice sounding almost gentle and human.

"Help me get them on the back of the horse."

Grunting with effort, she managed to tug Danny Wexler up from his chair, which made him gurgle in fear and sent a stream of warm drool across her arm. She got him up and then the Lord of the Forest did the rest. He put one massive arm under Danny's feeble flabby ones and lifted him as easily as if he were made of straw. The other two followed and were perched on the back of the horse, although Durban couldn't quite see how they fit; the Lord of the Forest seemed to take up all the room.

"What will you do with them?" she asked once the wheelchairs were empty and the horse was full.

"I will fix them," the Lord said, his voice husky and for the first time nearly inaudible. "If I can."

"Wait, before you go. Why can't I be a werewolf?"

"I told you. You need to tell the story of what happened here. So that it is not repeated."

"But—"

"I thought you were a good choice. I *could* go to CNN."

"No, no, but . . . why do you need me at all? This has all been on live TV."

"There is some question as to whether I can appear on camera or on film. It is quite possible that I did not. If not, the viewers have been treated to some interesting but incomprehensible viewing. I would like for you to fill in the blanks."

She had no camera, no notebook, no tape recorder, but figured she could get some film from the show and patch something together.

"Can I at least have an interview, then? Who are you, really?"

"I don't need publicity. Tell Monty Allen's story. Tell of his fear and his hate."

"But how—"

"There is a CNN reporter in a hallway of this casino. I could convert her back. . . ."

Durban was really annoyed. Men were all the same, even if they were supernatural.

"No, dammit, I'll do it. But with no film and no tape, I'll just seem like a kook."

The Lord of the Forest reined his horse around and clomped to the edge of the stage. He tossed a gray skin over the three teen-agers, and they seemed to almost disappear from view. The Lord himself, and the horse, were getting harder to see, too, as if a tiny patch of night had crept in to surround them.

"Your daytime talk shows should prove a suitable venue," he said, and then boomed his voice out across the auditorium. "Bobby! Margaret!"

Two of the werewolves in the back of the auditorium came alive and bounded down the stage left aisle.

"Bobby?" Durban said quietly. "Chesty?"

The Lord of the Forest chuckled, and the two scruffy-looking creatures hunkered down before him.

"You didn't think Chesty was her real name, did you?"

He extended a hand out over them, and they began to change suddenly, their coats becoming a little sleeker, their eyes brighter, their color lighter, their muscles more taut. They dropped from two legs onto all fours, and then into a crouch. They appeared to be an interim step between the regular werewolves in the audience and the dog-like Paul Moreau.

"I am pleased to see you among our number, Margaret. You have both done well. I will advance your lycanthropic evolution a little bit. Bobby and Margaret, arise."

The souped-up werewolves raised themselves on four new legs and stood waiting, furry sprinters ready for a race.

"Take these new creatures into the desert and show them how to live," the Lord of the Forest said. "And when you are done tonight, help Paul Moreau in his quest. He has done this alone for far too long. Good night."

The horse executed a quick quarter turn, and suddenly both were gone.

The hairy Bobby and Chesty looked at each other for a moment, and then raised their sleek snouts toward the ceiling and howled. Durban fell on her rump in surprise and then began scooting rapidly backwards; the place had come alive with werewolves, and they were making a lot of noise. She crabbed her way over to the broken window and could hear howling echoing down the street, coming from all over Las Vegas. She closed her eyes and waited to be an appetizer, but the creatures ignored her. With playful yips in her direction, Bobby and Chesty bounded up the aisles and out the studio doors, and the other werewolves, some tottering on uncertain legs, rose as one to follow them into the night.

THIRTY FOUR

Ashly Durban shivered in the desert air and wrapped her arms tighter around her shoulders. So much fur in town tonight, and she still hadn't been able to find a good coat. She had picked up a yellow windbreaker left behind by a newly lycanthropic audience member of the Henry Hull show, but it wasn't doing a very good job.

She had driven close to the top of one of the foothills of Mount Charleston, where she could look down onto the amazing sight that spread out below her in the valley—wolflike creatures, as far as the eye could see, running around and howling their heads off. In time, the night would have an unexpected effect. Some of the townspeople, having been given a temporarily better understanding of the natural world they lived in, would vote to halt a planned development on the outskirts of the city. They communicated with an endangered desert tortoise and learned what it needed to survive, and one month to the day of that Halloween night the Las Vegas City Council voted to suspend work on an upscale suburb and set aside a parcel of land for the tortoise. But that was all in the future. On this night, the entire population of Las Vegas, minus Ashly Durban, was running around, sniffing every bush and cactus, howling its head off and enjoying itself very much.

Everyone but Ashly Durban and Paul Moreau. He was leaning against her right shoulder, his lustrous white hair providing a little extra warmth. He looked at her face from time to time, but mostly kept his eyes focused on the pack below. She ruffled the hair on his thin head.

"Would you like to be down there with them?"

He looked at her and whined questioningly, and she gave him another quick pat and then shoved him forward a few inches, making his paws scuff in the dirt.

"Oh, go on. You know you want to."

The white dog bounded down the hill and melted into the pack.